"My father badmouthed George Cummings at every turn. You do know that hiring me will make your father angry."

"Sometimes anger is good for a man," Wade replied.

Abby's eyes widened, as if she were surprised by his statement, but then she nodded. "Sometimes anger is good for a woman." She met his gaze boldly, daring him to disagree.

The brief time he'd spent with her today proved she wouldn't back away from a fight. No doubt sparks would fly between her and his father.

He'd achieved what he'd set out to do. But before he'd gotten the first sense of satisfaction, disquiet took root in his mind. A quick glance at the woman in front of him affirmed the feeling. If he wasn't careful, Abigail Wilson might ignite something within him. A Wilson and Cummings might be oil and water, but that combination could ignite a blaze.

Had Abby sensed that attraction he felt? Did it alarm her as much as it did him?

Books by Janet Dean

Love Inspired Historical

Courting Miss Adelaide
Courting the Doctor's Daughter
The Substitute Bride
Wanted: A Family
An Inconvenient Match

JANET DEAN

grew up in a family that cherished the past and had a strong creative streak. Her father recounted wonderful stories, like his father before him. The tales they told instilled in Janet a love of history and the desire to write. She married her college sweetheart and taught first grade before leaving to rear two daughters. As her daughters grew, they watched *Little House on the Prairie,* reawakening Janet's love of American history and the stories of strong men and women of faith who built this country. Janet eagerly turned to inspirational historical romance, and she loves spinning stories for Love Inspired Historical. When she isn't writing, Janet stamps greeting cards, plays golf and bridge, and is never without a book to read. The Deans love to travel and to spend time with family.

JANET DEAN

An
INCONVENIENT
Match

Love Inspired

Recycling programs
for this product may
not exist in your area.

LOVE INSPIRED BOOKS

ISBN-13: 978-0-373-82900-2

AN INCONVENIENT MATCH

www.LoveInspiredBooks.com

Printed in U.S.A.

Dear Reader,

Welcome to Love Inspired!

2012 is a very special year for us. It marks the fifteenth anniversary of Love Inspired Books. Hard to believe that fifteen years ago, we first began publishing our warm and wonderful inspirational romances.

Back in 1997, we offered readers three books a month. Since then we've expanded quite a bit! In addition to the heartwarming contemporary romances of Love Inspired, we have the exciting romantic suspenses of Love Inspired Suspense, and the adventurous historical romances of Love Inspired Historical. Whatever your reading preference, we've got fourteen books a month for you to choose from now!

Throughout the year we'll be celebrating in several different ways. Look for books by bestselling authors who've been writing for us since the beginning, stories by brand-new authors you won't want to miss, special miniseries in all three lines, reissues of top authors, and much, much more.

This is our way of thanking you for reading Love Inspired books. We know our uplifting stories of hope, faith and love touch your hearts as much as they touch ours.

Join us in celebrating fifteen amazing years of inspirational romance!

Blessings,

Melissa Endlich and Tina James

Senior Editors of Love Inspired Books

To teachers everywhere, those in the classroom and those in the home, who instruct, not only from textbooks, but by word and deed. God bless you.

* * *

The Lord is my strength and my shield, my heart trusts in him and I am helped.
—*Psalm* 28:7

Chapter One

New Harmony, Iowa, 1901

One glance at the rogue across the way curled Abigail Wilson's gloved hands into a stranglehold on her skirts. She couldn't dispute that Wade Cummings was handsome, rugged—

Her heart stuttered in her chest. *And,* a ladies' man who took pleasure in toying with a woman's affections.

Abigail should warn that bevy of giggling young females surrounding him, all vying for his attention. Not that they'd believe falling for the Cummings heir entailed a risk. No doubt each hoped he would bid on her box lunch and spend the afternoon, better yet, a lifetime, plastered to her side. Their plan for the future—a wedding ring.

She'd seen how well that worked out in the best of circumstances, but tied to a Cummings that would be a jail sentence without end.

She turned away from her nemesis and joined the throng pouring into the small park bordering Main Street. Inside the park's gazebo a table held dozens of gaily wrapped box lunches. She handed hers to Oscar Moore, the fundraiser's auctioneer.

Oscar doffed his straw hat. "Afternoon, Miss Abigail."

Donned in his usual garb of a plaid flannel shirt and bib overalls even on this warm Saturday in May, Oscar lined her box up with the others on display, a colorful mix of paper, silk flowers and ribbon.

"I'd give Leon a run for his money and bid on your lunch exceptin' I make it a point to never come between lovebirds."

Abigail bit back a grin. Lovebirds hardly described her and Leon.

A sudden grimace marred Oscar's placid plump face. "Land's sake, they're at it again."

Up ahead, young people circled a commotion. Abigail rose on her tiptoes. Why, inside that ring, two of her students hunched, clenched hands reared back, ready to strike a blow. Within seconds bystanders took sides, egging them on, as if they needed encouragement. Paul was a hothead, but Seth normally had a level head on his shoulders. What had happened?

Abigail strode toward the ruckus, using her collapsed parasol to clear a path, and pushed her way between the two glowering teenagers. Not wise considering each stood a head taller than her, and outweighed her by a good fifty pounds.

"She's mine, you hear!"

"Like you own her!"

"You two are behaving like tantrum-throwing toddlers," Abigail said. Chests heaving, eyes sparking, knuckles white, neither boy appeared to hear. "Seth! Paul! Unfold those fists!"

Looking slightly dazed, both boys lowered their arms and took a step back.

Seth Collier, his dark hair curling with perspiration, dropped a sheepish gaze to his feet.

Paul Roger's face was contorted in anger and as red as his hair, his icy-blue eyes shooting daggers. He reached around

Abigail and shoved a palm into Seth's shoulder. Seth staggered, almost losing his balance.

Abigail slapped her parasol against Paul's forearm. "Stop that!" Finally both boys turned toward her. "What's this about?"

"Seth's going to bid on Betty Jo's lunch. Everyone knows she's my girl."

"Then outbid him. The box social is about raising money."

Snarling, Paul took a threatening step toward Seth. "No one bids on Betty Jo's lunch but me."

"If sharing a meal with another boy will damage your friendship with Betty Jo, then face the truth, Paul, you don't mean much to her in the first place."

Betty Jo Weaver, the object of the boys' hostility, sashayed over, dainty hands planted on hips, lips flattened in a disapproving line. "I wouldn't share my lunch with either of you blockheads, not for all the tea in China!" She spun away, petticoats and blond curls flying.

"As you can see, gentlemen, the way to a lady's heart isn't through your fists."

"Now look what you've gone and done," Paul groused to Seth then took off at a run. "Betty Jo, wait up!"

With the fight over before it started, bystanders lost interest and dispersed.

Abigail took in Seth's familiar faded shirt, the elbow she'd patched one afternoon after school. Motherless with a father who drank, the boy didn't have an easy life.

"You need to watch what you say to Paul. You know his temper." She smiled to soften her words. "Plenty of other girls would like to share their lunch with you."

"Maybe," Seth said but didn't look convinced.

Did he really care about Betty Jo? If so, he was bound to get hurt. Betty Jo Weaver had bigger pickings in mind. Already she'd joined the circle of Wade Cummings's ardent admirers.

Foolish girl.

Off to the side, face downcast, Paul stood watching. Young love hurt, she knew, but dismissed the thought and turned away from such silliness.

"Seth, the school board agreed to pay someone to stoke the schoolhouse stove this winter. Would you like the job?"

His eyes lit. "Yes, ma'am, I sure would."

"It'll mean getting up early."

"I can manage."

"I know you can. Now have a good time today. And no fighting."

"Yes, ma'am," he said then trotted off.

Seth was a good kid. A bright kid. And weighted down with responsibility. With a father who saw any act of kindness toward him and his son as interference. The best way to help Seth was to get him out from under his father's influence and into college next year.

"This box social reminds me of a meal we once shared."

At the sound of *his* voice and the implication in that tone, the hair on the back of Abigail's neck rose. She whirled to face the speaker, tripping on her skirts, and stared into the eyes of Wade Cummings.

He steadied her, his touch firm and warm through her sleeve. A lazy grin rode his chiseled features, as if he found her reaction amusing. When he knew perfectly well she wouldn't share a meal with him if he were the last person on earth.

She jutted her chin. "I don't know what you're talking about."

"Are you saying you've forgotten the school picnic? I'll never forget the strawberry pie you brought."

A flash of memory of Wade capturing a speck of filling

with his tongue, then declaring the pie the best he'd ever eaten as her stomach had roiled. Not from the dessert, but that he'd spoken to her at all, considering the trouble between their families. Worse when he'd asked to join her on the blanket, she'd nodded, unable to refuse the allure of those deep-set indigo eyes. That afternoon they'd strolled through the park, talked for hours. For weeks they'd spent every minute together they could. Not easy when her family adamantly refused to let Wade come calling.

That had been a long time ago. Before Wade dumped her like a sack of rotten potatoes. Before Pa died. Before she fully grasped the Cummings family treachery and suffered the consequences. She dealt with them still.

As she pivoted on her heel to avoid him and the heartache those memories awakened, Wade stopped her with a gentle hand on hers. "Did you make strawberry pie for today's lunch?"

"No." She shook off his touch, grateful she spoke the truth, but if she had prepared his favorite dessert, she'd never admit as much to Wade. "Leave me alone."

Oscar Moore's brother Cecil, self-proclaimed mayor of New Harmony, sidled up beside her. Long-faced and tall, the exact opposite of his rotund brother, Cecil lifted a brow. "From the looks of it you two could use a referee. My rheumatism's been acting up but I ain't too feeble to handle the job."

"No need, Cecil. Mr. Cummings was just leaving," Abigail said with a finality Wade couldn't miss. And from the stubborn set of his jaw, he hadn't.

"Well, in that case I'll mosey on back to my post." Cecil shook his head. "Too bad you two mix about like oil and water. Cause you look right well together. Better'n Pastor Ted's matched team of Percherons."

With a jaunty wave, he hobbled off, leaving Abigail with flushed cheeks.

Wade chuckled. "Hope you don't mind being compared to a horse. In Cecil's view there's no higher compliment."

"He's mistaken. Nothing about us matches."

"Sometimes an unlikely pair works well as one." Wade's gaze drilled into her. "I noticed how you stood up to those young troublemakers looking for a fight. I'd like to discuss—"

"We have nothing to say to each other."

"Please, hear me out."

"Why should I? Hasn't your family done enough damage?"

Wade gave Abby a long lingering look, letting his eyes roam her blond hair, the color of honey, worn in a pouf around her face in what he'd heard called the Gibson Girl look. Her dewy peaches-and-cream complexion, flawless except for a pale birthmark near her left ear, flushed with anger. At his perusal she lowered her gaze, the sweep of her dark lashes leaving shadows on her cheeks.

For a short time that face had occupied his dreams.

Truth be told, he'd never managed to purge her from his mind. "Can we get past the trouble between our families even for a moment?"

"You'd like that, wouldn't you?"

Under slim brows, her arresting eyes, a luminous blue, blazed with antagonism, no doubt the same look that had halted those hot-tempered adolescents in their tracks.

Abby had spunk.

Clearly, she despised him.

What difference did it make? Wade didn't seek a relationship with Abigail Wilson. Or anyone for that matter.

But after witnessing the feisty schoolmarm rebuke Seth

and the Rogers' kid, even whack Paul with her parasol, Wade knew he'd found the perfect candidate for the job. *If* he could get her to listen to anything he said.

Well, he wouldn't create a scene by insisting, not with everyone gawking. He tipped his hat. "You look mighty pretty in blue."

Though her eyes narrowed, her hand sought her hair, fiddling with a strand near her ear. Whether she'd admit it or not, he affected her.

As he sauntered off, those within earshot put their heads together, no doubt wondering why a Wilson and a Cummings had exchanged words.

How could he make his offer if she wouldn't talk to him?

The solution came. A solution so simple he wondered why he hadn't thought of it sooner.

A soft chuckle rumbled inside him. He wasn't a schoolboy she could intimidate. She didn't know it yet, but Miss Abigail Wilson had met her match.

Heart-pounding memories tore through Abigail. Memories of Wade sitting beside her in Sunday school, walking her home from class, always parting before they reached Cummings State Bank and the Wilson apartment overhead. One day he'd given her a pink hair ribbon, a memento of his affection, he'd said.

Why had she believed him?

Refusing to give the scoundrel another thought, Abigail moved through the park, pulling into her lungs a faint whiff of smoke. The acrid odor sparked memories of the fire that had swept through New Harmony two weeks earlier, leaving behind destruction and suffering.

As she recalled the unbearable heat, the thick smoke, the terror of that night, her stomach knotted. But then the underlying scent of fresh lumber reached her nostrils and its promise of new beginnings eased the tension inside of her.

Thank you, God, no one lost their life or would be permanently disabled.

A miracle or so it seemed to Abigail.

With a thankful heart, she greeted friends and neighbors in the crowd milling around the gazebo. An amazingly festive crowd considering the town had gathered to raise money for her sister's family and five other households who'd lost everything in that fire.

Mother Nature smiled upon today's festivities, bestowing glorious sunshine, puffy clouds and a gentle breeze, belying her earlier tirade—the lightning strike that turned a thunderstorm into a one-block inferno.

Up ahead, Rachel Fisher waved, a straw boater tilted at a coquettish angle on her raven hair.

Rachel reached Abigail's side and slid an arm through hers. "Papa said if no one bids on my lunch, he would." Her brow puckered. "I'll die of mortification."

"Wearing that pretty dress and hat—why, you'll have loads of admirers clamoring to share your lunch."

"You say the sweetest things. No wonder you're my best friend in the world." Rachel leaned closer. "Speaking of admirers, did you see the girls fawning over Wade Cummings earlier?"

Against her better judgment, Abigail turned toward her foe. He met her gaze, and then had the audacity to tip his hat, but not her world. Five years ago, the gesture would've quivered in her stomach. No more. She was done with that man.

"With all the eager contenders for the position, why isn't he courting anyone? Do you suppose he feels too good for us?"

"Yes, I do."

"Too bad." Rachel sighed. "Wade's handsome and rich and—"

"A Cummings," Abigail said, hoping to put an end to where the conversation led.

Abigail's hand sought the slender chain around her neck that held the tiny gold ring Pa had bought the day she was born. He'd called her his baby girl…until everything changed. Pa most of all.

Rachel rose on her tiptoes and searched the park. "Is Leon at the bank?"

"He'll be here before the bidding starts."

"Guaranteeing *your* lunch will be snapped up," Rachel moaned. "I've got to find Papa before he humiliates me." She gave Abigail a hug then scurried off in search of her father.

Mr. Fisher adored his daughter. Rachel didn't appreciate what she had. But then, Abigail hadn't either until she'd lost it.

Oscar Moore motioned her over to the gazebo. "What triggered that scrap between the Roger and Collier boys?"

"Betty Jo Weaver."

"Should'a known." His face crinkled in a grin. "You gotta be grateful school's out and you're free as a bird."

In reality, Abigail had eight mouths to feed. The fire made her search for a job difficult, as those who'd lost everything scrambled for additional income, all vying for the few available openings. "This bird is looking for a summer cage. If you hear of a job, let me know."

"Reckon something'll turn up iffen you pray about it."

She'd prayed about it, but wouldn't sit idly by when God had given her a good brain and the education to help herself.

"Well, time to get this here show on the road." Oscar lumbered up the gazebo steps, slipped two fingers in his mouth, releasing a shrill whistle that quieted the crowd. "Reckon you all know why we're here," he called out. "Let's plan on going home with full bellies and empty wallets. Show those folks, who lost everything, that we not only care, we share." He pumped a pudgy fist. "Are you ready?"

A cheer rose from the throng. A huge grin spread across Oscar's plump face, swallowing up his eyes.

The community had pitched in to help, exactly as Abigail would expect. Single women put up their box lunches to the highest bidder while married ladies handled the bake sale, offering pies, cakes and cookies, along with iced tea and lemonade, at tables already lined with buyers.

After explaining the rules, the auction began. Oscar accepted a bid made by the blushing box owner's beaming suitor who opened his wallet and withdrew bills. "The best money I ever spent," he said, handing the cash to Oscar.

At his side, his young love giggled. "I'm a terrible cook."

"When I can feast my eyes on you, Lora Lee, I don't care what I eat," he vowed, taking the box and offering his arm.

"You'll change your mind about that, sonny, when your belly meets your backbone," someone quipped.

Those within hearing distance chuckled. The suitor merely gave a goofy grin. Abigail couldn't remember seeing such adoration in anyone's eyes. Not that she wanted what they appeared to have. Her teaching contract forbade her to marry. Fine with her—especially now. She desperately needed that job.

As Oscar held up another offering, this one wrapped in toile and covered with tiny silk flowers, Abigail's gaze traveled down the block to where six empty lots left a cavernous gap on the tree-lined street, as unsightly as missing incisors in a mouth full of teeth.

Her sister Lois's family had crowded into the apartment over the bank with Abigail and her mother. Cozy hardly described four adults, four active boys and a newborn baby crammed into four tiny rooms.

Laid up with a broken leg and arm, injuries Joe sustained falling down the stairs while escaping the fire, her brother-in-law could barely get around, much less work.

Oscar raised a beribboned package to his nose. "A whiff of this lunch suggests roast beef with horseradish. Who'll give five dollars?" A hand shot up. "Yip! I've got five. Who'll give six?"

A nod.

"Yip!" Oscar turned back to the first bidder. "Do I hear seven?"

If this spirited bidding continued, the auction would raise enough money to purchase the building supplies. Every able-bodied man in town had volunteered their labor. They'd cleared the debris. But with none of the modest houses insured, the burned-out homeowners needed assistance.

One man could handle the loss with a mere nod of his head, but George Cummings did nothing unless he benefited. What else could she expect from the ruthless banker who'd brought about her father's death?

A nudge of conscience reminded her that the senior Cummings had burned his hands fighting the fire and no doubt suffered. But then, hadn't he brought suffering to others often enough?

Leon Fitch stepped to Abigail's side. Tall and thin, a thatch of russet hair parted in the middle, Leon rested gentle hazel eyes on hers. Not like the intense, unsettling eyes of that rogue across the way.

"Sorry I'm late," he said slightly out of breath. "Right before closing time folks lined up to withdraw money for the auction. I haven't missed your lunch, have I?"

Abigail assured him he hadn't.

For several months, Leon had escorted her to an occasional dance and church social. Not that she'd call their outings courting. Leon was far too deliberate to take such a momentous step in haste. Their companionable relationship suited her. She wasn't looking for love.

As they watched, two more boxes sold, one for eight dollars, the other for ten. Rachel's lunch came next.

Across the way, Abigail's friend stood beside her father, her hand rested on his arm as if to ensure he wouldn't bid. Rachel needn't have worried. Two men vied for the privilege of sharing her lunch. Jeremy Owens, the owner of the livery, and Harrison Carder, the new lawyer in town, a Harvard friend of Wade Cummings.

One glance at Wade and her heart lost its rhythm. A sudden longing rose up inside of her. Refusing to ponder the absurd reaction, she forced her attention back to the bidding.

The attorney won the bid at nine dollars. Rachel beamed while her father looked bewildered, as if he couldn't fathom his little girl stirring the interest of a man.

Oscar held aloft a box she recognized as hers by the blue-and-white checked cloth and red bow. She'd packed a hearty lunch for two of crispy fried chicken, golden biscuits, bread-and-butter pickles, potato salad, deviled eggs and slabs of blackberry cobbler, all Leon's favorites.

And not a single bite of strawberry pie.

Oscar inhaled. "Just take a whiff of this, gents. I'd say whoever wins the bid is in for a feast of fried chicken. Who'll give me five?"

"Is that yours?" Leon whispered. "It's red, white and blue like you said."

At her nod, Leon raised his hand, fingers spread wide.

Oscar pointed at Leon, taking his bid.

Abigail shot him a smile. Not the highest bid today but generous. Especially for a man who kept a firm grip on every dollar.

A smug expression on his face, Leon leaned back on his heels. "I know the contents will be worth the cost."

"It's for a good cause."

With a grin, he patted his flat abdomen. "That too, but at the moment, my stomach wins hands down."

"Who'll give six?" Oscar called.

"Ten dollars!"

Abigail spun to the speaker, her heart slamming into her throat then plunging to the pit of her stomach with the weight of a boulder.

Wade leaned against a gaslight lamppost, loose limbed, his expression unreadable on his Stetson-shadowed face.

A face she'd like to slap.

How dare he ridicule her in front of the entire town? Why did he bid? What did he want?

Oscar whirled to Leon, seeking a raise in the bid.

Beside her, Leon huffed. "Eleven dollars," he said in a voice that croaked, as if he might do the same.

Wade straightened, his gaze pinning Leon as if he were a frog in a science experiment. "Twenty-five."

"Well, praise be!" Oscar hooted. "If that ain't a bid that'd curl a pig's tail."

Around her folks murmured, a few chuckled nervously, aware no Cummings and Wilson shared a conversation, much less a meal.

Ever. Well, almost ever.

Abigail folded her arms across her torso and glared at Wade. Surely he had no intention of actually eating the food she'd prepared.

With her.

Not when their families had been at loggerheads for eons. Not when they'd never communicated more than a look in years. Until today.

"Leon, this here's your chance to be one of them knights in shining armor. Are you going to twenty-six?"

Abigail met Leon's baffled gaze. Why didn't he raise the bid? Surely he could see the entreaty in her eyes. Would he turn her over to Wade?

Leon shoved his hat down and kept his mouth nailed shut. Obviously she wasn't worth such an exorbitant sum. Her heart skipped a beat. Not to him.

Or perhaps Leon feared losing his job. The Cummingses owned much of the town, including the bank where Leon worked. Heat filled her veins. She wouldn't put such malice past a Cummings.

"I've got twenty-five. Do I hear twenty-six? Twenty-six?" Oscar chanted, scanning the throng. As if anyone else in town had the wherewithal to match the bid. "Going, going, gone. Sold!" Oscar beamed. "Wade Cummings paid twenty-five dollars for the privilege of sharing lunch with the young lady who prepared it. Reckon with Leon bidding we all know that's Abigail Wilson."

Around her a few people clapped but far more spoke behind their hands. Everyone was aware of the feud and did what they could to keep the Wilsons and Cummingses apart. Agnes sat them in opposite corners of her café like prize fighters in a ring. Tellers at the bank opened a new window rather than let Wade and Abigail wait in the same line. At church the families occupied pews on far sides of the sanctuary.

Before Abigail had left the one-room schoolhouse for a position in the high school and Wade's sister Regina and her husband had moved away, rumor had it George Cummings would refuse to let his future grandchildren sit in Abigail's class.

As if she'd take out the bad blood between their families on innocent children, real or imaginary.

She gulped. Wade was no child, far from innocent and nowhere close to imaginary.

He took out his billfold and handed the money over to Elizabeth Logan, the pastor's wife and president of New Harmony's Ladies' Club, the woman responsible for organizing the fundraiser and pretty much everything else in town. Whatever Elizabeth got involved in flourished. The feisty blonde had made a huge difference since she'd arrived at the depot two years ago to marry Ted Logan, a total stranger.

Abigail admired Elizabeth and wanted to help her sister's family and the others who'd lost everything in the fire. But nothing could make her eat one bite of food with that man.

With long strides Wade sauntered to the gazebo, took the box Oscar handed down, his bicep bulging beneath the white shirt he wore, then strode toward her, his eyes locking with hers. Her insides quaked like the leaves on an aspen tree, but she lifted her chin, refusing to look away.

Leon slinked off, leaving her to fend for herself. Not that she needed him—or anyone— to fight her battles.

But as Wade moved closer, she recalled from history that retreat was sometimes the best strategy in battle.

Determined to escape, she held up her skirts and dashed toward the park's entrance. The sound of footsteps propelled her on, raising the hair on her neck and drawing laughter from the onlookers.

She'd never outrun him.

Chapter Two

One glance over Abigail's shoulder confirmed Wade's long legs had swallowed the distance between them. Apparently this skirmish required hand-to-hand combat. She whipped around and faced him.

Wade swept the Stetson off his head, his brown sun-streaked hair gleaming. "I paid a princely sum for the privilege of sharing your lunch. Surely you don't mean to refuse my bid."

Her hands knotted at her sides. The urge to throw a punch slid through her. Gracious, she was conducting herself like Seth and Paul. *Lord, help me hold the reins on my temper.*

Composed, she met Wade's gaze, a gaze sparkling with humor. She shot up her chin. If he found this standoff amusing, she'd use the tone reserved for disorderly students. That is, if she consented to speak at all.

"A sum that will benefit your family, I might add." His indigo eyes issued a challenge. "Mrs. Logan won't take kindly to reneging on your word."

"Elizabeth will understand I couldn't possibly share my lunch with a Cummings."

"Is the prospect of joining me for one meal in the comfort of a shade tree that terrible? When your sister's family and five others in town will benefit?"

Her gaze darted to the six empty lots. Wade knew exactly how to manipulate her, had from the beginning, roping her in with his phony interest then discarding her with the malice of a cold-blooded rattler.

Cecil Moore, his knobby hands looped around his red suspenders, edged between them. "You ain't looking none too happy about these here proceedings, Miss Abigail. Reckon you know putting your box up for auction is same as promising to eat with the highest bidder." He jerked a thumb, strap and all, toward her nemesis. "That means Wade here. Don't you worry none. I'll keep an eye peeled. See he treats you proper."

Abigail sighed. What choice did she have? Cecil was right. Hadn't she said much the same to Seth and Paul? That the highest bidder deserved to share Betty Jo's lunch. She'd go through the motions, but wouldn't surrender, wouldn't eat a bite with the enemy.

She thanked Cecil, assuring him she didn't need his protection. Then cheeks burning, she marched past smiling onlookers toward a cluster of trees, Wade bringing up the rear.

Once she reached a shady spot, she removed her hat and gloves, an attempt to cool herself and her temper. While he tossed his hat aside and sat leaning against the tree, one booted foot stretching within inches of her skirts. She unwrapped the lunch, laying out the contents on the checkered cloth, ignoring, or trying to, his long-legged presence. With trembling fingers she loaded his plate then shoved it into his hand.

"Thanks. Looks delicious." He had the audacity to pat the spot beside him. "Join me." He scooted over, as if she'd consent.

"You'll enjoy your own company far better than mine."

"You underestimate yourself." He laid his plate aside, rose and filled the other, then handed it to her. "I insist." That stubborn look in his eye said he wouldn't tolerate refusal.

Glaring at him, she accepted the food and then sat on the far side of the checkered cloth, as if that scrap of material could provide a barrier between them.

"I hope you get indigestion," she said, ramming a fork into the mound of potato salad on her plate.

He chuckled. "You've changed."

The accusation scorched her cheeks. If she had changed, the fault could be laid at Cummings's feet. "Why would you bid on *my* lunch when half a dozen young ladies would've swooned over the privilege of dining with New Harmony's most eligible bachelor?" She'd laced her tone with sarcasm though her meaning probably had bounced off his inflated ego.

The corners of his mouth slanted up. "Maybe I wanted to save you from that timid beau of yours."

"Leon is not my beau." She shot him a blistering look, surely hot enough to ignite green, water-soaked timber. He didn't flinch.

"I see him squiring you around town. What do you call him then?"

Why did *timid* ring true?

"It's none of your business."

He munched on the chicken leg then licked his fingers like a mannerless child. Yet the sheer power of those broad shoulders, the length of his legs, the sinewy forearms made it abundantly clear, Wade was no child.

"Delicious," he said then cocked his head, studying her. "I suspect I'm lucky you didn't know you were cooking for me, instead of Mr. Timid."

"You know perfectly well that his name is Leon Fitch. He works for the Cummings State Bank." She arched a brow.

"But you're right about one thing. If I had known you would share my lunch, I'd have been tempted to season the food with a laxative."

Eyes alight with amusement, even approval, he chuckled. The absurdity of her claim even had *her* giggling. "That spunky attitude of yours is exactly why I want to talk to you," he said.

Abigail had no idea what he meant, but whatever Wade Cummings wanted she was having no part of it.

The chuckle died in Wade's throat. Too much hinged on Abby's answer. The resentment he read in her eyes and knew he'd caused socked him in the gut. "To answer your question—I had to bid on your lunch to get you to talk to me."

As he watched, the truth of his words flitted across her face, a most attractive face even dappled with patterns of sunlight and shade. His fingers itched to free her hair, to see her fair tresses cascade over those slender shoulders as they had the day of the school picnic.

Expression wary, she fiddled with a delicate chain she wore. "What on earth would you want to talk to me about?"

This feminine female possessed a forceful attitude—exactly why he required her assistance. "I'm in a bind."

She gave a snort. A flush climbed her neck, no doubt reacting to what she'd see as unladylike behavior. "As if a Cummings doesn't have everything he could possibly desire."

Her erroneous claim gnawed at him. Wade could think of many things in his life he'd like to change, but he merely shrugged. "I'm not the only one in a predicament. To be blunt, your family's mired in trouble."

"Yes, along with five other families. The reason for this fundraiser."

"The fire isn't your only problem. Everyone in town knows Joe's up to his neck in gambling debts."

The sudden flash in her eyes promised she'd support her brother-in-law with her last breath.

"Joe found the Lord and turned his life around. I couldn't be prouder of anyone."

Family loyalty, they were both drowning in it.

"So I heard. But his faith in God hasn't solved his financial mess, has it?"

Her gaze dropped to her hands. "If he had an education, Joe could pay off his debts faster, but all he knows is farming."

"Joe's a hard worker. If he were able-bodied, he'd climb out from under that mountain of debt eventually. But he's banged up and unable to work for what…weeks, maybe months? Add the loss of everything in the fire and money's got to be a problem."

Eyes sparking with fresh indignation, she scrambled to her feet. "Do you get some perverse pleasure out of enumerating my family's troubles?"

In an attempt to point out the gravity of her situation, he'd gone too far and ruffled her feathers. Not an approach that would gain her cooperation. "I couldn't be happier that Joe's turned his life around." He laid his plate aside, his appetite gone. "I'm not the villain you make me out to be."

Those crystal-blue eyes hardened until they glittered like multifaceted diamonds. "You and your family have—"

"Does everything have to come back to that?"

Her hands fisted on her hips as she bent toward him. "Pretend you're faultless if you want. Pretend nothing stands between us if you want. Pretend the feud between our families is juvenile if you want. But that doesn't change the truth." She took a deep breath. "I don't care about our relationship. But I do care what your father's done to my family.

Thanks to George Cummings calling our loan we lost our farm, land that had been in my mother's family for two generations." Her voice broke. "Losing the farm destroyed my father."

Abby's allegations gnawed at Wade. His father maintained he'd done nothing illegal, nothing any good banker wouldn't have done. Wade had been at the bank long enough to believe his father spoke the truth, but Abigail saw smart business decisions as treachery. To make things worse, she hadn't forgiven him for breaking off their brief courtship years before.

Whether Abby realized it or not, he'd done her a favor. Not that he could ever explain.

"I'm sorry you lost your farm," he said, "but I can't undo the past. None of us can." Wade plowed a hand through his hair, seeking some way to get past the feud. "Will you sit down and hear me out? Please?"

Her mouth narrowed into an uncompromising line, but then she gave an almost imperceptible nod.

Once she'd plopped down as far from him as she could get, he said, "The night of the fire my father entered a burning house trying to save someone trapped inside."

By the startled look on Abby's face, she was as surprised as he'd been that George Cummings would risk his life trying to save another's. How well did he know his father?

"I assumed he'd been injured fighting the fire."

"Turned out he was mistaken. The house was empty. But during the search, he burned his hands and inhaled smoke that damaged his lungs. He's getting his strength back and dealing with the pain. But he can't feed himself, can't hold a book, can't do anything but stare out the window. The lack of activity is driving him crazy." He let out a sigh. "Along with what little staff we had. Our housekeeper comes once a week but refuses to enter his sickroom. Cora got so upset with his behavior that she left and won't return."

Everyone in town loved the Cummingses' cook, Cora. If she couldn't abide the man after years in his employ, who could?

"So hire a nurse."

"We did. She quit."

"Take care of him yourself."

"I'm overseeing operations at the bank and other holdings in town. He needs more attention than I can give."

"If he wasn't such a—" She sighed. "I'm sorry. The fire and Joe's injuries have me as jittery as a new teacher on the first day of school. What your father did was heroic." She worried her lower lip with her teeth. "Why not ask the Moore brothers? They're footloose."

"My father would prefer a beating over their homilies."

"Pastor Ted might know someone."

"Actually, I have someone in mind."

"Who?"

In her eyes he saw no sign of awareness. She had no idea, even yet, what he wanted.

"I'm looking at her."

Abigail's jaw dropped. Wade wanted her to nurse the man who'd destroyed her father? "That's ridiculous."

"Think about it. School's out until September. You need money to help your sister's family. I've got money to pay you." He leaned toward her. "What do you have to lose?"

Everything. Her family's approval, her sense of loyalty to those she loved, her certainty that working for the Cummings would fuel town gossip—

Shouldn't Wade share the same concern? Why did he want *her* of all people? She couldn't stomach the idea of being in George Cummings's presence and knew he'd feel the same. "I'm the last person your father would want in his sickroom."

"Perhaps, but I know you can handle him. I saw you walk between those hotheads about to throw a fist. From what I've heard, you managed the one-room schoolhouse with students of every age and temperament and tolerated no sass. And you're equally proficient in your classroom at the high school."

Apparently Wade had kept tabs on her. Why not be honest, her ears perked up whenever his name was mentioned. Not that she cared. He wasn't a man she could trust.

"That makes you the perfect companion for my father."

At the prospect of overseeing George Cummings's needs, she gave a derisive laugh. "You can't be serious."

Frustration rode his face. Closing his eyes, he battled for control until his features softened, as if he'd corralled them to do his bidding. Had he counted to ten or higher, as she'd trained herself to do in the classroom?

He met her gaze. "This isn't a joking matter."

Abigail couldn't agree more. Perhaps George Cummings had another side if he'd risked his life looking for a victim of the fire, but he hadn't shown mercy in his business dealings with her father. Losing the farm had destroyed Frank Wilson and impacted all their lives. A day didn't go by without thinking about the penalty the Wilsons paid for George Cummings's greed. Nothing could make her spend time with that heartless man. "I wouldn't look after your father," she said, forcing the words between clenched teeth, "if it was the last job on earth."

Unable to abide Wade's presence a moment longer, she struggled to rise but caught a heel in her hem. He leaped to his feet and strode to her, reaching a hand of assistance, his eyes pleading, as if...

As if he needed her.

She backed away, avoiding his gaze. She wouldn't be needed by a Cummings. Not by the father. Not by the son who'd tossed her aside as if she were unworthy of him. The only explanation for the abrupt, cruel way he'd broken off the relationship.

"Are you sure about that, Abby?"

At the use of such a personal nickname, she jerked up her head, about to take off his. But something in his gaze stopped her. Something dejected, even desperate, as if he believed she held the key to his future.

"Please. It's only for a couple of months, three at the most. You'll get the money you need. And I'll be able to handle the obligations my father's injuries have roped me into." He met her gaze, his eyes soft with understanding. "You and I are in the same boat. We do what we must for the sake of our families."

Was Wade's life as weighted down as hers?

The idea seemed ludicrous. Still…

She glanced toward the table where her sister sat, wrapped in a shawl, barely recovered from delivering her baby, yet selling baked goods, doing what she could to help. Most women would still be confined to bed.

Tears stung the back of Abigail's eyes. Lois had endured years of Joe's gambling, yet lived each day with courage and faith. While steadfastly praying for her husband, she'd headed her family, determined to care for her sons. Now she had to endure the loss of her home, her possessions, along with an injured husband who couldn't work.

With everything they owned destroyed, how would the Lessmans furnish the new house? This job offered a way to equip their home, exactly what Abigail had prayed for.

No matter how badly she wanted to refuse Wade's offer, what choice did she have? She'd do whatever it took to bring a new beginning to her sister's family.

The collar encircling her neck felt like a noose. And Wade Cummings had just tightened the rope.

Wade watched the wheels turn in Abby's pretty head, now bowed as if burdened by the load of responsibility she carried. She'd take the job, no doubt about it, yet the air practically crackled with her resistance. Resistance evolving to assent as she recognized he spoke the truth.

She had no choice.

Not that she liked the decision.

Well, he didn't either. After all the troubles between their families, one of which she laid at his feet, to ask Abby for help hadn't been easy.

Though Wade felt certain she could handle his father, he had another reason why he wanted her to take the job. A reason he'd never explain to her, to anyone.

Nothing George said or did could make Abby's bad opinion of his father sink lower. While someone else in the community, someone who held George Cummings in esteem, or at the very least respected his success, might resent his father's bad temper and add fuel to the storm swirling around his family.

Weary from the scandal that started with his mother's desertion, intensified with his father calling the Wilson loan, and pinnacled at Frank Wilson's death, Wade craved peace.

He wanted a new beginning. To be a part of the community, not as a Cummings, but in his own right, to have the satisfaction of crafting beautiful furniture, a dream of his for years. To tell Abigail all that would make him vulnerable, an easy target for the Wilson archery.

She looked up at him, her eyes as chilly as blue-shadowed snow. "I'll do it."

Her expression, her tone, the stiff way she held her body

told him she despised the decision. Yet he knew from the determined slant of her chin that she'd keep her word.

"Thank you," he said, hoping she heard his gratitude.

"My father bad-mouthed George Cummings at every turn. You do know that hiring me will make your father angry."

Frank Wilson had taken pleasure in launching barbed arrows at the Cummingses, hitting their bull's-eye dead center. Anger was the armor Wade's father wore. "Sometimes anger's good for a man."

Her eyes widened, as if surprised by his statement, but then she nodded. "Sometimes anger is good for a woman." She met his gaze boldly, daring him to disagree.

Had it been? Or had the cost of that anger imposed a steep price Abby still paid?

Whatever suffering that anger had brought, the brief time he'd spent with her today proved she wouldn't back away from a fight. No doubt sparks would fly between her and his father.

"With you two in the same ring, I have to wonder who'll be left standing when the bell sounds."

"Comparing us to opponents in a boxing match isn't farfetched." She released a soft sigh. "I suspect we'll go several rounds before we determine the winner."

He smiled at her gumption—and at his victory. He'd achieved what he'd set out to do.

Before he'd gotten the first taste of satisfaction, disquiet took root in his mind. A quick glance at the woman in front of him affirmed the disturbing feeling.

If he wasn't careful, Abigail might ignite something within him. As Cecil had said, a Wilson and Cummings were oil and water. A combination that could go up in flames, creating a blaze he couldn't quench.

She took a step back. Had she sensed that attraction he felt? Alarming her as much as it did him?

"Just what are you paying me?" she said. "Whatever it is, it's not enough. Not nearly enough."

She didn't say why, but it didn't take a genius to guess. Being around him—and his father—demanded a price too high to pay. For the hundredth time, he wondered if his plan made perfect sense or if the venture would blow up in his face.

Chapter Three

In the bedroom she now shared with her mother, Abigail stood before the mirror, putting the finishing touches on her hair, then opened a bureau drawer in search of a handkerchief.

A scrap of pink caught her eye. Without her consent her hand sought the silky band, transporting her back through the years.

To the day Wade had given her the ribbon, a token, he'd said, of affection for his princess.

To the gentle grip of his hand on hers.

To the time when she'd been a frivolous young girl who'd believed in Prince Charming.

As if the satin seared her hand, she dropped it then slammed the drawer shut. On memories that brought a lump to her throat.

Swallowing hard, she pasted a smile on her face and strolled toward the kitchen. Hoping to eat breakfast and leave with no one questioning her plans. She wouldn't tell her family about her job. Not yet. Not when she didn't know if George Cummings would see her fired.

Painted a cheerful robin's-egg blue and bedecked with little-boy drawings partially disguising dingy floorboards, cracked ceilings and chipped sink, the kitchen hummed with activity.

"Good morning," she said, careful to let none of her misgivings about her day creep into her tone.

A chorus of "Morning" drifted back to her.

From the open shelves, Abigail grabbed a bowl, squeezed by her mother at the stove to help herself to the oatmeal, and then opened the icebox. The jug of milk was all but empty. She'd do without.

At the table she sat beside her oldest nephew, Peter, his dark-haired head bowed over his food, his spoon scraping the bowl as he shoveled oatmeal into his mouth.

Ma, her lean frame sheathed in a faded floor-length cotton wrapper, thick braid hanging midway down her back, poured coffee from the enamel pot, then handed a cup to Abigail. "You're dressed early."

Abigail thanked her then took a sip, avoiding her mother's perceptive gaze. "Mmm, coffee's good."

Across the table, his broken leg elevated on a crate, the cast on his arm cradled in a makeshift sling, Joe hunched over his Bible. His flaxen hair still tousled from sleep, his boyish good looks belied his courage. Some would say his audacity that on the night of the fire, he'd dropped his family at the apartment, then had gone back to their burning house to save what he could. Instead he'd tumbled down the stairs, breaking bones.

Joe looked up and shot her a smile. "From the way you're dressed, if I didn't know better, Ab, I'd think school was in session."

"Gracious, I must look a sight most summer mornings."

Grinning, he shook his head. "I'm privileged to be surrounded by three of the prettiest females in New Harmony." But he only had eyes for Lois sitting at his side, holding two-week-old Billy in the crook of her arm.

Fair skin rosy with the compliment, Lois gave her husband a teasing grin. "Me? Wearing this frayed robe, my hair a mass of tangles and puffed up with baby weight? You must need spectacles, Joseph Lessman."

Joe leaned close and kissed Lois square on the lips. "You've never looked more beautiful, wife."

The love between Joe and Lois didn't mean Abigail had forgotten the years her sister's marriage had kept Abigail awake at night. "He's right, you know," she said to Lois. "You look wonderful."

Survivors of his gambling addiction and of the fire, Lois and Joe had learned what was important. God had given them a new start. She prayed nothing would happen to bring them harm.

Her mother glanced at Abigail's bowl. "Are we out of milk?"

"The boys need it."

Lois tucked the blanket around baby Billy's exposed toes. "They've eaten. Help yourself, sis."

"Nursing the baby, you need milk more than I do."

Abigail said a silent prayer then dug into the bowl. When she'd finished, she poured the last of the milk in a glass and took it to Lois. Trailing an index finger down the sleeping baby's velvety cheek, Abigail relived the night when the panic of the fire sent Lois into labor. With Doc tied up caring for the injured, Ma and Abigail delivered this precious baby. An incredible moment Abigail would never forget. "I only heard Billy cry twice last night."

Lois kissed the newborn's forehead. "He's a good baby. At this rate, in a few weeks, he'll be sleeping through the night."

Abigail had barely slept herself, trying to think of a way to help Lois's family and handle the expense of feeding eight mouths that didn't involve working for a Cummings.

But no idea had come.

Huddled close to his mother, four-year-old Donnie sucked his thumb. Something he'd reverted to since the fire. Or perhaps his new baby brother was to blame. Abigail kissed the top of Donnie's fair head. "Love you."

Donnie popped out his thumb. "Luv you, Auntie Abby," he said then stuck his wrinkled thumb between sweet rosebud lips.

She knelt beside six-year-old twins Gary and Sam stretched out on the floor wearing their rumpled nightshirts, playing with metal farm animals. Survivors of Abigail and Lois's childhood, their paint was chipped and worn. "How's the livestock this morning?"

Sam's soft brown eyes twinkled. "Dogs got into the chicken house."

"Oh, no. Did you lose many?"

Though he tried not to smile, a dimple appeared in his cheek. "Six."

"So sorry."

"I'm feeding the cows," Gary said.

"And they appreciate it."

"The chickens didn't die, Aunt Abby," Gary whispered. "Sam made that up."

"Did not!"

"Did so."

She tousled both blond heads. "Making things up is part of the fun, Gary," she said, then carried her bowl toward the sink.

"If you boys are going to be farmers, you'll need to build secure chicken coops so dogs and foxes can't get at them," Joe said.

"When they grow up, I hope they'll further their education, prepare themselves for another line of work."

"Nothing wrong with farming," Joe said in a sharp tone.

"Of course there isn't," Abigail hurried to say. "But we've seen that land can disappear."

Joe harrumphed. "Can't live life expecting the worst."

She hadn't meant to offend her brother-in-law, but when they'd lost the farm, Joe'd lost his job too. His gambling started not long afterward.

At the sink, Ma poured hot water from the teakettle then worked up some suds. "I've been thinking about asking Martha Manning for a job clerking at the Mercantile."

Her mother didn't have the energy to handle a job and oversee her grandchildren. "Lois needs your help with the boys. I'm going to spend the day checking possibilities."

Not exactly the truth, but not a lie either. If she was fired, she'd look for something else.

"I talked to Agnes about waitressing in the café," Lois said. "She doesn't need more help."

"You've no business working with a two-week-old baby," Joe said, his brow furrowed. "I thought I'd ask the Moore brothers if I could clean their house."

Lois shook her head. "How would you handle the work with a broken leg and arm?"

"I'd be slow, sure, but I'd manage."

"To sweep and mop floors? Burn the trash? Wash windows? Doc said to stay off that leg so it can heal."

Eyes bleak, back rigid, Joe closed the Bible then glared at the crutch propped in the corner. "I can't sit idle while bills pile up."

Lois patted her husband's arm. "God will take care of us."

"I know He will."

Abigail wouldn't wait on God to provide. She plopped her straw hat in place, then jabbed the crown with a hatpin.

Peter wrinkled his nose, lightly sprinkled with freckles from time in the sun. "A pile of bills is a bad thing."

The boy had seen that early on.

"Don't worry, son. God created us with an amazing ability to heal. Why, I'm better already. Won't be long till I can race you down the stairs," Joe said.

"I'll beat you, Pa!"

A tingle of gratitude ran through Abigail. *Thank You, God, for healing Joe's broken bones.*

Her breath caught. With that power to heal, how long before George Cummings would no longer need her assistance and she'd lose that income? Even if Joe could work, the Lessmans' needs exceeded his potential earnings.

On the floor Sam and Gary mooed, clucked and baaed at the top of their lungs.

Lois raised a finger to her lips. "We can't hear ourselves think."

"Animals don't know to be quiet, Ma," Gary said.

"In that case, why don't you take them outside?"

"Yes, ma'am." Their smiles revealing missing teeth, the twins scooped up their flocks and herds and plopped them in the box.

"Play on the back steps," Lois reminded them.

Donnie popped his thumb out of his mouth. "I wanna go. Can I, Mama? Can I go too?"

"Sweet lamb, you can't go outside without an adult."

Donnie let out a shriek of protest.

Joe waggled a finger at him. "That's enough, Donald William."

"I want my yard," Donnie wailed, tears welling in his crystal-blue eyes.

With her free arm, Lois scooped her son close. "Shh, you'll make Billy cry," she said, though the baby continued to sleep peacefully. Lois's eyes glistened. "We'll get our yard back, Donnie. House too. In time."

Abigail heard the wobble in her sister's voice. Joe patted Lois's arm. She looked pale, wrung out, no doubt exhausted and concerned about their future. The fire had left them all shaken.

She hoped nothing happened to tempt Joe to return to the poker tables.

God, I don't understand why things have only gotten worse for Joe after turning away from gambling and claiming You Lord of his life.

"I've meant to ask, Ab." Lois's gaze met hers. "Why did Wade Cummings bid on your box lunch yesterday?"

Ethel whirled toward Abigail. "You shared a meal with a Cummings?"

"He won the bid, Ma. I had no choice."

"Isn't that just like that family, using their money to force others to bend to their will."

Joe frowned. "Didn't Leon bid?"

"He went as high as eleven dollars before he stopped." Abigail cleared the table and carried dirty dishes to the sink. "He was probably afraid of losing his job at the bank."

Face flushed, Ma scrubbed the oatmeal pot, sending suds flying. "I wouldn't put it past a Cummings to fire someone for crossing them. Nothing that family does would surprise me."

"Wade jumped the bid to *twenty-five* dollars," Lois said. "No one else in this town has that kind of money."

"Stay away from that man, Abigail. Like father, like son. Wade Cummings will bring you nothing but trouble. Most likely would enjoy it too." Ma took the dishtowel from Abigail's hands. "You'll ruin your nice clothes."

"Not sure God approves of this feud," Joe said, voice low, almost as if he was talking to himself. Since Joe found God and turned his life around, his perspective on everything had changed.

Ethel's wounded expression conveyed her displeasure. "I

can't believe you'd take a Cummings's side, after what they did to Frank."

Joe dropped his gaze. "You know whose side I'm on, Ma."

Changing the subject, Abigail said, "Peter, don't forget to practice your reading. You too, Gary and Sam."

"I'll see that they do." Lois turned to Abigail. "I'll pray you find a job, sis."

Her conscience pinching like ill-fitting shoes, Abigail thanked her sister. "Ma, I may visit Rachel so don't worry if I miss dinner."

No point in telling her family about working for the Cummingses and getting them riled up, when most likely she'd be fired before the day ended.

A shiver slid through her. What had she let herself in for?

Wade rapped on the bedroom door, steeling himself for the confrontation sure to come once his father knew he'd hired a Wilson for his companion.

A cough, then "Who is it?"

"Wade." He waited but heard nothing, then opened the door and entered the bedroom. Spotless, organized with nothing frivolous, nothing personal, not a picture, trinket or toiletry in sight. The decor was stark, shades of brown and black, dismal.

Like the man.

The one exception to the barren room—the ancient hound sprawled at the foot of his father's bed. Lazy, sad-eyed, long ears drooping, attached to his father with a steadfast loyalty Wade admired. With a welcoming wag of his tail, Blue raised his head for the expected scratch behind his ears.

George Cummings, face etched with pain, sat propped up in bed, his white hair blending with the pillowcase, his bandaged hands resting palms up on the sheet.

Wade's gaze settled on those motionless hands. Those

hands normally darted and swooped, punctuating his father's words.

"How was your night?"

His father shrugged.

"You know Doctor Simmons left a bottle of laudanum to help you sleep."

"And end up addicted? No thanks."

At forty-nine, his father was lean, muscular, a man with energy that came from vibrant health. That is until the fire left him with a cough and short of breath. Doc said in time his lungs would heal. How long?

Like every able-bodied man in town, Wade and his father had fought the fire. He hadn't seen George enter a burning house. Not surprising with the thick smoke and the extent of the blaze. With herculean effort they'd been able to save the next block from destruction, not much comfort for those less fortunate.

"Before I leave for the bank, would you like to sit near the window?"

"I can manage." His claim ended on a wheeze. "Question is—can you manage things at the bank?" his father said, his lack of confidence in Wade grating on every nerve.

"I'm taking care of things."

"My son, the craftsman, happiest surrounded by wood shavings and sawdust."

Wade didn't answer, merely held his father's gaze, refusing to rise to the bait. George delighted in starting an argument, as if only then did he feel alive. Yet the knowledge his father held him in disdain bored into Wade's confidence like an oversize auger. He blurted, "A craftsman for a son must grate against the family image you take such pride in."

"I couldn't care less about impressing anyone. Enjoy your little hobby—as long as you have time to handle the Cummings holdings."

Once his father's body healed, Wade would reveal his plan to craft one-of-a-kind furnishings, to turn a pastime into a dream. George would despise the decision. Not that Wade needed approval.

He bit back a sigh. Whether he wanted to admit it or not, underneath he wanted his father's support. Support he'd never give.

George glanced at the clock. "Shouldn't you get going?"

Where was Abigail? "I've hired someone to keep you company. Fetch what you need. Prepare your meals."

"A man would think his daughter could handle that job, but at the first excuse Regina skedaddled. Your sister is cut from the same cloth as her mother."

Wade's stomach twisted. What did it say about a man that his daughter fled his sickroom in tears and refused to return?

What did it say about a man that his wife left him for the stage years before?

His heart stuttered in his chest. What did it say about a woman that she hadn't taken her children with her?

"Please tell me you didn't hire one of the Moore brothers."

"What?" Wade forced his thoughts back to the present as his father's words penetrated his mind. "I didn't."

"Thank you for sparing me that." His father rolled his eyes toward the ceiling. "Nothing could be worse than spending my days listening to their countrified homilies."

The Moore brothers might be rough around the edges, but they were good men who cared about everyone in the community, even someone on the fringe.

Would Abby suit his father's persnickety taste in caregivers?

George studied Wade's face. "What's wrong? You look like you're heading to your own hanging."

Perhaps he was.

How would he manage having Abby in and out of the house day after day? When he'd seen her foil that fight, she'd seemed like the perfect choice, but now—

Now he wondered if her presence would bring more trouble than it solved.

"For Pete's sake, spit it out. Who'd you hire?"

"Abigail Wilson."

"If that's your idea of a joke, I'm not laughing."

Wade met his father's gaze. Their eyes locked. George's filled with comprehension. "You're not kidding."

"No, sir, I'm not. You've already chased off the only nurse in town. Most of the staff has found employment elsewhere. No one is eager for the job—"

"Except someone desperate, someone with a family member up to his eyeballs in debt, and no doubt, like all the Wilsons, blaming me." He chuckled. "Well, well, Frank Wilson's daughter is going to wait on me. That should make life a lot more interesting." He snorted. "She won't last a day."

Wade knew what his father didn't. Abigail Wilson was made of stronger stuff than that.

A coughing fit seized him. As George struggled to catch his breath, Blue scrambled to his feet and waddled to his master's side, then plopped down, draping his head over George's chest.

Wade gave his father a sip of water, then grabbed a towel to mop up dribble that ran down his chin.

"Frank condemned me for calling his loan, yet he signed the papers," George said as soon as he could speak. "Knew what he'd signed too. Trouble with people like Frank Wilson—they don't own up to their responsibility. Lay the blame on others for their own failure."

"No point sullying the name of a dead man."

"He didn't hesitate to besmirch my name. Instead of finding a job to earn money that would've taken care of his family, Wilson did nothing except bad-mouth me, turning public opinion against us, the big, bad Cummingses gobbling up the Wilsons' eighty acres. The Panic of 1893 would've ruined the bank had I not called the Wilson loan and others like it. Everything was legal and within my rights."

"Legal, but was it ethical? You bought the Wilson farm then made a huge profit from selling a part of their land a few months later to the Illinois Central Railroad."

His father glanced at his bandaged hands. "The railroad's interest in the land had nothing to do with calling that loan. Time you understood that this family wouldn't be where we are today if I hadn't paid attention to earnings. If I'd extended charity to those who couldn't pay, I'd have gone down in the same sinking ship."

Countless times his father had drummed into Wade the importance of making tough choices to ensure a profit, emphasizing that the debits and credits on a balance sheet determined if a man lost everything or emerged a winner.

Wade wondered what his father had won.

That fortune he prided himself on accumulating hadn't given him happiness. His father's bad temper kept others at arm's length, even his own family. Valuing money more than human beings made a man hard. So hard that a son couldn't get close.

He hoped Abby fared better.

Chapter Four

Abigail shot up her parasol, angling it against the morning sun then strode up the block, her skirts swishing at her ankles.

The Cummingses' mansion wasn't far in distance, but as far from her life as she could get here in New Harmony. She wouldn't be welcome there.

"Abby! Wait up." Holding on to her hat with one hand, Rachel bustled across the street to Abigail's side. "I'm on my way to look after the Logan children. Elizabeth wants to divvy up the money from yesterday's auction in peace. But, quick, tell me about your lunch with Wade."

"There's nothing to tell, really."

Rachel's eyes glittered with excitement. "Of course there is! Why did he buy your box lunch when you two barely speak?"

"I'll tell if you promise not to try to change my mind."

Rachel lifted her right hand as if taking an oath on the witness stand. "I promise."

By the time Abigail finished the explanation, Rachel's eyes were the size of silver dollars. "What did your mother say about working for a Cummings?"

"She doesn't know." Abigail tightened her grip on her

parasol. "I may be fired before noon. No point in telling my family until I see if I'm keeping the job."

"How can you work for George Cummings after what he did to your father?"

If only she had another way. "I want to help Joe and Lois. The auction should supply the lumber, maybe even the building materials, but nothing else. Right now, neither of them can work."

"You're brave to do this. Everyone in town stands in awe of Mr. Cummings." She gave Abigail's arm a squeeze. "I'll pray for you."

"Thank you. Something tells me I'll need it."

"Stop at my house on the way home. I want to hear all about your day."

As they exchanged a quick hug, Abigail promised she would. Rachel turned toward the parsonage while Abigail moved toward she knew not what. But she had the intelligence and backbone to handle whatever guff George Cummings threw at her.

Outside the Cummings gate, wrought of iron, tall and imposing and all but shouting Keep Out, Abigail gulped, lifting her eyes to the three-story structure looming over her. Brick exterior, wood cornices and brackets supported the eaves. A boxy cupola with windows rose above the roof, a watchtower of sorts.

Abigail had never been inside the mansion, for surely no other word described this commanding house. Yet nothing about the structure was pretentious. The house reflected George Cummings, a man with the money to build a solid house that never let down its guard. Never let others near.

She unlatched the gate that swung open on well-oiled hinges, then refastened it and marched up the lane circling the front of the house. At the top of the porch steps, she ran a gloved hand along the iron rail. The letter *C* had been carved into the lower panel of the solid oak door. Above the entrance, the transom's stained glass sparkled in the morning sun.

Everything was in perfect condition. Unlike the apartment they rented from the man. Obviously the Cummings put their money where they would benefit.

To build and maintain this grand house required a great deal of money. Some of that money had come at her family's expense. How did the man sleep at night?

Since moving to town as a child, Abigail had attended the same church as George Cummings, walked the same streets, yet she'd never exchanged more than two words with the financier.

Now she would be his paid companion.

If not so appalling, the idea would be laughable.

Yet the money she'd earn would help her sister's family furnish their home and purchase clothing. No laughing matter. Perhaps even help pay some of the gambling debts crippling them.

Lord, I need this job. Give me courage.

She'd handled bullies before, at least of the school-age variety. She hoped George Cummings was up to her presence.

Pulling in a deep breath, she lifted the lion's-head knocker and dropped it against the metal plate.

The door opened, putting her opposite of Wade. At the sight of him, her heart scampered then tumbled. In a tailored black suit with vest, a tie matching his indigo eyes, he looked leaner, taller and more broad shouldered than the day before.

From his attire, Abigail assumed Wade was on his way out, probably headed to the bank. Nothing could please her more. The less time she spent around the rogue the better.

So why was a bevy of butterflies dancing low in her belly?

His dark gaze swept over her hat, gloves, the simple skirt and frilly high-necked blouse she wore in the classroom. The intensity of his regard rippled through her. Her attire wouldn't compare to the fancy garb of the female students at Harvard.

Not that she cared.

He stood staring at her, as if transfixed. "Good morning, Abby," he said finally.

Abby was what he'd called her during the days she'd hung on his every word, memorized his every gesture. She couldn't abide hearing the pet name on his lips. "I prefer Abigail."

He opened his mouth but then clamped it shut and stepped aside to let her enter. "Right this way, Abigail."

She hadn't missed his displeasure, but gave no sign of noticing.

With a no-nonsense nod, she stepped into a marble entry and a world like no other. More reception hall than foyer, a huge marble fireplace dominated the room. A thick wool rug, silent and soft underfoot, covered gleaming parquet floors bordered with a braided design in darker wood. Imagine the craftsmanship needed to produce the intricate inlay. And the cost.

In the apartment over the bank, planks sagged and squeaked. Gaps between boards collected dust. Over the years Ma had braided scraps of fabric and sewn them together into colorful rugs. She'd quilted coverings for the beds, knitted an afghan for the sofa—done what she could to make the rooms cozier. Last summer Abigail had put a fresh coat of paint on all the walls.

Their apartment wasn't stylish, but not all that different from Rachel's home.

But this…

At her sides, Abigail's hands trembled. Her family had lost everything. The Cummingses lived like kings.

A crystal chandelier glittered overhead, lit even on this sunny morning. Sconces added to the ambience, throwing patterns of light on the walls. At home, kerosene lamps enabled them to read the newspaper or stitch a hem but would never illuminate this enormous space. Nor leave a ceiling free of traces of soot.

Lace curtains covered the large curved window on the landing of a grand staircase. Suddenly aware Wade was watching her, her face heated. She'd been standing there, mouth gaping like a kid at a candy counter.

The money used to furnish this house could've helped those in need. Those who'd lost everything in the fire. When had George Cummings given a dime to help anyone?

As she followed Wade to the stairs and climbed, they passed bucolic landscapes painted in oils, prints of ships sailing the high seas, watercolors of botanicals—all in gilt frames hanging from the picture rail by dainty chains.

Few pictures adorned their apartment walls—an image of their family taken by a traveling photographer mere months before Papa died, a sampler Grandma Wilson stitched as a young woman, a Currier & Ives print of a steam-driven paddleboat.

This house made Abigail feel small, out of her depth, flailing for footing in a world so unlike her own.

No wonder Wade had broken off their relationship. He'd understood what she hadn't…until now.

She didn't fit in his world.

Well, she might not have much in material things but she had a good mind and an education enabling her to provide for her family at no one's expense.

Lord, I've never cared that much about material things.

Yet this grandeur hurts. Forgive me for my anger and jealousy.

Aware that Wade waited for her, she hurried up the stairs. Even on the second floor, pictures and furnishings lined the walls. An elegant mahogany highboy, rose damask loveseat with tufted back, tiger maple sideboard flanked by carved armchairs. Why, more furniture graced this wide corridor than they had in their entire apartment.

She followed Wade to the far end of the hall. Wade knocked then opened the door into an enormous paneled bedroom. She looked in on the man himself as he sat in a wheelchair in front of the window, his back to them.

No drapes graced the windows. The dark walls were void of artwork and knickknacks, and heavy furniture, grand in scale, made the room intimidating.

"Dad, Miss Abigail is here."

George Cummings said nothing, not even acknowledging his son's presence. Yet she knew he'd heard, could feel his intensity, see it in his rigid posture. She clenched her trembling hands in front of her and threw back her shoulders.

A hound lay stretched in a patch of sunshine, emitting a loud yawn that ended on a squawk, either too tired or too indifferent to investigate a newcomer.

"Well, I'm off to the bank." Wade turned to her, his eyes remote. As their gazes held, she saw something else, an apology, perhaps. Or some hurt that never went away.

Abigail thought of her family. They might not have a grand house but laughter and chatter filled their rooms. Yes, an occasional disagreement too, but she'd never experienced the stilted impasse that she felt between Wade and his father. What had happened to put that wall of animosity between them?

"The kitchen is stocked with whatever you might need to prepare lunch and dinner for you and Dad."

That Cora had quit and Wade's sister Regina refused to oversee her father's recuperation didn't bode well for Abigail's day.

"Don't hesitate to summon Doc Simmons if my father's breathing alarms you."

"I'm sure we'll be fine."

"Ah, she speaks" came from the chair, as it whirled on casters and she faced the man who had destroyed her father.

Handsome, with a full head of snow-white hair and a commanding bearing, George Cummings watched her as if seeing her for the first time. The fire in his eyes, eyes the exact color of his son's, promised trouble. She had an urge to look away, yet held his gaze. Never show a bully you're intimidated.

Closer inspection revealed lines of pain etched in his face. A prickle of sympathy ran through her. A man who'd run a bank and a host of businesses must be frustrated at finding himself an invalid. Frustration he took out on others. Her stomach lurched. And no doubt would on her.

Wade glanced at his father. "I'll check on you at lunch."

"Don't bother. You've done quite enough."

Nothing in Wade's father's derisive tone held affection. Abigail had been raised on the importance of family. How could he speak that way to his son, especially in front of a Wilson?

Her hand found the chain at her neck as images flitted through her mind—her father bouncing her on his knee, giving her piggyback rides, playfully tugging on her braids. The father she'd adored. He'd called her his baby girl. Before he'd faded away, becoming a shadow of his former self, a man who'd barely functioned.

This man had caused that change in her father.

Wade motioned for her to follow then led her into the hall.

"Except for the housekeeper coming in on Fridays, you're alone in the house."

Even good wages weren't enough incentive for his staff to remain on the job. Was his bad-tempered demeanor a façade meant to hold others away? Including his son? If so, why?

"I'll stop in at noon." Wade's forehead creased as if he worried about her survival. "Make sure you're okay."

"It might help if you didn't."

His frown vanished, replaced by a stiff smile. "As you wish."

Without a backward glance he strode off, leaving her to deal with his father alone.

If not for Lois and Joe's desperate need for a new beginning, no amount of money would make her deal with George Cummings.

Yet as much as the man had ruined her father's life and his presence reminded her of all the suffering he'd brought her family, she'd earn her wage. Make him as comfortable as she could, help him pass the time, prepare his meals. Work as if working for the Lord.

She breathed a quick prayer for strength and stepped into the room.

Mr. Cummings observed her with shrewd eyes, evaluating her as he would a business rival. "My son picked a puny gal to handle his old man."

"God chose a shepherd boy to handle Goliath."

He snorted. "You think highly of yourself, young lady, but just so you know, I'm not about to lose."

"This is a sickroom, not a battlefield." She leaned toward him. "But just so you know, I'm not in the habit of losing."

"Well, that's about to change." He gave a cold smile. "You're fired, Miss Wilson."

She planted her hands on her hips. "The only person who can fire me is the person who hired me."

"This is my house. I'm ordering you to leave."

"In good time, but for now, you'll have to put up with me."

He shot up, sending the chair careening against the wall and him into a fit of coughing. As he gasped for air, his face turned blotchy, then purple.

Abigail rushed to his side on limbs hot with panic. His hound dog beat her there, stationing himself at his owner's feet, whining as if his heart would break.

Unsure what to do, Abigail pounded on his back with her fist then steered him to the open window, praying the breeze enabled him to catch his breath. Finally the coughing eased then stopped, leaving an eerie quiet almost as unnerving.

With shaking hands she filled a glass with water and held it to his lips. He drank deeply, then dropped into the wheelchair she'd shoved near, leaning back, eyes closed, appearing exhausted. Yet the tone of his skin looked good.

"Are you okay?"

"For a schoolmarm you ask stupid questions," he ground out. "You're trying to kill me with that sassy tongue."

"Your temper is to blame for that coughing spell, not me."

"I suppose you'd point the finger at a man for dying, too."

"You might faint from coughing, but you won't die." At least she'd never heard of such a thing, but she'd ask Doc Simmons to be certain.

"In that case, I may keep you on merely to relieve the monotony. But don't get the idea you're a giant-slayer."

"Whatever you say," she said with enough sweetness to make sour cherries appetizing.

He frowned. Obviously disappointed she hadn't gone on the attack. Not an auspicious beginning. She might need to get a slingshot and start practicing. If she hoped to keep this job, she had to gain George Cummings's respect. That meant giving him a dose of his own medicine. She wouldn't allow an aging, ailing Goliath to ride roughshod over her.

Chapter Five

Silence greeted Wade as he opened the front door and entered the entrance hall. Smiling, he removed his suit jacket and hat and tossed them on a chair. Apparently God had answered his prayers for a truce between Abby and his father. Or did the eerie quiet mean they'd knocked each other out cold? He grimaced. A joke, but somehow not that funny.

The entire day he'd struggled to concentrate, wondering how Abigail was getting along with his father, not an easy man anytime, but especially now. He'd left the bank early. Early enough that he hoped to find time to work in his shop before Abby left for the day.

But first he'd see how she'd managed. He took the steps two at a time and strode down the hall toward his father's room.

Abby appeared in the doorway. Only then did he admit he hadn't expected her to last the day. Feared his father would kick her out or she'd make a run for it.

This woman had grit as he'd predicted. But what toll had a day with his father taken on her?

She held a forefinger to her lips then moved toward him. He took in the spring of her step, the tilt of her chin. She didn't look worse for wear. Her regal beauty surpassed the splendor of her surroundings. That Abby graced his home socked him in the gut. Five years earlier he'd pictured her here, but held no such delusions now.

"Your father's napping," she said when she reached him.

Upon closer inspection he noted the weariness in her soft blue eyes, as if spending time with his father had sapped her energy and strained every nerve. As he'd assumed, her day hadn't been an easy one.

"Pain has kept him from sleeping well."

"Perhaps that explains some of his crankiness."

What did a man say to that? No, cranky is the norm?

"To get his mind off his troubles, I offered to read several books from your library, but he had no interest. I persevered and selected *The Red Badge of Courage*. I'd read only a few pages when he fell asleep." The corners of her lips turned up but the smile didn't reach her eyes. "I suspect he prefers doing battle himself rather than listening to a fictional account."

"Dad thrives on verbal sparring and relaxes with balance sheets. Fiction holds little appeal for him."

"I can't imagine life without novels."

Evidently she appreciated a good book as much as he prized a fine piece of wood. "I suspect most teachers would concur."

Her eyes lit with the glow of an activist. "Books open us to adventure, revealing a host of ideas and cultures to explore, bringing romance—" She cut herself off, pink tingeing her cheeks. "I thought reading might enlarge your father's interests." She sighed, the sound laden with frustration. "He's like some of my bullheaded students who don't welcome my efforts to expand their minds and aspirations."

"He does share the traits of a stubborn adolescent." He grinned. "Find a way to mature him and I'll increase your pay."

An infectious twinkle danced in her eyes, as if they shared a private joke. "I'll work on that," she promised with a giggle.

Imagine, someone who wasn't intimidated by George Cummings.

"I suspect my father is too set in his ways to change, but hopefully your students can."

"If only they could understand that education is the path to a good life."

Education had merely postponed his plans. But for some, education opened the door to opportunities.

Clearly Abby cared about her students' futures and took an interest in all facets of their lives. "They're lucky to have you," he said and meant every word. A startled look flitted across her face. Not surprising with their history. "My father is fortunate too."

She shook her head. "He wouldn't agree."

"You're not planning on quitting, are you?" he said in a rush of words.

"I never run from a commitment."

Despite her claim, she hadn't met his gaze. Would she keep the job? The prospect of not seeing her each day slammed into him. Absurd. His concern about her quitting had to do with his father.

She glanced down the hall. "I'd better check on him."

Well, at least she'd last the day. He removed his pocket watch from his vest. With a touch of a finger, sprang the lid. "Would you mind if I head out to the carriage house? I'd like to work in my shop."

"As we agreed, I'm here until six." She raised a slender brow and nailed him with a steely stare. "Not a minute more."

"Yes, ma'am," he said, feigning a salute.

Carrying her grin with him, he trotted down the stairs

then made his way to the workshop built onto the back of the carriage house. The prospect of returning to his passion after a two-week absence lightened his steps. Without a piece of wood under his palms he'd felt less somehow, not whole.

He left the door ajar to catch the afternoon breeze and walked inside. In this shop he felt at peace, in charge of his realm. His gaze roamed the tools of his trade—hammers, miter boxes, levels, a host of planes and saws, his lathe, emery cloth, sandpaper, everything spotless and in its place. A broom rested in the corner, ready to sweep up sawdust and shavings, anything that might mar a damp finish.

As a young boy he'd watched Grandpa Brooks's rheumy eyes shine as he'd talked about the satiny feel of polished wood under his palms. Something Wade understood.

Surrounded by the scent of wood, he donned the leather apron and reached for fine grit sandpaper. With each stroke, the last bit of tension eased from his neck and shoulders cramped from hours hunched over paperwork on his desk.

As he ran the sandpaper along the grain, he admired the beauty, the solid strength of the cherry buffet. A piece that would give years of service—could be passed down through the future owner's family, a treasured heirloom.

Once his father got back on his feet, Wade would create furniture full-time. The empty warehouse they owned off Main Street would be a perfect location for his cabinetmaker shop. Soon he'd produce functional unique pieces.

Everything would be perfect except—

He had no one to share his dream with.

His thoughts flitted to Abigail but he quickly tamped down the notion of sharing his life with her. He'd seen how a dream could evolve into a nightmare. Surely his parents had once been united in their goals. What had happened to destroy the accord of earlier days?

A knock on the door frame startled Wade out of his reverie. Seth Collier stood on the threshold.

Wade smiled. "Afternoon, Seth."

In need of a haircut, the hem of his pants barely reaching his ankles, his shirt rumpled, the lad could use a mother's touch. Yet shabbily clad or not, Seth carried himself with a dignity Wade found remarkable considering the boy's upbringing.

"I could use a break. Want to take over?"

A fierce longing crossed Seth's face. "You sure?"

"You've sanded enough boards to handle this buffet. You know where to find the emery cloth."

"Yes, sir." Seth moved toward the supply cabinet, a smile softening his angular face.

"The Johnsons have selected this piece for a wedding gift for their daughter. Once the finish is smooth I'll apply the last coat of varnish."

Seth bent to the job. He had a light touch. A gentle way with the wood, as if he found contentment reshaping boards into a thing of function and beauty.

In that, Seth Collier reminded Wade of himself. But the comparison ended there. Seth lived with burdens Wade could only imagine. "How's your dad?"

The boy's hand slowed. "Tolerable."

Giving way more information than he probably intended, the response twisted in Wade's gut. Seth never complained, but in the months he'd been coming by the shop, Wade had pieced together a picture of his life. A boy without a mother, though Seth's had died, not deserted her family as Wade's had. More often than not Seth's father lived in a moonshine-induced haze, leaving cooking, chores and the responsibility for eking out a meager existence on their farm to his seventeen-year-old son.

Compared to Seth Collier, Wade had lived a life of ease.

He tried to relieve some of the financial burden by paying Seth for his help in the shop, but Wade wanted to do more.

Knowing what to do was the difficulty. Rafe Collier wouldn't take a handout, would as soon turn a shotgun on anyone coming on his property to—as he saw it—interfere with how he raised his son. While in reality Seth raised himself.

"Want me to talk to your father?"

"No, sir."

An uncomfortable quiet settled between them.

"I've been thinking—we could use a stable hand. The pay is good." He studied Seth's face. "The job would mean living above the carriage house."

Seth shook his head. "Can't leave my pa."

Loyal to his father—a man who barely functioned and surely didn't appreciate what he had in this boy. "The offer stands if you change your mind."

Seth straightened and met Wade's gaze. "Would you make me your apprentice? Teach me to be a cabinetmaker?" Words poured out of the boy with the force of an underground spring. "I know I'm asking a lot since I've got no money to pay you."

At the prospect of teaching Seth the trade, of sharing what he'd learned with someone captivated with woodworking, a spark of excitement took hold of Wade. What better way to help the boy?

"That's a great idea. I plan to open a shop. Not a factory per se since no two pieces would be alike. I'd create the design and handle detailed work like inlays, veneers and carving. I'd teach you to handle basic construction and finishes. Then later you could try your hand at more intricate work." His voice rose with excitement. "You'd be a big help. I'd pay you."

A wide smile took over Seth's face. "I'll be your first employee. I'll quit school. Work full-time—"

"What gibberish are you planting in this boy's head?" Abby stood in the open door, eyes steely, cold and turned on Wade. "Hasn't your family destroyed enough lives?" Her fisted hands tangled in her skirts as if the fabric were the neck of a chicken about to be wrung. "I won't let you destroy Seth's."

Heat sizzled through Wade's veins. A Wilson couldn't have a rational reaction to any idea stamped with a Cummings's approval. "How can you accuse me of trying to harm this boy?"

Eyes downcast, Seth dropped the emery cloth and stepped away from the buffet. "I need to get home," he mumbled then sped past his teacher.

As soon as he fled the shop, Abigail reeled on Wade. "Now look what you've done!"

"Look at what *I've* done? You're the one upsetting that boy with that ridiculous claim I'm trying to harm him." Wade's long strides swallowed the distance between them. He stopped mere inches from her skirts, catching the scent of roses, feminine, delicate—at odds with this strong-minded female. "Anyone can plainly see I'm trying to help him."

"By suggesting he quit school?"

"That's his idea, not mine. I don't condone—"

"Surely you can see this apprenticeship would be a mistake."

"Mistake? To learn a trade with good pay and a promising future? Hardly." He folded his arms across his chest and glared at her.

Slapping hands on hips, she leaned closer until they were inches apart. He'd never noticed the little flecks of gray in her eyes before. Gunmetal gray. Shooting him down. Or trying to.

"You're luring one of my best students away from getting his high school diploma and a chance for higher education."

"I'm doing no such thing. Seth helps out after school a few afternoons a week. He's shown the interest and aptitude of a craftsman."

"With your family's wealth behind you, you can risk a new venture. But Seth has no resources to ensure his future other than an excellent mind. I won't let you waste his potential."

Wade's pulse hammered in his temples to an unrelenting beat. "Are you insinuating woodworking is squandering one's intelligence?"

She glanced away. "Well, no, but Seth's really smart. Capable of much more than—"

"Than what?" Wade tried to tamp down the frustration roiling inside him and failed. "Working with his hands!" He raised his palms. "Do these calluses disgust you? Are you so biased toward education you have no respect for physical labor? No respect for a skilled craftsman?"

She stood mute, face flushed, eyes shimmering like sparklers on the Fourth of July. She'd never been more infuriating. Or looked more beautiful.

Every drop of his anger evaporated, leaving him with a sudden insight he couldn't stomach. This woman he'd cared about, this lovely, intelligent, capable woman was…exactly like his father. "Well, God has given some of us the desire—the gift—to create something beautiful, yet functional."

"You can't see the forest for the trees. No one job can provide security. I can't imagine what would have become of my family if a teacher hadn't encouraged me to pursue higher education. Seth needs to get out of that house. College will prepare him for whatever the future brings."

"Attending college isn't a solution for Seth. He needs to make money, not put his life on hold while he gets a degree."

"That he needs money is Rafe's fault. Once Seth escapes his father's influence, he'll make a good life for himself. Iowa State College of Agriculture and Mechanic Arts trains students in engineering, veterinary medicine. The University of Iowa provides instruction for lawyers, doctors—many professions."

"How do you suggest Seth pay college expenses?"

"Well, he couldn't go to Harvard like you did," she sputtered, "but state residents don't pay tuition."

"What about money for clothing, travel home and textbooks?"

"He can work in the summer as I did. If money's available to help students from impoverished families, I'll find it."

"Have you chosen his wife?"

Her nostrils flared. "What are you talking about?"

"Appears to me you've laid out Seth's entire life. Might as well pick his bride."

Splotches of red stained her cheeks. "I've done no such thing. I just want to do what's best for Seth."

"You think you know that boy and what's best for him. Seth loves working with wood as much as I do."

A look of disdain flashed across her face, quickly controlled but unmistakable, as exasperating as an account that wouldn't balance.

Every muscle in Wade's body tensed. "Not just anyone can make the kind of furniture you see in this shop." He swept his arm around the room. "The quality of my work takes practice, patience and respect for wood."

Her gaze traveled the buffet, the highboy, the table and chairs. "Your furniture is beautiful, but Seth is bright—"

"What does that make me?" Wade ground out between clenched teeth.

She took a step back. "I, ah…I don't mean to be insulting. Obviously you're intelligent. You graduated from Harvard, one of the finest colleges in the country. The very reason I'd think you'd understand my position. Education is the best assurance of happiness in this life."

"Are you happy, Abby?"

A flicker of unease dimmed her eyes. "I'm concerned for Lois's family but I'm content."

Whether she admitted it or not, Abby was far from happy. She served the community at church and in the classroom, she took care of her family, did all she could to make the lives of others better—even to the point of meddling—but inside she had a hollow spot that needed filling.

He ought to know. He had the same.

With a gust of air, he exhaled, releasing his frustration or trying to. "You mean well, but you don't know Seth Collier—at all."

"I saw Seth every day in English class. And you see him, what? A couple times a week?"

"What I know didn't take long to understand. Seth won't leave his father to go off to college somewhere."

"We'll see about that. But first, he needs to finish high school. Surely you agree about the importance of that diploma."

"Of course, Seth should finish school. Today's the first I'd heard of his plan to quit."

"Why not admit you're using Seth?"

She'd gone too far. Wade jabbed an index finger her way. "I'd never use that boy. I pay a wage for the work he does. I can't pay much until I get the shop off the ground, but I'd never take advantage of him. Of anyone."

The cold chill of her eyes slithered through him. That

chill told him she believed he'd taken advantage of her. Toyed with her affection. That's what this was really about. What defense could he give without hurting her more?

She took a step back. "You're using Seth to accomplish what you can't do alone. Well, this time you Cummingses won't win."

She whirled toward the door. Before she crossed the threshold she looked back at him, eyes issuing a challenge. "I'll see that Seth gets a college education if it's the last thing I do."

Wade wouldn't allow Abby to force her will on that boy. "If that's not what Seth wants, then it looks like we're going to be butting heads." He motioned to the hat she wore. "I hope that chapeau of yours is lined with steel."

"I plan on using my brain, not brawn. You might want to give that a try," she said, smiling sweetly. Then with that last jab to his pride, she flounced out the door.

Leaving him to grapple with the truth. Abby wanted to save Seth from the fate of being just like him. That she held him and his dream in contempt knotted in Wade's stomach.

No matter what she thought of him, how little she held him and his vocation in esteem, Abigail Wilson would soon learn she'd thrown down the gauntlet to exactly the wrong man.

Chapter Six

Abigail stalked off the Cummings property, every muscle in her body rigid. To deal with George Cummings was bad enough. He'd ruined her father, killing him as surely as if he'd driven a stake through his heart.

But to learn Wade tried to tie Seth, her most promising student, to the youngster's hand-to-mouth existence lit the wick of temper lurking inside her.

How could Wade take advantage of a boy struggling for the necessities of life?

She could understand that Seth would see an apprenticeship as a solution to his problems. That thinking was shortsighted. How likely was it that Wade's new venture would succeed? Few people in town could afford expensive furniture. Seth would abandon a high school education for a risky undertaking, losing the chance to attend college.

Heat slid through her veins. She wouldn't allow such foolishness. Yet what could she do to stop it?

Talking to Seth's father, a loner who never allowed anyone on his property, was impossible. She'd talk to Seth. But what if the boy wouldn't listen? He'd shown no sign of wanting to hear her out. Instead he'd dashed out of the shop, avoiding her eyes, avoiding her guidance. As much as she wanted to track Seth down and convince him that she had his true welfare at heart, he'd probably gone home. She couldn't do anything tonight.

With everything bottled up inside, if Abigail didn't talk to someone, she'd explode. Her family would take her side but even admitting she'd spent a single day under the Cummingses' roof would open wounds.

The Fisher house came into view. This morning, Abigail had promised to stop at Rachel's. Her best friend would understand.

At Abigail's knock, Rachel opened the door, a welcoming smile on her face. "I thought you'd never get here." Mouthwatering aromas from the kitchen permeated the house, pulling Abigail in as surely as her friend's tugging hands. "Can you stay for supper? Papa's already eaten and off framing houses."

Was he working on Lois's house? After a hard day at work, Mr. Fisher had to be tired. Once her father had lost the farm, he hadn't possessed the energy to come to the table much less help someone in need. "You've got a great dad, Rachel."

Nodding, Rachel smiled. "Please say you'll stay."

That morning, Abigail had mentioned she planned to stop at Rachel's. Her mother wouldn't worry. "I'd love to."

As they walked to the kitchen, they passed the homey parlor Abigail could describe with her eyes closed. Not one knickknack or furnishing had been changed since Lily Fisher's death.

The kitchen's butter-yellow walls, white curtains, oak icebox, table and cupboards invited visitors to linger. A bone china teapot, a reminder of Rachel's mother's English ancestry, presided over the round oak table. Her bibbed floral apron hung on a hook, an apron Rachel had grown into.

At nine years of age, Rachel had lost her mother to cancer.

Abigail had lost her father at nineteen. In reality she'd lost him the year she turned thirteen and they were forced off the farm. Pa grew morose and kept to his room. Ma was hired on at the canning factory and came home exhausted. Abby and Lois did what they could to make life easier for their mother. And tried to keep their voices down so as not to disturb their pa.

One good thing came from that difficult time. She and Rachel became inseparable. Both knew the heartache of losing a parent. Both dealt with realities forcing them to grow up fast. Rachel became the family homemaker and Abigail became the family breadwinner. If sometimes those roles pinched like too-tight shoes, they shared the strain with each other, shielding the surviving parent from their struggles.

As Rachel bustled around the kitchen, setting out two glasses and filling them with milk, she rattled off one question after another. "What's the inside of the Cummingses' house like? How did Mr. Cummings treat you? I want to hear everything about your first day."

"Maybe my last." Speaking the words aloud surprised Abigail as much as they appeared to shock Rachel.

Eyes wide, Rachel plunked the glasses on the table, splashing milk. "Really? What happened?"

As familiar with Rachel's kitchen as her own, Abigail laid out silverware and napkins. "I got lulled into joining forces with my adversary. I should've known nothing good would come from that alliance."

Still as much as she longed to quit the job, she couldn't lose the chance to help Lois and risk running up bills at the grocer. Feeding a houseful of boys took money.

Rachel's brow furrowed. "Was Mr. Cummings cruel?"

"Not cruel. Short-tempered, but I managed to hold my own with him."

"Then why would you want to quit?"

How could she explain? Gathering her thoughts, Abigail dropped into a chair and sipped from her glass. "After what they did to my father, seeing the rich life the Cummings enjoy—" Her voice broke and she took a steadying breath, fingering the chain around her neck. "The grandeur of that house compared to our apartment—an apartment we rent from *them*—stung like vinegar on a gash."

"That doesn't seem fair."

"We both know life isn't fair. But seeing that house brought back Pa's despair." She swallowed hard, fighting the tears that threatened.

Rachel set in front of her a plate of chicken and dumplings, mashed potatoes oozing butter and fresh-shelled peas. The enticing aroma elicited a rumble from her stomach.

Rachel laid a gentle hand on Abigail's shoulder. "I'm sorry," she said, then crossed to her seat and offered a prayer, thanking God for the food and asking for wisdom for Abigail.

After the emotional ups and downs of her day, Abigail was surprised by the intensity of her hunger. "Everything's delicious."

"Papa still tells me how grateful he is that I took over the cooking." Rachel snickered. "Remember how he used to burn everything? I had to learn to cook or starve."

Abigail grimaced. "I can still see his fried chicken, burnt skin on the outside. Pink inside."

"Many a night we filled up on bread and butter." The humor in Rachel's eyes dimmed. "I miss Mama." She reached out and caressed the teapot with gentle fingers, as if the delicate china somehow connected her to Lily. The wistful expression on her face tore at Abigail.

She laid her hand on Rachel's wrist. "I wish I'd known your mom."

"She would've loved you. Been proud of who you are."

"Not the way I'm feeling today." Abigail sighed. "God is probably unhappy with me too. No matter how much I pray to live as Scripture teaches, I don't succeed. Today I let my temper get away from me."

"I understand. Visiting the Cummings house is like rubbing your nose in the mess they've made." Elbows on the table, she plopped her chin on her hands. "Is being around Wade hard?"

If she admitted how hard, Rachel would believe she still cared about Wade. "Wade and I had an argument over Seth Collier's future." She went on to explain what had transpired, including Wade's plans to open a cabinetmaker shop.

"I know you care about Seth, but..." Rachel's brow knotted. "I don't understand what's wrong with him working for Wade."

"He's got one more year of school before he graduates. He's talking about quitting."

"Can't he work for Wade while he's finishing high school?"

"Perhaps, if he wanted to, but the more hours Seth works, the more money he'll make."

"You can't blame him, can you?" Rachel said softly.

"I understand the pressure to make money, but a college education will give him far more potential for a good-paying job." She sighed. "And if that's not enough reason to oppose this plan—an apprenticeship means Seth will stay in New Harmony instead of getting out from under his father's influence."

"Does Wade understand your concerns?"

She harrumphed. "Nothing I said fazed him. He's dangling an apprenticeship under Seth's nose, not because it's good for Seth, but because he needs trained craftsmen." She slapped the table. "Well, if he's determined to use that boy,

Wade Cummings can find another lackey to deal with his cantankerous father—if he can."

Abigail's shoulders slumped. She'd told Wade she kept her commitments. But surely he wouldn't expect her to remain on the job after this standoff.

"If you quit, how will you help Joe and Lois?"

"Something will turn up," Abigail said with a confidence she didn't feel. All previous attempts to find work had failed.

Her conscience twisted the food in her stomach into one huge lump. She pushed her plate away. She couldn't leave Joe and Lois in the lurch when they needed her most.

But how could she keep the job? George Cummings stirred up childhood memories that stung like a swarm of vicious yellow jackets in August.

Worse, Wade's voice, his touch and his scent reawakened memories of tender moments they'd once shared before he'd discarded her like an outdated textbook.

Now he intended to ruin Seth's life.

Well, she wouldn't let him hurt that motherless boy.

As she and Rachel cleaned up the kitchen, an idea took hold that held promise. "Perhaps appealing to Seth's interest in Betty Jo Weaver might make him see that quitting school wouldn't impress her."

"Yeah, but having money to spend on her might."

Abigail sighed. She hadn't thought of that. Poor Seth. She'd talk to the boy before Wade ensnared him in a venture with as much chance for success as Seth's father, Rafe, had of separating himself from a jug of moonshine.

Rachel handed Abigail a glass to dry. "I'm not sure quitting the Cummingses' job is the right thing to do."

"What do you mean?"

"Keeping an eye on the enemy might be a better strategy."

At the prospect of spending endless days at the Cummingses' house, Abigail's throat tightened.

"Especially if that enemy is good-looking, rich and available," Rachel added with a satisfied smirk.

"When will you stop trying to play matchmaker? You of all people should understand I can't trust Wade."

"You were kids. As a teacher you deal with the ups and downs of young love. See firsthand how flighty adolescents can be." She smiled. "I know you, Abby. I can see things in your eyes you don't want to admit, even to yourself."

More memories flitted through Abigail's mind. Of dark blue eyes locking with hers. Of strong calloused hands cradling hers. Of that one stolen kiss that branded her mind as much as her lips.

She sighed. Even five years since he'd hurt her, she remembered everything they'd shared. Wade had been an oasis in a parched season, bringing joy into her life.

Yet look where that had led. To a tear-soaked pillow, a shattered heart and a resolve to never get close to Wade Cummings—or any man—again.

Yet only one day on the job proved he still made her react. Still drew her like metal filings to a magnet. As if she had no will of her own.

"I know I should keep the job but—"

"Abby, you knew the feud and the breakup would be issues. So what's changed? George Cummings isn't responsible for the trouble over Seth and by working there you might help soften the crusty old codger. Something the entire town would appreciate."

Though she wouldn't admit it, Abigail had seen a flicker of something vulnerable in Wade's father. The same wounded expression she'd seen in her father's eyes. Perhaps guilt for past actions destroyed Mr. Cummings's peace. Whether it did or not—and she doubted it—the man suffered from burns and inflamed lungs, the price he'd paid for trying to save another—a heroic act. For that, he deserved a helping hand.

"He must not be all bad," she said with reluctance. "His dog loves him."

Eyes sparkling, Rachel giggled. "Reason enough to keep the job."

The front door banged shut. Mr. Fisher appeared in the kitchen, looking tired but content. He took in their smiling faces. "From that giggling, I'd say you two enjoyed your evening."

"Hi, Mr. Fisher."

"How did things go, Papa?"

"Ten men showed up and worked till dark. The ladies kept the coffee flowing. Wade Cummings helped me nail lath. That young man can work. Keeping up with him tuckered me out." He gave Rachel a one-armed hug. "I'm calling it a night, sweetie. Lock up when Abigail leaves."

"I will. Night, Papa."

With her father out of earshot, Rachel turned to Abigail. "See, Abby? Wade's doing his share to help folks get back on their feet. Not everything a Cummings does is bad."

Abigail shivered. She'd sat in judgment of others. God would not approve. "I suppose not."

She'd come looking for Rachel's support. Instead her friend had questioned the wisdom of quitting the Cummings job. Even praised Wade and commiserated with his father.

Not what she'd wanted to hear.

But as much as Abigail wished she had another option, as much as it went against her principles to work for a Cummings, she didn't have an alternative.

Maybe Rachel was right. Staying near Wade's workshop might be her best chance to influence Seth.

Rachel walked Abigail to the door. "I'll sleep on the decision, but if I keep the job, it's not because I have one iota of interest in Wade Cummings."

"Whatever you say," Rachel said, her tone laced with amusement as if she doubted Abigail's claim. "Sleep tight."

With Rachel's implication churning through her mind, Abigail doubted she'd sleep a wink.

Wade trekked past the carriage house. The sun had risen with shades of pink streaking the eastern sky. Abby's favorite color and the reason he'd bought her that ribbon. His sister had kept dance cards, dried petals and trinkets, every memento her husband had given her. Could Abby still have that scrap of satin? With all that stood between them that was unlikely.

Inside the stable, he inhaled the pungent odor of hay and manure, oddly comforting, and went about the task of feeding and watering the horses. His father—intolerant of the slightest mistake—had fired the groom for some lapse. Wade could've hired someone, but he enjoyed coming out here. Or would, if not for the quarrel with Abigail heavy on his mind.

As he filled Beauty's and Rowdy's feedboxes and water buckets, he admitted the worst part of this squabble—he needed her. To need a woman who looked down her nose at his dream chafed against his pride. Yet, even if Abigail couldn't respect him or his work, how could she believe he'd harm Seth? Had the breakup destroyed everything she'd once seen and valued in him?

With the animals fed and watered, Wade plopped down on a bale of straw to clean tack, a job he'd put off too long.

Across the way, Beauty snuffled oats. Rowdy shoved his water bucket along the straw-strewn planks. A dove cooed from a perch in the rafters above him. All was tranquil. Except him.

If only an ointment existed that would soften him, keep him pliable like this leather, instead of hard and brittle. He wasn't the man he wanted to be. But had no idea how to fix his world. Not with his father, not with the feud, not with Abby.

Finished with the task, he hung the bridle then checked his pocket watch. He had an hour before he had to prepare his dad's breakfast. Time enough to add the last coat to the cherry buffet he'd promised Jim Johnson, a wedding gift for his daughter.

Odd that others appreciated his work, but his father and Abby scoffed at his passion. They'd both eat those words once his furniture was in demand all over the country. Then Abby would see that working with one's hands could bring both financial security and contentment.

In the shop he inspected the work Seth had done. Pleased with the boy's sanding, Wade grabbed a cloth, dampened it with solvent and cleaned the finish.

"Good morning."

Wade jerked up his head and looked into the kind face of Pastor Ted, a brawny, blond giant of a man who appeared better suited to stand behind a plow than a pulpit, but God had called him to preach. Ted had overcome gambling, led Joe to repentance of the same compulsion and never gave up on anyone, including George Cummings.

"I figured I'd find you out here." Ted leaned against the workbench. "How are things going?"

"Dad's hands are healing with no sign of infection." Wade grimaced. "His lungs are about the same."

"How's his heart? Don't mean the organ pumping his blood."

"Can't say his injuries have improved his attitude. I suspect Abby Wilson could use your prayers more than Dad. She's seeing to his needs while I'm at work."

A smile spread across Ted's face. "That may be God's answer to healing the feud."

Wade snorted. Even from an optimistic preacher, those words rang hollow. "The bad blood between the Wilsons and Cummingses is years in the making and merely the beginning of the trouble between Abby and me."

"Mind my asking what the problem is with you two?"

Wade's mind traveled back five years. "The spring of my senior year—Abby's junior year—she got beyond the feud and we got close. For weeks, we spent every moment we could together, talking, taking strolls in the park, sitting in Sunday school." He glanced at Ted. "Always with Rachel as chaperone, but seeing each other wasn't easy. Her family refused to let me come courting."

"I can imagine."

A lot had changed since they'd hung on each other's words, Abby most of all. What had happened to the sweet, tenderhearted girl? His stomach lurched. He'd caused that change in her. "She cared about me and I tromped on her heart."

"What did you do?"

"Sat in a different row in Sunday school, stopped meeting her and Rachel in the park, quit seeing her home from school."

"Why did you pull away?"

Wade hadn't had a choice. He'd ended the courtship to protect Abby, but he'd never tell her the reason. And he sure wouldn't tell Ted. "My father insisted I attend Harvard that fall. To tie Abby to me when I'd be half a continent away didn't seem fair." He looked at his feet. "I was young and stupid." He released a gust of air. "Now she sees me as trouble."

"Trouble pretty well described me and Elizabeth in the first weeks of our marriage. Look at us now. Well, don't look too closely. We have our spats. My wife has strong opinions and an iron will. A man doesn't always know how to react to an independent female. But the Good Lord knew what He was doing when He brought Elizabeth into my life. She's made me a very happy man." He shot Wade a smile that revealed how much he loved his wife. "Take it from me. The right woman can be the last one you'd expect." Ted chuckled. "Elizabeth wasn't even the mail-order bride I sent for."

Wade recalled the switch of brides that had had Ted reeling for weeks and the entire town in an uproar. "I don't doubt God knew the perfect wife for you and sent Elizabeth. But I'm not meant to settle down." His parents' marriage and his mother's abandonment had taught him plenty. He'd rather face a stampeding herd than risk falling in love.

"Don't close yourself off from others. Not from this town. Not from that irritable father of yours. Not from the woman God has in mind for you."

Wade believed closing himself off had saved his sanity. But saying as much would not please the pastor so he said nothing.

"No matter what you plan, Wade, God may not intend for you to go through life alone."

"Are you saying God cares about the details of our lives?"

"Yes, I am." His gaze locked with Wade's. "Don't transfer your dad's aloofness onto the image of our Heavenly Father."

Wade frowned. Had he done that?

"God cares about all of us, even those who don't acknowledge Him. Even those we may feel don't deserve His love. And He's working in our lives. Talk to Him about everything, He wants to hear from you."

With a brisk nod, Wade kept his gaze on the task, rubbing the cloth along the crevices of the buffet. The silence stretched as neither man spoke. "Abby's upset with me for agreeing to teach Seth Collier cabinetmaking," he found himself saying.

"Why? That boy could use a way to earn money."

"She believes Seth should attend college, not apprentice with me."

"Putting the two of you at odds."

Wade huffed. "That's stating it mildly."

"I suspect that's tied to the bad blood between your families. You know, Wade, the feud is contrary to Scripture. We're to love others as Jesus did, no matter how difficult that may be. Or the faith we claim is just so much talk."

A yearning to love and be loved twisted through Wade like a spiraling cyclone. How could he risk such a thing? His parents' marriage proved happiness was unlikely if not impossible. When a marriage ended, children's hearts were broken.

Through the years he'd seen there was more than one way, one path in this life. A man had to find the route he could walk in peace. Some like him were meant to walk that path alone.

He hadn't fought for Abby. Even if he had, she would never accept who he was. He couldn't spend his life with a woman who didn't respect his dream, didn't respect him.

Ted rose and laid a hand on Wade's shoulder. "Never doubt God can change hearts and circumstances. But He expects us to know His word and obey His commands. If we don't, He sometimes uses circumstances to get our attention."

The weight of the pastor's words rested on that gentle hand, nearly driving Wade to his knees. This feud was unacceptable to God. The grudge was sin.

Scriptures ran through his mind verifying he must try to heal the rift between the Cummingses and Wilsons. He may have played no part in starting the feud, but Wade wanted what God wanted. He wanted the enmity to end.

How could he impact the situation for good when Abby didn't trust him? How could he make her understand he had Seth's welfare at heart? That he'd had the same concern for her when he'd broken off their relationship.

Ted gave a gentle smile. "Prayer changes things." He pushed away from the workbench. "Better head to the house to see George."

"Tell him I'll be in to prepare his breakfast as soon as I finish here."

"Will do." Ted strode off, a man on a mission. No doubt hoping he could soften Wade's father. If anyone could do it, Ted Logan and his prayers could.

Hadn't Ted just done much the same with him? In a few words, the pastor had planted a seed that had taken root in Wade's mind. He'd do what he could to heal the feud.

Yet he couldn't keep his support of Seth's dream to himself. Wade had never had anyone to encourage him and had lived with the pain of indifference, even opposition. He would be there for Seth, even if that meant opposing Abby.

Ted had said prayer was the answer. Wade had prayed countless times for others, for his father's health, Cora's back, Joe's healing—a long list. Yet for some reason he didn't understand, he'd held himself aloof from God, not voicing his feelings, his innermost thoughts. Such foolishness when God already knew everything about him. Was he ashamed of needing God, seeing his dependence as weakness?

But the pastor's insinuation that he and Abby might have a future—nothing could be more ludicrous.

She viewed his position with Seth as reason to continue and expand the feud. Odd she didn't understand the boy couldn't leave his father when she had stayed in New Harmony, as he had, out of steadfast loyalty toward family.

That loyalty both connected and divided them. Somehow he had to find a way to strengthen that connection and heal the rift. Though Wade suspected nothing he could do would heal the pain of the breakup.

Wade opened the can of varnish and found his best brush. He applied the last coat to the buffet, letting the finish flow from his brush as he swept it along the grain.

Pleased with the result, Wade hurried to the house. The time had gotten away from him. His father wouldn't be happy to have to wait on breakfast.

For a moment when Ted had talked about Elizabeth and how unlikely their relationship had been, Wade had believed he could have Abby in his life. But the memory of his mother's desertion cooled the flames of that fantasy like cold water drenched glowing embers, leaving behind cold, gray ashes.

He'd do all he could to mend the feud as long as the actions he took didn't involve putting his heart at risk.

Surely God understood a man could only handle so much.

Chapter Seven

Face flushed from the heat of the stove, Ethel whirled toward Abigail, the spoon in her hand splattering oatmeal. "I forbid you to work for that family!"

Abigail grabbed a rag and stooped to wipe up the mess. "We need the money."

"You're always fretting about money. Money isn't everything."

"No, but it pays the bills."

"I can't let you do this. I'll ask the Moore brothers if I can clean their house while Lois is recuperating."

Ma needed less, not more work to do. Saying as much would hurt her pride. "The job at the Cummingses pays far better than Cecil and Oscar will. Besides, Lois needs help with the boys."

"How can you forget what the Cummings did to your pa?" Ma asked, dishing oatmeal into two bowls.

Taking up every inch of space, Gary, Sam and Donnie lay on the floor coloring. Abigail lowered her voice. "I haven't forgotten. Look at my wages as compensation for what he took from us."

"A few dollars doesn't balance losing our farm." Ma's mouth twisted. Blinking away tears, she quickly straightened her shoulders. Wilson women didn't cry. "I can't believe God wants you working for those people."

"I felt the same at first, but now I think it's fitting the Cummingses will help us handle our bills." She motioned toward the table. A column of figures in his hand, Joe sat, head down and shoulders slumped, as if the weight of his debt crushed him.

Ma's gaze darted to her son-in-law. "All right, but if that man does one thing to upset you, promise you'll quit."

No point in sharing George Cummings's cranky disposition. Her mother, a woman who didn't mince words, wouldn't hesitate to march into that house and have it out with the man. "I promise."

Bowls in hand, she and Ma joined Joe at the table.

Joe's dark eyes clouded with misery. "This is my fault."

Abigail shook her head. "We're family. That means we're in this together."

Ma sprinkled sugar over her oatmeal. "You held two jobs before the fire, Joe. You'll do what you can once you heal."

"It's what I did in the past that brought this on." Joe fiddled with the pencil in his hands, twirling it between his fingers, staring at the paper in front of him. "I know God will help me find a way to pay these debts, but right now I can't see how."

Knowing Joe's resolve, he'd figure out a solution. Still, a farmhand didn't bring in much money. If he and Lois had furthered their educations, they'd make a better wage. But with a strong back and an even stronger work ethic, he'd do his best. No one could ask more. Abigail would help all she could.

Her attitude toward her brother-in-law had not always been positive. For seven years, she'd alternated between praying for and resenting Joe. His addiction to gambling had mired his family in debt and deprivation, forcing Lois to take in washing and ironing, to clean the Moore brothers' house, to do every job she could to feed and clothe four growing boys.

Yet as hard as she'd worked, Lois hadn't been too occupied to hear the gossip. Folks didn't blame her for Joe's conduct, but nevertheless Lois had lived with the humiliation of Joe's gambling. Abigail knew how much that had hurt her.

Eleven months ago, Joe repented. From that moment on, as if God Himself had reached down and plucked the desire to gamble from Joe's body, her brother-in-law was a new man.

Joe and Lois not only had survived, their marriage had thrived. Joe had made headway toward paying off his gambling debts when a bolt of lightning had destroyed everything the Lessmans had, including Joe's ability to work.

Why had God allowed this tragedy so soon after Joe had returned to Him and walked a new path?

The only explanation Abigail had came from the book of Job. Life wasn't easy, never had been, not for Job, not for the Wilsons. She didn't know what God had in store for her sister's family. But Abigail dared not question God.

As discouraged as Joe appeared, she feared he'd be tempted to return to gambling. Was this latest calamity some kind of a test? If so, she hoped he'd pass.

Abigail scooped up the last bit of oatmeal then pushed back her chair to rise.

Her mother took her hand. "I'll pray for you today."

"I appreciate that, Ma."

Buoyed by how well Ethel had taken the announcement, Abigail gave her mother a kiss and hurried to the door before she changed her mind and tried to stop her. As she took hold of the knob, her sister entered the kitchen, carrying Billy with Peter at her heels.

"Where are you off to this early, Ab?"

"She's taken a job looking after George Cummings," Joe said.

"What?" A frown puckering her forehead, Lois edged closer. "Does this have something to do with Wade buying your box lunch?"

Why bring that up? "Well, yes. I refused to talk to him. So he had to win the bid to get me to listen to his offer."

"I remember the summer Wade hung around you like a bee in a flower garden." Lois's eyes narrowed. "Is something going on between you two?"

"No! I'm working in that house to help with expenses."

"Are you sure?" Joe frowned. "If I thought for one minute that taking that job could get you hurt—"

"Abigail Wilson, what are you hiding?" Ethel fisted blue-veined hands on her hips. "Your pa forbade Wade to come courting. Did you sneak behind our backs?"

When had Lois become a tattletale? "We sat together in Sunday school. Strolled in the park—nothing that even came close to courting. Rachel was always along."

"Did he kiss you?"

Heat flooded Abigail's cheeks. "Ma!"

"I want to know. Did he kiss you?"

After Lois and Joe's marriage floundered, her parents had increased their control until Abigail felt suffocated. "I'm twenty-two years old. Yet I can't breathe around here without someone questioning me."

"That's nonsense. I'm your mother. You shouldn't keep things from me."

"Abby's done nothing wrong. I shouldn't have brought that up. It was a long time ago." Lois tucked a wayward curl behind Abigail's ear. "Forgive me?" she whispered.

Abigail nodded. Still, the time had come to sever the apron strings. She took a step back. "I'm old enough to make my own decisions. I've decided to work for the Cummingses. You all should trust me to know what I'm doing."

Lois turned to their mother. "Let's give Ab some breathing room. Though heaven knows we don't have much around here to give." She chuckled, obviously trying to lighten the mood.

"This argument is all the Cummingses' fault. They continue to hurt us as they always have," Ma said.

Was everything the Cummingses' fault? Could the Wilsons have played a part in their own downfall? Abigail quickly tamped down the thought, unable to consider the possibility.

"Got to go or I'll be late." She hugged her mother, inhaling the familiar scent of honeysuckle. "I love you, Ma." She pulled away and let her gaze roam the faces that held her heart. "All of you."

"I love you too, dear. I don't mean to sound like I thought you'd done something wrong. I just—" Ethel sighed. "Talking about the Cummingses brings back memories I'd rather forget."

"For me too," Abigail said.

Joe smiled. "Proud of you for lending the Cummingses a helping hand. Jesus met everyone's needs, not just the deserving."

A flash of annoyance sparked in her mother's eyes. "If you remember, Jesus had plenty to say to hypocrites. George sits in church every Sunday, yet robbed us."

Joe sighed. "They had legal right to call that loan."

"Not a moral right." Ethel dropped her gaze, fidgeting with her apron. As if she'd warred with herself and the good side of her nature had won. "The man did help put out that fire."

"What an irony," Lois said. "With Abby working for them, the Cummingses will be beholden to a Wilson."

To assist her sister's family, to regain her family's self-respect, Abigail needed this job, as much as the Cummingses needed her. But she couldn't help wondering if Lois had it all wrong.

Abigail stood in the open door to George Cummings's bedroom, watching Wade attempt to feed his father. Surely father and son could find a better time than breakfast for a battle of wills. Eyes averted, neither man spoke, as if embarrassed by the small act of service.

Wade lifted a fork to his father's mouth, jostling the utensil. A bite of scrambled egg bounced down George's shirt, landing on his knee.

"You're not much of a nursemaid," George grumbled. "Abigail knows enough to tuck a napkin on my lap."

"I forgot." Wade tossed the bite of food onto the tray. "This would be easier if you kept your face turned toward me."

George raised bandaged hands and nudged the bowl aside. "The eggs are dry."

"If you hadn't chased Cora away, she'd be fixing your breakfast, not me."

"I'm finished," George said glaring at Wade. "Better to go hungry than eat your cooking."

At the cutting remark, Abigail flinched, sympathy for Wade rising within her. George found fault with everything his son did. Yet Wade merely shrugged, a mask of indifference hiding the frustration she'd glimpsed on his face.

Compelled to smooth rough waters, Abigail strode toward the window where they faced off like two fighters in a ring.

"Good morning," she said cheerfully, and then peered inside the bowl Wade held. "A toddler eats better than that."

George's flinty eyes softened. "Toddler, is it? Well, in that case, I hope you're prepared for one of my tantrums."

"You don't scare me." She took the bowl and fork from Wade who'd vacated the chair beside his father. Abigail sat in his place, and with a flick of her wrist, she unfurled the napkin and tucked it under George's chin. She popped a bite of egg into her own mouth. "Nothing's wrong with these eggs."

On the tray she found a spoon and filled it. "Want to try handling this yourself?"

"I won't make more of a mess of it than Wade." George grasped the handle in his bandaged palm, grimacing in pain. "Doc said to keep my fingers moving. They aren't excited by the idea."

"Sorry, but you should obey doctor's orders."

"Looks like I'm not needed here." Wade nodded to Abigail then turned to his father. "See you later, Dad."

The senior Cummings didn't respond.

Abigail arched a brow. "Did the fire affect your hearing?"

Deep blue eyes settled on her, blinked then lifted to his son. "Hope you can manage the bank better than you managed these eggs."

Color climbed Wade's neck. "That's my intent," he said then strode out of the room.

Not a cordial exchange. Wade's tone had been as sharp as his father's. What stood between those two?

As George struggled to bring the spoon to his mouth without spilling the contents, Abigail rose and stepped to the window. Blue lifted his head from his paws to watch her, but remained curled alongside his master's feet.

"How did you sleep last night?"

"When a man does nothing but lie around all day, he doesn't sleep well."

She turned toward him, watching him maneuver the spoon until he succeeded in getting the contents into his mouth. The next bite didn't go as well. George dropped the spoon into the bowl and leaned back, breathing heavy.

Abigail filled the spoon, lifting it to his lips. Red-faced, he opened his mouth like a baby bird. Not that she'd mention the resemblance, but his helplessness and the obvious embarrassment it caused him tugged at her heart. "What do you say we go outside today? Fresh air would do us both good."

"Not a bad idea for a stuffy schoolmarm," he said, then allowed her to feed him another bite.

"You know a lady has the privilege of changing her mind." She wagged a finger at him. "And this lady just might."

"In my house, she doesn't," he said, eyes rock hard and daring her to disagree. "I'm holding you to it."

"Then you might want to be nice."

He looked away. "Giving orders is my way," he said quietly.

"Well, sugar works far better than vinegar. And not merely with me. You might give that a try with your son."

"Don't get the notion you're going to remake me, young lady."

"God is the only one who can do that." She chuckled. "I'm praying for that very thing."

He shot her a scowl. "Let a man eat in peace."

She snapped a salute. "Yes, sir."

"That's more like it." But his testy tone ended on a chuckle. He finished the last bite of egg. She gathered the bowl and spoon. "Thanks," he said, trying that sugar she'd mentioned.

Blue rose and meandered over to Abigail for a pat. "You're a good dog."

"Don't believe Blue likes you better than me."

Smiling, she gave the dog's ear a scratch. "You like me better than your grouchy master, don't you, Blue?"

George harrumphed.

Abigail merely chuckled at his little-boy antics. Why he didn't rile her today, she had no idea. In fact she found his conduct oddly amusing. A good thing since wit proved the best way to get along with the man.

She hadn't forgotten what he did to her family. So her attitude made no sense. Except she knew Rachel and Ma were praying for her, probably Joe and Lois too. The only explanation she had for today's sense of peace.

With his breakfast finished, Abigail picked up the tray and stepped out of the room.

Wade leaned against the wall, arms across his chest, his sapphire eyes dismal. His dejected expression tore at her.

Within seconds he smoothed his brow and relieved her of the tray. As they walked down the hall and descended the stairs, she was all too aware of his physical strength, yet underneath that rugged exterior lived a wounded man.

"How do you do that?" he asked.

"Do what?"

"Keep that rapport with my father."

"I refuse to let him intimidate or offend me—at least today. A dash of humor keeps the mood light. You might want to keep that in mind."

They reached the bottom of the staircase and Wade turned toward her. "Too much stands between us."

"A rock the size of Gibraltar stands between your father and me. I'm sorely tempted to speak my mind about what he did to my family, but good wages make guarding my tongue easier." She grinned. "If you want to get along with George, try viewing him as an employer, not a father."

His lips curved up. "I admire that sense of humor of yours. Now you're using it on me."

With a single smile that lit his eyes, Wade captured her with his mesmerizing gaze, drawing her to him like a moth to a flame. Abigail's heart skipped a beat then fluttered like a bevy of delicate wings, shooting a surge of longing clear to her toes.

Appalled by her reaction to this man, a man she couldn't trust, she turned away by the sheer strength of will and led the way into the kitchen. Wade set the tray on the counter near the stove. A counter strewn with a bowl of broken egg shells, a crock of butter, a breadboard littered with crumbs. The stove didn't look much better with two dirty skillets and a pan with slices of burnt toast and a charred lump that might've been eggs. Maybe.

"Sorry about the mess." Hands on hips, Wade motioned to the stove. "I despise that monstrosity. If Dad thought my scrambled eggs were dry, he should've seen these, the ones I burned."

That twinkle of humor in Wade's eyes only partially masked the hurt beneath his words. An urge to pull him into her arms, to offer him words of comfort gripped her, forging a connection she couldn't deny.

Their gazes locked, dilating his pupils and wrapping the two of them in intimacy. His eyes dropped to her lips. He lowered his head, his intention clear. As his lips met hers, her heart tumbled, leaving her wobbly on her feet.

A knock. Abigail stumbled back. With one last lingering look at her, Wade crossed to answer the door.

Seth stood on the other side, holding his cap and squinting in the sunshine. "Morning, Wade. Is it okay to clean up the shop? The finish on the buffet should be dry."

"Sure. You know where the key is."

A smile broad on his face, the boy nodded then dashed off toward the carriage house.

How could she react to this man when they didn't agree

on anything? "You've done nothing to discourage Seth from working here."

"I pay him to help whenever he can. He needs the money."

"He'll see that money as proof he doesn't need to further his education."

A muscle in his cheek jumped. "Would you be battling me about Seth's future if my name wasn't Cummings, if I hadn't broken off our relationship?"

She grabbed a washcloth, scrubbing the counter. "What relationship? What we had was mere infatuation." She scooped up the mess on the stove, a reminder of the mess he'd made of her life when she'd trusted him. "Your assumptions are insulting. I'm thinking of Seth's welfare. I don't want him to end up like my mother and sister."

His brow furrowed. "What are you saying?"

As if he didn't understand. Refusing to answer, she gathered the dishes and skillets and stomped to the niche, lowering them into the sink.

He followed. "I asked you to explain."

She flung the washcloth into the sink. "When your father called that loan, he took our home, our livelihood, my father's life. Joe started gambling, hoping to win a pile of money. Instead he wound up with a compulsion and a pile of debt." Breathing heavy, she leaned toward him. "To put food on the table, Ma and Lois worked their fingers to the bone, all but ruining their health. If not for my education, I'd be doing the same." She slashed a hand. "You've had an easy life. So don't tell me you know what's best for Seth."

Wade laid a hand over his heart. "I'm sorry you and your family suffered from the loss of the farm." He took a step closer until his booted toe brushed her hem. "But I can promise you Seth will never leave his pa to go off to college. Let the boy choose his own path."

Wade pretended concern for Seth. In reality he only cared

about his dream. He continued to toy with people's lives, as he had hers. Making moves as if people were pieces in a chess game.

She took a deep breath, and then released it in a flood of words. "You make working here too difficult."

"Please don't quit. My father needs you. Think of him." His hand reached for her then fell away. "I need you," he said, his voice raspy.

The desperation in his tone melted something cold and rigid within her. A desire to lean into his touch, to rest against that broad chest, to forget the past battled with her common sense. She steeled her spine and drew back.

"No one else can handle him but you."

All that mattered to Wade was his father. He didn't care that his presence, his touch, scorched like a hot sadiron.

No matter how much she told herself otherwise, she was falling under his spell. How could she stay in this house when every day brought her closer to the web he spun?

She wouldn't care for a long list of reasons.

He belonged to the family that had destroyed her father.

He opposed her over Seth's future.

He'd tossed her away like a useless trinket years before.

And no doubt would again if given the opportunity.

And *now* he claimed to need her? Asking her to overlook all that stood between them?

She shook her head. "Too much has happened. Too much happens still."

"If it would help make things easier, I'll stay away, work late at the bank. Return home after you've left for the day."

Had he read her mind? Knew she dared not risk being in his presence? Or was he as uneasy in her company as she in his? With every fiber of her being she resisted his entreaty. He was asking too much of her.

And yet...

Deep down she knew no matter how much she wanted to, no matter how much she should, she couldn't refuse. Not that she trusted Wade, but his loyalty to his father—the same loyalty she felt toward her father, bridged the chasm of their past.

"Please," he said.

What choice did she have? They needed the money and she couldn't refuse to help an injured man. The parable of the Good Samaritan made God's position clear. She was to love her neighbor. Even if that neighbor was an adversary.

"Not seeing you at every turn would make my job easier. I'll stay."

His eyes warmed with gratitude. "Thank you."

She planted her hands on her hips. "For what it's worth, I suggest you take a long hard look at yourself. At the first sign of conflict with your father, you run. Running doesn't solve a thing."

"I may run from trouble. But isn't it possible you see trouble where none exists?"

With that he left the kitchen.

The front door opened and closed.

Wade had gone.

Was he right? Was her anger over Seth not about his welfare? Her stomach clenched. Her temper defeated her good sense and God's teachings.

Lord God, I'm sorry. What have I become?

As soon as she could, she'd apologize to Wade.

She hoped her hostile attitude wouldn't get her fired.

Chapter Eight

❧

As Wade trudged toward town, the morning sun beat down on him. He removed his suit coat and slung it over his shoulder, then gave his tie a yank, loosening the stranglehold on his neck.

Down the way, Martha Baggett hustled one of her three daughters along the walk...maybe Theresa, hard to tell from here. He suspected the family had selected him for a suitor and didn't care which daughter he favored. Once Mrs. Baggett caught his ear, she'd delay his arrival at the bank.

He trotted across the street, weaving between passing buggies and wagons. Out of the Baggetts' reach, he slowed his pace.

No one interested him except Abby. Perhaps he liked playing with fire. For underneath that proper exterior resided a wounded woman ready to erupt, to spew red-hot anger.

He was to blame. Why not admit it? Abby wanted nothing to do with him. She took care of his father for the pay, nothing else drew her. Not him. Not anything but money. His stomach twisted. Wasn't that the usual reason to interact with a Cummings?

Outside the bank Wade shrugged on his jacket and tightened his tie, a vise-like grip that intensified every day he spent behind that desk. In the lobby he greeted the staff, including Leon Fitch. The man was capable enough, but lacked the initiative to advance beyond the position of teller.

What did Abby see in Fitch?

He frowned. Perhaps a man she could manage.

Outside his father's office he stopped at the secretary's desk. Reed thin and erect, Miss Detmer handed him the mail, opened and sorted.

"Nothing urgent." She gave a polite smile.

He thanked her, and then turned the knob on the door with President etched on the frosted glass. A title he didn't want, at least not here. Others did. Their cashier, Gene Bishop, was capable of handling the job. As was Regina's husband, but tired of his father-in-law's watchful scrutiny, Lawrence had accepted an offer in Waterloo. Perhaps he could be convinced to return, once Wade's father understood he had no alternative.

A glance at his calendar confirmed he had no appointments until three o'clock. Dropping into his chair, he flipped through the correspondence then tossed it aside.

Leaning back in his chair, he plowed a hand through his hair. Would Abby leave? Cora had quit. His sister refused to step foot in the house.

No one stayed.

Not his sister. Not his mother.

Why had he?

He could open his cabinetmaking shop anywhere. Why did he plan to start here? In a town that sided with the Wilsons over the Cummingses. In a town where his father had the opportunity to criticize him, showing not one semblance of respect. In a town where Abby opposed him.

And made him want to disregard his vow to stay clear of women.

With all that uproar, why had he remained in New Harmony? A thought unfurled in his brain.

Love for his father did not keep him here.

Debt did.

George Cummings hadn't shirked his parental duty to his children as their mother had. Wade owed his father, the one who stayed. Wade would stay too, as long as his father needed him.

He'd pay the debt no matter the cost.

True, Wade hadn't confronted his father about the feud, about his mother leaving, about his father's aloofness. That might be running as Abby claimed, but Wade wasn't leaving.

Not that he feared going out on his own. Life would be simpler if he did. But remaining in this town didn't mean he would give up his dream. He'd take action today. With some work their empty warehouse off Main Street would be the perfect location for his shop.

A knock at the door brought him to his feet. Harrison Carder poked his head in the door. Tall, with blond hair and beard, Harry oozed boyish charm. "Got a minute?"

Wade came around the desk. "Sure, what's on your mind?"

Harry gave a crooked grin. "Money. Why else would I bother a banker during his workday?" He closed the door behind him. "Got any?"

Chuckling, Wade clapped a hand on his friend's back then perched on the corner of his desk, motioning to a chair. "Money I've got—with interest, of course."

"Of course." Harry took a seat, propping an ankle on his knee. "I'm in the awkward position of requiring a small loan to tide me over."

Harry's new law practice had a shaky start, but he'd assured Wade that every town needed a lawyer and he intended to get in on the ground floor in New Harmony. In a few months that ground floor had slid to the cellar.

"Before we discuss that loan," Wade said, "I'm glad you stopped by. I need your services."

"You do?" Harry straightened, his foot dropped to the floor. "Doing what?"

"I'm opening a business. I'd like you to do the legwork."

Harry's gray eyes lit with interest. "You're finally going to make furniture full-time."

"As soon as my father can direct this desk."

"So how can I help? New Harmony doesn't have complicated zoning ordinances or other legalities that could impede your plans."

"True, but we've both heard of the mistreatment of workers in big cities. I want you to research what I can do to ensure employees' health and safety."

"You don't need a lawyer for that."

"I need advice from someone I have confidence in. That's you. Unless you don't want the work."

Harry rubbed his hands together. "I want it, all right."

"I'd like you to start today." Wade rose. "Better yet, now. Come with me to look at the site I'm considering."

"Glad to. If you're paying me, I'll postpone that loan, at least for another month." He frowned. "You sure this offer isn't about keeping a fraternity brother off the dole?"

"You'd take a job shoveling manure before you'd accept charity." He raised his brows. "Actually I could use some help in our stable doing that very thing."

Harry rolled his eyes toward the stamped-tin ceiling. "Makes a man thankful he got a law degree."

"I wish Abigail Wilson could hear say that."

"Why? She got something against lawyers?"

"She's got something *for* education, as if education guarantees an idyllic life."

"I'd be happy to fill her in." He shot Wade a speculative look. "Why care what this woman thinks?"

"We hold opposing opinions on what Seth Collier should do with his life."

"I know the boy. He cleaned my office before I moved in. Did a good job. Heard his father drinks."

"Rafe is the main reason I've taken Seth under my wing. Abby would no doubt like to sever the appendage."

"Ouch." A wide grin rode Harry's lean face. "Sounds like you two are setting off fireworks. I noticed sparks the day of the auction."

"Yeah, but these explosives aren't pretty."

"She sure is."

Wade's gut clenched. Was Harry interested in Abby? "I noticed you bought Rachel Fisher's box lunch."

Harry huffed. "Her father glowered at me all through lunch. She's a sweet young thing but not my type."

"Which is?" Wade forced out, feigning indifference or trying to.

"I like a woman with spirit. One who goes after what she wants." He tugged on his neatly trimmed beard, watching him. "Someone like Abigail Wilson."

Jaw clenched, Wade leaned toward Harry, taking his measure.

Harry chuckled. "I can see I'm treading water off your shores."

"Your evidence is weak, Counselor."

"The jury is still out." Harry rose with a grin. "But I know when to rest my case. Let's take a look at that property."

Welcoming the change of topic, Wade grabbed a ring of keys from the middle drawer of his father's desk. Out on the street, they turned left. A short block later, they reached the empty warehouse that Wade hoped would house his shop.

The third key Wade tried opened the door. They entered, looked around.

"If you ignore dust, cobwebs and evidence of nesting varmints, you can see the potential." Wade motioned to a bank of windows along the right wall. "Plenty of light and ventilation. Huge elms shade the building in summer. A working pump provides water. Once I'm making a profit, I'll modernize with indoor plumbing." He let his gaze roam the interior. "I'll put a showroom and small office up front. Furniture production will take place farther back."

"Sounds like a viable plan. You'll need an area for employees to eat their lunch and take breaks."

"You're already earning your wage." Wade smiled. "I know the perfect solution for getting the place cleaned up. I'll ride out to the Collier cabin. Ask Rafe and Seth to clean and paint."

"From what I hear, you could get yourself killed."

"Unlikely. But if I should disappear never to be heard from again, I expect you to prosecute."

"You've got my word, ole buddy." Harry smirked. "Don't fret about Abigail Wilson. I'll see she doesn't miss you for long."

Underneath that teasing exterior, Wade suspected Harry was dead serious. "Very funny."

Well, he wouldn't let Harry's banter ruin his excitement. If Seth and Rafe took the job, in a matter of two weeks, maybe less, Wade could have the location ready. In the meantime, he'd order equipment and build those to-scale replicas. The work would be tedious and time consuming, but salesman samples would bring in orders.

Until his father healed, Wade couldn't leave the bank, but he had set his plan in motion.

Everything would be perfect if not for the trouble between him and Abby.

Trouble he longed to ease. With God's help and his own persistence, he'd find a way.

Not that he held any hope of a future with Abby. Yet the prospect of seeing his friend squire her around town didn't sit well with Wade. He'd warn Abby that Harry was a charmer, a ladies' man. Not that she'd appreciate it, but he couldn't stand by and let her be hurt. His lungs squeezed. *Again.*

Abigail leaned against the counter and let her gaze sweep the large, well-equipped kitchen. A mammoth stove, the vast work space and two enormous iceboxes could easily handle food preparation for lavish dinner parties.

Off to the side, the butler's pantry's floor-to-ceiling cabinets displayed silver serving pieces geared to lavish entertaining. Entertaining this house hadn't seen. Or if it had, the Wilsons hadn't received an invitation.

No matter how often she came in here, Abigail couldn't get over the luxury. Proof she and Wade lived in different worlds.

Turning back to the tiled niche holding an enormous divided porcelain sink and faucets with hot and cold running water, she prepared dishwater. As she worked up suds and washed the dishes, tension eased from her shoulders and neck.

Once she'd put the dishes away, she took the dishrag and cleaned the stove and counters, working at a leisurely pace, giving George opportunity for a nap.

A knock at the back door startled her. Who could that be?

Cora poked her head in, her salt-and-pepper tresses pulled into a tidy bun. "Abigail Wilson, I never expected to find you here."

"I'm your replacement." Abigail gave a weak smile. "A poor substitute."

The cook glanced at her laced no-nonsense shoes. "Not likely to fill these clodhoppers," she said with a grin. "Consider yourself lucky."

With an air of authority, she stepped to the counter. Not surprising considering she'd cooked for the Cummingses for as long as Abigail had lived in town, maybe longer. "I'm here to make the mister a rhubarb pie, one of his favorites."

Perhaps Cora's presence would give Abigail an opportunity to learn more about the trouble between Wade and his father and the reason she'd quit.

Cora wagged a finger. "Not that you're to tell him I'd do such a thing. The man doesn't deserve it. But..." She met Abigail's gaze. "I can barely sleep at night for worrying he's starving. I'll rest easier knowing you're fixing his meals."

"He's eating better."

"Thank the Good Lord." She removed the towel from the bowl she carried. "I brought the rhubarb."

Without further to-do, she tied a crisp white apron around her bulky middle and lit the stove. "Has his cranky disposition improved along with that appetite?"

"Cranky doesn't begin to describe him."

"Never thought I'd say this, but I'm glad he's his old prickly self." Cora grabbed a blue-banded crock from the cupboard and then poked about, gathering ingredients. "The first week, that man had me frantic. His tray returned to the kitchen untouched. Didn't have any fight in him."

"Yet you left." Abigail raised a brow. "Why?"

"After the crisis passed, I had to. Not for the way the mister treated me—heaven knows I'm used to his barbed tongue—but I can't abide the way he treats Wade. Wade nearly killed hisself filling his daddy's shoes all day and sitting at his bedside all night. I warned the mister I'd leave if he didn't change his ways." She gave a lopsided smile. "Hard to bully a bully."

"Well, his fight's back, especially with Wade."

Cora sifted the flour, added lard then water. As she tossed the mixture with gentle fingers, her warm brown eyes locked with Abigail's. "I'd hoped with me gone, they'd find a way to get along. Perhaps you'll smooth the waters between Wade and his pa."

Abigail heaved a sigh. "I don't see how, especially with the trouble between our families."

With flying fingers Cora floured the countertop, plopped the dough in the center and began rolling out the crust, her large bosom bouncing with her movements. "Maybe that's why God planted you here."

"I'll earn my wage, but a Wilson bringing peace to a Cummings…?" Abigail snorted. "I'd have more success controlling the weather."

Chuckling, Cora draped the dough over the rolling pin and onto the pie plate, then filled the shell with sugared rhubarb. "Listening to that mule bray is enough to make a grown woman weep," she said, adding the top crust, trimming the excess with a knife and then twisting thumb and forefinger to crimp and seal the edges.

"You make that look easy."

"Been making 'em since I was eight." She winked. "Wish I could twist, crimp and seal the mister as easily."

Abigail giggled and Cora joined in.

Abigail glanced at the clock. Almost eleven. "I'd better get back upstairs before Wade returns for lunch."

"He never leaves his desk till noon." Cora cut two slits in the top, spread milk over the surface and sprinkled the crust with sugar, then cocked her head at Abigail. "Are you avoiding my boy? Not that he's mine but since his mama left I claim him."

Before Abigail could harness her tongue, she blurted, "You can have him."

The cook slid the pie into the oven. "There's a story in there somewhere. Keep an old lady company and tell it."

Curiosity about Wade made Abigail stay, but she wouldn't appear too eager and give Cora the wrong impression.

While Cora put away ingredients and cleaned the counter, Abigail washed the bowl and utensils.

With the kitchen in order once again, Cora motioned to the table in the corner where the help took their meals. "Let's have a cup of tea and one of my cookies."

"I will as long as you understand I have no story to tell."

"Always is. Always is."

Once they'd sat with the teapot and a couple of those enormous cookies Cora had unearthed, Cora stirred two teaspoons of sugar into her cup. Then took a sip and sat back with a satisfied sigh. "Nothing soothes like a cup of tea. From the sound of it you could use some soothing yerself. If you don't want to see Wade, then my boy must be the reason. I may be poking my nose in, but what's he done?"

The tea brewed at just the right temperature and strength hadn't soothed, not with Cora asking the questions. But if Abigail opened up, perhaps Cora would do the same. Yet how could she explain to this woman who obviously adored Wade?

"We're in disagreement over what's best for a student of mine, Seth Collier."

"Two hounds fighting over one bone. I pity the boy."

Recalling the uneasy expression on Seth's face as he ran out of the shop, Abigail's heart lurched. In her effort to help had she behaved that badly?

"I reckon a bone's better off fought over than abandoned."

Abigail bit into Cora's cookie, moist, soft and delicious. "I'm not sure what you're saying."

"Seth's got two people caring about him. Even if that

caring puts you at odds and the boy in the middle, that's better'n neglect."

Neglect described Seth's life with his father, the reason he should leave.

Across from Abigail, Cora thrummed an unnerving tune on the table with her fingers. Apparently the calm of that tea had vanished. Why would talking about Seth upset her? Who besides Seth was neglected—?

Her breath caught. Cora was referring to Wade and his sister Regina. Abigail had heard about Wade's mother's desertion. The entire town knew. When a traveling opera company hit town, Ernestine got acquainted with the actors. When the troupe moved on she went with them, leaving her children behind.

Abigail loved her nephews and couldn't conceive of such a thing. "Do you know why Mrs. Cummings left?"

Cora sighed. "I've thought on it and thought on it, but I'll never understand her leaving."

"You don't think her husband's conduct drove her off?"

"The mister treated Ernestine just fine. Gave her this grand house, every comfort, but I could see she wasn't happy."

"If she was treated well, how could she leave her children?"

Cora's cup clattered to the saucer. "The day Ernestine left, I watched some lackey haul out her trunk while she stood by wringing her hands, fretting about her children. But no matter what she said, she was giddy too, as if she'd found something exciting she couldn't live without.

"I pleaded with her to wait for the children to get home from school. Those younguns loved their mama and I knew her leaving would break their hearts. But she wouldn't wait. Said the opera company had to make their next performance and she couldn't bear saying goodbye. Said to tell her babies she'd only be gone a little while, a week at most, only long enough to fill in for the leading lady who'd taken sick."

She and Wade had lost a parent, difficult anytime, but especially when the parent made the choice to pull away.

"I sent word for the mister to get hisself home." Cora's voice broke and she swiped at her eyes. "But those young-uns got here before he did."

Wade had dealt with heartache even grown-ups couldn't fathom. Appetite gone, Abigail put the cookie aside. "What happened?"

"They stopped in the kitchen for a snack, like usual. Wade chattered on about winning the fourth-grade spelling bee. Before I could stop him that boy trotted upstairs to tell his mama the news.

"I gave Regina a cookie and followed him to Ernestine's bedroom. His eyes had this wild look. 'Where's my mother?' he asked. I said, 'She'll be back in a week.' Maybe he read something in my face he didn't like 'cause he ran to her bureau, looking for her clothes. He turned to me, his eyes as empty as those drawers.

"Right then the mister come in. 'Where is she?' Wade asks in this high-pitched voice. 'Where's my mother?'"

Abigail remembered the panic of watching her father fade away. For a small boy to learn his mother left with no warning... Goose bumps rose on her arms.

"The mister plops on the bed, a note dangling from his fingers. 'She's gone.' Wade stood there waiting for an explanation, but the mister doesn't give any. He just sits there like he's in a trance.

"I gathered that boy in my arms and hugged him tight. 'She said she'd be back. She'll be back.'

"The mister says, 'She isn't coming back. Not ever.' Wade pulled away from my arms and stomped over to his pa.

'Would you let her?' He grabbed the mister by the lapels. 'Would you let her come home, Papa?'"

Suddenly chilly in the cozy kitchen permeated with the aroma of rhubarb pie, Abigail wrapped her arms around her middle, unable to take her eyes off Cora.

"The mister says, 'Once she gets a taste of the stage, she won't give it up.' Then Wade says, 'I want to live with Mama.' Wade choosing his mama over his pa, well, I reckon that made things worse too. The mister's face kinda crumbled then got hard like stone. 'Traipsing around the country with an opera troupe's no place for a child. She made her choice. She picked her dream over her duty.'

"Those words destroyed that boy's hope. Wade ran out of the room. I found him in the stable, crying. Grabbed him up, sat on a bale of straw and rocked that weeping boy in my arms." Tears slid down Cora's cheeks. "I took Wade into my heart that day. Why I claim him as mine. Land's sake, that was years ago, but the memory still makes me weep like a baby."

Cora blew her nose on a handkerchief she pulled from her bodice. "His pa shoulda been comforting his son, not me. I'm not blaming the mister for his anger. He loved Ernestine. Her leaving nearly killed him." She sighed, fiddling with her cup. "Killed her for sure. The manager of the opera company said she performed on stage once before she took sick."

Abigail remembered the talk. Ernestine came down with influenza and in a matter of days, died.

"How old were Wade and Regina?"

"Wade was nine. Regina six."

When Ernestine Cummings deserted her family, she erected a barrier between Wade and his father that they couldn't hurdle.

When Abigail could speak, she took the older woman's plump hand. "Thank God you were there for Wade."

Cora straightened her shoulders. "The mister's stubborn as they come and won't make that first step. I reckon he's scared Wade's like his mama."

"How so?"

"Wade's what I hear called artistic, always has been."

"Why do you think Ernestine chose to leave?"

"Her dream of becoming an actress was part of it." She sighed. "The mister was good to her but wasn't no Prince Charming."

Abigail gulped. Underneath, wasn't Prince Charming what she wanted? As if any such man existed. Fairy tales were for children.

"Reckon he did the best he could, trying to handle his work, his home, his children. But he didn't know how to give Wade and Regina what they needed. Regina's made a new life for herself, but Wade… I'm hoping you'll bring those two hardheads close."

Abigail gave Cora's hand a squeeze then stood. "I'll try."

How could she help Wade and his father reconcile when the rift between her and Wade was even wider?

Chapter Nine

Rhubarb pie and a sandwich waiting in the kitchen was probably as close to Abby as Wade would get. She'd avoided him since their encounter that morning.

At the first opportunity, he'd apologize. Not that a simple "I'm sorry" would fix the trouble between them, but he'd sleep better knowing he'd tried.

He stepped out the back door, munching on the cheese and ham and ambled toward the carriage house. He spotted Abby in the garden, gathering an armful of iris. Tendrils of her hair had pulled loose from their moorings and peeked beneath her wide-brimmed straw hat. She met his gaze. Gone was the anger he'd last seen, replaced with a vulnerability that drew him closer.

A smudge of dirt marred the soft curve of her cheek yet he'd never seen her look lovelier. With those guileless eyes resting on him, he couldn't get his mind to work. He couldn't get his tongue to move. *Cummings, you're behaving like a moron.*

He swallowed hard and forced out "Thanks for making my sandwich and the pie."

"Cora gets the credit for the pie."

"Cora came by the house?"

"Yes." She released a sigh. "Wade, I...I need to apologize for this morning."

"I'm at fault for riling you."

"Of late, that's easy to do." Those soft blue eyes of hers darted around the garden, as if she didn't know where to put her gaze. "I thought these flowers might cheer up your father."

"No more than the lovely woman delivering them."

"Thank you," she said, then gifted him with a stunning smile, a beautiful and for him, rare occurrence. That smile danced over his defenses and slammed against the protective wall he'd built around his heart. Something frozen inside him softened, sliding into lonely crevices he didn't know existed.

Yet hadn't he seen with his parents, with himself, that love brought pain? Fighting the connection between them, he took a step back.

Abby dropped her gaze to the bouquet in her hands, fidgeting with a torn leaf then ripping it from the stem. As the leaf fluttered to the ground, she lifted her eyes to his. "I've seen the strain between you and your father. Not that I'm blaming you. George isn't an easy man. Still, if you tried, perhaps you two could forge a new beginning."

That she cared soothed like butter on a burn. But to fix the trouble between him and his father meant knuckling under and giving up his dream. "Other than following the path he's planned for my life, I can't please him." Her puzzled expression said she didn't understand. "He wants me to take over our holdings. But sitting at a desk all day, working with numbers is as arduous to me as dragging a ball and chain."

She pursed her lips, no doubt pondering a solution. Those sweet lips had him thinking all right, thinking about kissing her. *Whoa, Cummings. You're not ready to take that risk any more than she is.*

Yet his hand moved to her cheek. With the soft pad of his thumb he wiped the smudge off her cheek. At his touch, she inhaled sharply. "Just a little dirt," he said.

"I must look a mess."

"You look perfect."

His praise bloomed in her cheeks. She lowered her lashes like a flustered schoolgirl. "Perhaps if you and George could find a pastime to share, that would help."

Work was all his father knew. "I don't know what that could be, but I'll think on it." Instead an idea for a pastime to share with Abby came to mind. "I'd like to enlarge this garden, add some plants, but I have no idea what."

Her eyes lit. "Several perennials would do well in this sunny location. I'd love to help."

Abby lived in an apartment with only a scrap of a yard. Yet she enjoyed digging in the soil, fiddling with plants. Something he wanted to share with her. "Round up the plants you'd like. Put the expense on the Cummings account. When you're ready, I'll dig up the grass."

"No need. Perennials like to crowd together."

Wade knew nothing about gardening, but when it came to Abby, crowding together definitely appealed. Their gazes locked, those soft blue eyes of hers danced with excitement. When had he seen her look happier?

"I know several women who'd share a cutting or plant."

"Whenever you're ready, let me know. I'll dig the holes."

"You'd do that for me?"

That and so much more. "It'll be fun."

Such simple things. Plants, fresh-turned soil. Yet she behaved as if he'd given her a priceless gift. When all he'd done was to observe the pleasure gardening gave her and offer his time and muscle. Perhaps Abby was right; perhaps an activity could connect him and his father.

"Wade, I…" Her eyes sobered. "Thank you for forgiving me for my temper."

"Thank you for forgiving me for riling you." If only she could forgive him for hurting her all those years ago. Yet to explain, he would have to reveal his father's cruel plan and hurt her more.

As much as he wanted to stay, to spend the afternoon with Abby in this garden, if he hoped to get his shop underway, he had to get out to the Collier cabin. "I need to get a move on."

"Where are you off to?"

Once she knew his destination that smile would fade. Temptation to evade the question slid through him, but he wouldn't lie. "I'm heading out to the Collier place, to talk to Rafe about a job."

Her eyes dimmed. "About a job? Or Seth's apprenticeship?"

"I see no point in talking to Rafe about Seth's plans."

"Thank you," she said, laying a gentle hand on his arm. "Be careful. Rafe's not known for hospitality."

"I will."

With a nod she turned away, carrying that basket of flowers to his father, a lucky man.

As Wade saddled Rowdy, he whistled a tune, feeling a smidgeon of optimism that he and his father could find a way to get along. More importantly, he had the first hope he and Abby could have a future. Moving beyond the past would take time. He wouldn't push.

Meanwhile, he'd talk to Rafe about cleaning the empty storefront. And handle the myriad of details of getting a business underway.

With a splendid sunny afternoon ahead of him, unshackled from a desk, he gave a gentle tug on the reins, turning the horse toward open country. A flick of the leather and Rowdy clopped along at a trot, leaving behind a trail of dust.

In every field he passed, slender shoots stretched to the sun. Farmers had plowed and planted in narrow precise rows appealing to Wade's methodical nature and desire for order.

If only he could control his life as well as farmers did these crops, but as perfect as they looked now, disease and pests riddled yields, drought and hailstones destroyed the harvest. Life was not without trouble.

At the lane leading to the Collier cabin, Wade tugged on the reins, then dismounted and tied Rowdy to a fencepost. Keep-out signs on the barbed wire fence, on the gate, even on a tree, a lone sentry in an adjoining field, all forbade entry. To Wade those signs banning entry suggested Rafe had something to hide.

Would Rafe take the job? Or would a jug hold more appeal?

Wade tried the gate. A padlock hung from the chain, giving him no choice but to walk from here. Rafe could be half-soused or working. Either way, Seth's father didn't tolerate visitors and wasn't above pulling a gun on trespassers, most likely a bluff. Still, Wade wasn't fool enough to disrespect the barrel end of a shotgun.

He scaled the gate and loped along the hard-packed ground. Halfway up the lane the blast from a shotgun stopped Wade in his tracks.

"You're on private property. I aimed at the sky. Next time I won't be as tolerant."

"Wade Cummings, Rafe."

"What do you want?"

"I've got a job offer for you and Seth, if you're a mind to take it." He took a step forward.

"That's far enough."

Wade froze.

Rafe emerged from a clump of trees and motioned with his shotgun. "Move back to the gate. I'll send Seth out to hear what you've come to say."

"You're the one I want to talk to."

"What you want doesn't matter."

With no hope of changing Rafe's mind, Wade pivoted on a booted heel and retraced his steps. That he'd be talking to Seth not his pa didn't set well. A man ought to supervise the job.

When he reached his horse, he gave Rowdy's nose a rub, listening to the quiet, broken only by a buzzing insect and the call of birds. Did Rafe appreciate the peace of his farm? Or was he too busy slugging down whiskey and warding off intruders to notice?

In the distance, Seth approached. Alone.

Rowdy nudged Wade with his muzzle, almost knocking him off balance. "You're not shy about asking for what you like, are you?" As he rubbed between his ears, Rowdy stood stock-still, except for his tail, swishing flies.

Seth scaled the fence exactly as Wade had, evidence that gate rarely swung open. "Pa said you had a job."

"I do. Your pa should've come to hear my proposal."

"Pa isn't much for visitors."

An understatement if Wade had ever heard one. "I've selected an empty warehouse we own off Main Street as the location for my cabinetmaking shop."

"That's great!"

Seth's enthusiasm made Wade smile. "It is. But the place is dirty, infested with varmints. A few windows need replacing and the roof needs patching. Not a job for one man."

Especially a boy.

"Our fields are planted. Crops are up," Seth said, his voice filling with pride. "Nothing to hold us here. I'll ask Pa."

"If your dad wants the work, tell him to meet me at the warehouse tomorrow at noon."

"I'll do what I can to get him there."

"I can't think of any nice way to say this, Seth, but your pa can't drink on the job. That's not something I can tolerate."

A flush climbed Seth's neck. "Yes, sir."

"I hope it works out."

Seth bobbed his head.

"Your dad's a fortunate man to have a son like you."

The boy met Wade's gaze. "I'm fortunate to have him for my pa."

Yeah, right. A gun-toting, liquor-guzzling recluse was everyone's aspiration for a father. Rafe Collier made George Cummings look like a perfect parent.

"Hope to see him tomorrow."

With a nod, Seth scaled the gate and leaped to the ground, then jogged toward home.

To what?

Wade didn't know. That uncertainty bothered him. Not that he believed Rafe would harm his son.

As he untied Rowdy then swung into the saddle, the possibilities gnawed in the pit of Wade's stomach. Seth was a good kid. He deserved a good life. If only education was the answer for Seth as Abby believed. But the boy's steadfast support of Rafe didn't give Wade one glimmer of hope Seth would leave his father.

Wade's hand knotted on the reins. Under Seth's cheerful exterior surely lay a hurting boy. A boy needing approval, affection, a good example, someone he could look up to. Not a heartbroken drunk for a father.

If Rafe refused the job cleaning up the warehouse, Wade

would see that Seth earned money to handle their expenses until harvest. But money didn't replace a parent.

Wade knew that as well as anyone.

Cora's sugar cookies should entice a few volunteers to lend a hand. Not that Abigail relished taking men away from rebuilding houses destroyed in the fire. But George Cummings's shortness of breath kept him from handling the flight of stairs. A man accustomed to overseeing his realm perceived his second-floor bedroom as a prison. In this heat a torture chamber.

That morning Abigail had come up with a simple solution. Moving George's bedroom to the front parlor would enable him to access the kitchen and the outdoors, at least as far as the front porch. She couldn't manage the four-poster. No one person could. The image of Wade's bulging biceps rose in her mind. She gulped. No doubt he could wrestle the bed and mattress downstairs alone. But once she'd explained her plan, George wouldn't abide one moment's delay.

If the move lifted George's spirits and improved his attitude as Abigail expected, then perhaps he'd treat Wade better. And they'd take the first step toward healing the impasse between them.

Before the building site came into view, Abigail heard the rat-a-tat of hammers, a discordant but gratifying sound promising a new beginning for her sister, for all of those who'd lost everything in that fire. Two newly framed houses came into view. Square two stories with a pitched roof. One of those houses stood on the Lessman lot. Abigail laughed with sheer joy. Soon Lois would have her home restored.

Abigail patted her brow with a hankie and watched a dozen men nailing shingles on the rooftops. A nasty job in this heat. On down, crews secured wood siding. All four houses were almost enclosed.

Wade was nowhere in sight. Not surprising when he had a bank and half-dozen businesses to run. She couldn't wait to tell him she'd gotten promises of several plants for the Cummingses' garden. Some would have to wait until fall or at least cooler temperatures.

Pastor Ted approached, a nail pouch tied around his waist and toting a hammer. "Afternoon, Abigail. Finished Sunday's sermon and thought I'd lend a hand."

"Nice of you to help." She offered the silver tray piled with cookies. Fancy for a construction site, but all she could find in the Cummingses' kitchen. "Have a cookie."

"Mmm, Cora's?" At her nod, he grinned. "Better get one before they're gone." He helped himself and took a bite. "Delicious. Thoughtful of you to bring a treat."

"Actually the cookies are a bribe. I need help moving Mr. Cummings's bedroom downstairs."

A grin spread across his face. "That's a fine idea. Being in the middle of things should ease that impatience of his." He shoved up the brim of his hat. "Is he giving you much trouble?"

"He tries but I don't scare easily." She chuckled. "Actually he's coming around." With a start, she realized she spoke the truth. George had tempered his attitude, at least toward her. "Probably because he's feeling better."

"Good to hear. Can I help round up the men you need?"

"Thanks but I'll manage."

"Well, better get up on a roof. I suspect you'll have plenty of volunteers, eager to stretch their legs. If not, give me a holler." He strode off munching on the cookie.

One nice thing about a pastor who'd left farming for the ministry, the man knew how to work when the need arose.

Oscar Moore plodded toward her, pushing a wheelbarrow loaded with a galvanized tub of iced lemonade and a dipper and singing "Oh My Darling Clementine" at the top of his lungs.

When he reached her, he released his grip on the handles, jostling lemonade, then tipped his hat. "Afternoon, Miss Abigail. Cecil and me are on the drink brigade. Can't keep these men watered in this heat. The ladies at the Club made the lemonade."

"Considerate of them to pitch in."

Head back, Oscar watched men crawling on the roofs. "Not sure if we was dropped on our heads or what, but Cecil and me don't cotton to heights. Like our feet planted on terra firma." He turned to her. "That's Italian for 'ground.'"

Abigail bit back the chuckle trying to force its way out of her throat and offered Oscar a cookie.

"I've thought about asking Cora to marry me," he said, taking a cookie. "Wish she could marry Cecil and me both, but with bigamy against the law and all, that ain't likely. If I was to propose, Cecil would resent me getting the drop on him."

"If Cora accepted your proposal, you could always invite your brother over for dinner."

"Yeah, we could, but then there's the matter of Cecil and me owning a house. Reckon I'll forget matrimony." He took another bite. "Sure is tempting though."

Abigail doubted Cora's cookies were a solid foundation for marriage. But perhaps no more apt to crumble than other motivations she'd heard.

"Might want to plug your ears," Oscar said then held his hands to his mouth, creating a megaphone of sorts. "Ice cold lemonade! Come get it, gents!"

Within seconds men eased off the roofs, tromping down the ladders leaning against the house, lumbering toward them. Faces flushed, shoulders drooping, wrung out from laying hot shingles. They gathered around the wheelbarrow, gulping a dipperful of lemonade then passing the ladle on to the next man.

How could she ask these tired men to do more? Perhaps they'd welcome a break. She carried the tray among them, offering Cora's cookies. They thanked her profusely then gobbled the cookies as if they were starving.

"Gentlemen, before you go back on that roof, could four of you haul a bedstead downstairs at the Cummings house? The second floor is hot and confining."

"Shingles are getting soft in this heat and could use a rest, same as me," Jim Johnson said then scratched his head. "Though a Wilson working for the Cummingses is about more than a man can digest."

Orville Radcliff whipped a red-patterned bandana out of his hip pocket and wiped his brow. "Never thought I'd see the day—God at work for sure."

Abigail had all she could do to keep her lips sealed shut. Mr. Radcliff meant no harm, but too much stood between the Cummingses and Wilsons to consider that a few days working in their house had somehow resolved the feud. Things were better between her and George, but to pretend a reconciliation she didn't feel would be dishonest, even self-deceit.

Dan Harper wiped cookie crumbs off his mouth. "Let's not keep Cummings roasting like a hog on the spit."

Harrison Carder, the new lawyer in town, shot her a smile as he twisted his neck and shoulders, working out the kinks. "Any excuse to get off that roof sounds good to me."

"Do you gentlemen know when the Lessman house will be livable?"

"We're aiming to finish them about the same time," Dan said. "Expect it'll take another month. Hard to say, since the number of workers varies each day, depending on a man's job and how long he can let the chores slide."

A month. "Lois and Joe could move in by early July."

Dan Harper grinned. "Yep, should have a humdinger of a Fourth of July party, celebrating the country's birth and that burned-out block's rebirth."

"That's a fabulous idea," Abigail said. "I'll talk to Elizabeth Logan. The Ladies' Club will ensure the celebration is the best this town's seen."

"Reckon our wives will get tied up in the planning." Jim Johnson shook his head. "We won't get a decent meal for a week."

"A big 'ole party will be worth the sacrifice, Jim. Well, I'd better wash this wheelbarrow down before the bees find it and me," Oscar said.

As the men set off, Harrison offered Abigail his arm. "Communities don't band together like this back East."

"I'm surprised New Harmony interests a man like you."

He wagged his brows. "A woman like you makes this town downright appealing."

"Thank you," she said, but knew flattery when she heard it.

At the Cummingses' house she led the men inside and up the stairs, listening to murmurs of admiration. None had been in the house before, a sad commentary on the Cummingses' connection to the community.

George greeted the men, his voice raspy with emotion, obviously touched by the turnout.

Unsettled by the confusion, Blue rose and hid behind George's leg as the crew took the bed apart and carried the headboard, footboard, slats and rails downstairs to the parlor. Jim and Dan reassembled the four-poster in the spot Abigail had emptied of furniture. Harrison and Orville brought down the mattress. Then all four tromped upstairs for the washstand, washbowl, lamp and wheelchair while Abigail remade the bed.

Within minutes they'd taken unneeded furniture to George's bedroom—with the exception of the grand piano—and converted the front parlor into a combination bed-and-sitting room with everything George needed at his disposal.

On the last trip, the men brought George, carrying him in a seat fashioned from their hands and arms. Blue plodded after them, ears flopping on each step.

"I could've handled the stairs," George protested as they deposited him in a rocker. "But your way was faster. Good to be in the heart of things. Thanks, men." He reached into his vest pocket and removed his billfold.

"Just being neighborly," Jim protested. "If you want to spend your money, donate to rebuild the burned-out houses."

George handed Jim a wad of bills. "Will you see that this gets into that fund?"

"Sure will! Thanks for the contribution, Mr. Cummings."

He flapped a dismissive hand. "Hear you're making progress."

"Yes, sir, the community's coming together to get it done."

An unsettled look in his eyes, George nodded.

Abigail walked the men to the foyer, thanking them again. As they traipsed out the door, Harrison lingered. "If you need help with anything, let me know."

"Thanks, that's nice of you."

"Contrary to what Wade may have said, I'm a nice fellow."

Biting back a smile, she cocked her head at him. "Sorry to disappoint you, but Wade hasn't told me anything about you."

"Once he hears about our conversation, he will. The man's the jealous type." A grin on his face, he tipped his hat then jogged down the steps and caught up with the others meandering down the drive.

Harrison implied Wade was jealous. Over her? Could that be true? She pictured Wade, handsome, broad-shouldered and those indigo eyes. Oh, my. She could lose herself in their depths.

Wade worked hard, was kind, even generous. More importantly, he loved God.

But he was a Cummings.

She refused to give such silliness another thought. Nevertheless she glided to the parlor, feet barely touching the ground. One look at George's impatient stare brought her down to earth and a chuckle to her lips.

"Why the delay, woman? Let's get outside."

"Yes, sir."

She took George's arm and helped him out of the house onto the porch, where there was only room for two chairs. From here he could watch the world go by, at least the part passing his house.

Once he was situated, Abigail stood soaking up the beauty of the shrubs and trees dotting the lawn, the drive curving around the bubbling fountain. Every room in the house had this lovely vista or a view of the garden and paddock where the horses grazed and the woods beyond.

Across the cinder alley behind their apartment, burning barrels rusted. Fire escapes clung to the backsides of buildings like vines.

George motioned to the other chair. "Sit."

Blue dropped down beside him.

Abigail plopped hands on hips. "Stop issuing commands as if I'm that dog of yours or I may start baying at the moon."

"Nothing wrong with that, is there, Blue?" Giving her a wink, he reached a hand and patted the top of the dog's head.

Grinning, Abigail sat and leaned back in the chair, enjoying the peace of the moment. She'd accomplished what she'd set out to do. Gratified George not only appreciated her efforts, he'd thought of others.

"You were generous to donate to the building fund."

He flapped a hand, as if shooing a pesky fly. "I'm one of many to donate."

"True, but from that fistful of money I'd say your donation was significant. I appreciate it. My sister and brother-in-law are one of the families that lost everything in that fire."

"I know."

Something closed about his tone made her wonder if he resented helping a Wilson. But then he smiled. That good mood of his suggested this might be the right time to broach the subject of Seth. "Someone else in this town could use your help."

Indigo irises lifted to hers, the resemblance to Wade unsettling. "Who?"

"Seth Collier, a student of mine. He'd do well in college, but his father can't afford the books, clothing and other expenses."

"And that's where I come in?"

"You catch on fast. If you agreed to pay his living expenses, Seth could manage the rest."

"Why this student?"

"Seth's bright and a hard worker. More importantly he needs to get away from his father's influence."

"I've heard about Rafe's antics. He doesn't appreciate meddling. Been known to back up his opinion with a shotgun."

"Another reason I want Seth out of there."

A shadow fell across the porch. "Seth won't leave his father."

Abigail jerked toward Wade. Eyes snapping, face grim, he pinned her with his gaze. She rose to her feet. "I'm merely trying to save Seth from—"

"From what? His father? Or from the fate of being just like me?"

George snorted. Wade turned hostile eyes on his father. The elder Cummings's smile faded.

She folded her arms across her chest. "I'm talking about protecting Seth. Rafe's no example for his son, could even bring Seth harm."

"Rafe may prize his privacy, but he'd never mistreat that boy."

She leaned toward him until they were nose to nose. "Rafe's example of using alcohol to handle problems could influence Seth, lead to his drinking."

"Rafe has a problem, sure. So did your brother-in-law. Would you suggest Joe's gambling made him unfit as a parent?"

His words slugged Abigail in the stomach. She sucked in a gulp of air, stunned by a comparison she couldn't deny. Anything done to excess could impede a man's judgment.

The scowl on his face faded. "I'm sorry if that hurt you, but we're not talking about abuse here. Plenty of children must cope with the parents God gave them."

Wade's gaze locked with hers. His words evoked memories from her childhood, no doubt his too.

"Abby, you mean well, but you're trying to shove your plan for Seth's life down his throat. Instead, pray for the boy's wisdom, give him gentle council—take the time to discover what's important to him."

She motioned to George watching them with hooded eyes. "Your father understands the importance of getting Seth out from under Rafe's thumb."

Wade's narrowed eyes drilled into her like one of those augers in his shop. "Perhaps you'd like to find another place of employment."

Abigail felt the blood drain from her face. She couldn't

earn the wage the Cummingses paid anywhere else…if she could even find another job.

George leaped to his feet, coughing with the exertion. "You're not firing her. She had the sense to relocate me downstairs while you haven't given my comfort a thought."

"What are you talking about? I hired Abby to handle your needs so I could focus on your business holdings."

"This young woman is thinking of ways to make me more comfortable. Ways to give me dignity. You're not firing her!" he said, ending on a wheeze.

Abigail couldn't believe she and George Cummings were on the same side of anything, much less this battle.

Red-faced, Wade turned glacial eyes on her. "I appreciate what you're doing for my father. But I won't tolerate you using Cummings money to maneuver Seth. I understand what's important to that boy."

"We'll see about that. I intend to talk to Seth."

Wade's features hardened, appeared carved from granite. "Do that. I expect him in the shop any minute."

"If Seth expresses a desire to attend college and your father wants to help, will you go along with Cummings money paying his expenses?"

"*If* college is what the boy wants. But Seth will never agree to leave his father."

She folded her arms across her chest. "We'll see which of us is right. Today."

Chapter Ten

Determined to escape that infuriating female, Wade stomped inside the house. Once he changed his clothes, he'd hightail it to the shop and release his frustration making the salesmen samples—miniature versions of his furniture he'd use to bring in orders.

As he strode through the foyer, he glanced into the parlor. The furniture had been rearranged to make room for his father's bed. Two wingback chairs had been pulled up near the bay window. Off to the side of the bed his wheelchair waited, ready if needed but unobtrusive. With easy access to the outdoors and kitchen, the move downstairs made sense. Wade sighed. A solution he should have thought of but hadn't.

Weighed down by the insight that no matter how hard he tried to please his father he always seemed to fail him, Wade left the parlor and took the stairs two at a time. As much as he valued Abby's practical ideas and the kindness she showed his father, that didn't give her the right to ask George to finance Seth's college expenses. Especially when she knew how he felt about pushing Seth into leaving town.

He had urged Seth to finish high school and hoped the boy would take the advice. But Wade had lived his entire life under that duress and wouldn't force his will on another.

He snorted. In truth, he wished he could control Abby. Whether she realized it or not, she put the boy in the awkward position of choosing between them when Seth wanted nothing more than to please them both.

As he barreled down the upstairs hall, he admitted Abby respected neither his opinions nor his dream. Whenever she talked about woodworking her attitude proved she held his life's work in contempt, the same as holding him in contempt.

Inside his room painted a soft blue-green, a blend of the colors of sky and paddock visible through his window and in stark contrast with his mood, he doffed his suit and tie and changed into faded Levis and an old shirt, finally at ease in his own skin.

Abby had forgotten what they'd once shared. Or perhaps those idyllic days he remembered meant nothing to her. If only he didn't remember. Perhaps then her disrespect wouldn't chafe like days in the saddle.

He jammed his feet into his boots then tromped down the stairs and out the back door. Each step of his booted heel ground the truth into his brain. Abby knew his relationship with his father was tenuous at best. Yet she'd gone to George behind Wade's back, adding another wedge between him and his father.

Together he and Abby could have accomplished much good for Seth. But the underhanded way she approached the situation told him what he already knew. He needed to keep his distance from Abigail Wilson.

His mother's desertion had taught him others let you down. Even those you thought loved you. He'd loved his mother with a little boy's trusting heart, soaking up her gentle touch; her soft breath on his cheek as she tucked him in at night; her acceptance of his assertion that one day he'd build furniture like her father, Grandpa Brooks. She'd smiled and encouraged him to follow his dream. Yet following her dream had devastated his family and resulted in her death.

He couldn't ignore what her experience taught. To temper one's dreams and avoid giving one's heart. Better that he never marry, never bring children into this world. When a marriage ended children's hearts were broken.

Abby would make someone a wonderful wife. With the trouble between them that someone wouldn't be him. The prospect of not having her in his life sunk inside him like a stone. As much as her attitude about Seth, about his life-work, irked him, he admired her spunk, her wit that deflected his father's guff, how tirelessly she worked.

Earlier she'd recruited volunteers from the job site to move his father's bedroom. Those men worked long hours day after day to restore what the fire had destroyed. Wade hadn't done his share.

Inside his shop, his gaze roamed the furniture lining the walls and landed on the oak head and footboards leaning in the corner in front of the slats and rails. An idea took hold in his mind. Plenty of men could nail a stud or shingle, but no one else in this town crafted furniture. He'd build beds, as many as he could manage in the time he had. From what he'd heard, he'd have a month. He'd order mattresses through the Mercantile.

The salesmen samples would have to wait.

The needs of others preempted his dream. His stomach lurched. Not that he was accomplishing much anyway. Rafe hadn't shown up at the warehouse at noon. He'd have to find someone else to repair the building.

Seth would arrive any time now to work in the shop. Wade wouldn't bring up his father. Though Seth probably already knew Rafe had missed the appointment and lost the chance to earn money they badly needed.

The boy could cut and sand slats and rails while Wade

worked on the head and footboards. As he calculated the beds' dimensions, figuring the cuts he'd make, the tension of his encounter with Abby drained out of him.

If she dared to show her face and try to talk Seth out of the boy's own plan for his life, Wade would keep his mouth nailed shut.

Though he suspected Seth would teach Abby a lesson on being true to oneself that no amount of college classes had prepared her for.

"I'm quitting school." Seth toed the ground, avoiding Abigail's gaze. "Going into crafting furniture with Wade."

This harebrained idea was Wade's fault. She'd like to stomp through the shop door, mere feet away from where she and Seth stood, and give Wade what he deserved—an old-fashioned tongue-lashing, but first she'd try to convince Seth to reconsider.

What could she say to convince her brightest student that education laid a strong foundation for a good life? "Seth, making money to help out at home is a worthy goal. But a college education will enable you to make *more* money." She took a breath. "If you're worried about the cost of college, I might've found a way to help with your expenses."

If Wade heard her he'd be furious, but his father's offer had been generous, something he should celebrate.

Seth lifted his gaze, his dark eyes resolute. "I don't see the point in going, Miss Wilson. I know enough to get along."

"You're not the first farm boy to consider dropping out of high school." She knelt beside the flower bed and scooped up a handful of loose dirt, holding it toward Seth. "Working the soil is an honest occupation, an admirable occupation. This nation would go hungry if not for our farmers. But you never know when that farm might disappear." She opened her hand and let the dirt slip between her fingers. "You can't rely on land."

Hadn't she seen that? Their farm had been there one day and gone the next. Education could not be taken away from you.

"We have a sheepskin deed signed by President Van Buren in 1840. Our farm isn't going to disappear."

Rafe, with his weaknesses, hadn't borrowed on his land? If her father hadn't, how different their lives would have been.

Seth's eyes lit. "Farming isn't what I want to do with my life."

"Do you think Wade's shop couldn't disappear? You can learn the craft of cabinetmaking, but if the orders don't come in, you'd be out of work. You're smart, capable of doing anything you put your mind to." She ticked off the possibilities on smudged fingers. "You could be a doctor, lawyer, professor, writer, scientist—the possibilities are endless. You need an education to fall back on."

Seth's mouth turned mulish. "Making furniture is what I want to do. *All* I want to do."

Wade appeared in the doorway. Arms folded across his chest, stance wide, expression stony—ready to leap to Seth's defense. If only they could be on the same side of this issue.

She turned to Seth. "Is that the main reason you don't want to finish high school and go to college next fall? Or is it that you don't want to leave your father…ah, shorthanded?"

Seth flushed. "I'm needed at home."

"If you go to Iowa State in Ames, you can get back home to see your dad." She studied him. "If you're concerned your father can't manage by himself, I'll find a way to help Rafe."

She had no idea how. Perhaps Wade could give Rafe a job in his shop. She sighed. Wade wouldn't tolerate an employee who drank, even if that employee was Seth's dad.

Seth took a step back, moving toward the shop, toward Wade. "You're a good teacher, Miss Wilson. You've always been nice to me—patching my clothes, giving us home cooking. I appreciate it, but I'm going to work in Wade's shop." He glanced at Wade. "As his apprentice," he said, voice filling with pride.

Wade laid a hand on Seth's shoulder. "Are you sure that's what you want?"

A smile lit Seth's face. "Making something special out of ordinary boards, pegs and glue—something solid enough to last for years is like sharing in the creativity of God." His face flushed either with embarrassment or sheer emotion. "With sandpaper, stain and varnish, I can produce a finish that glows like a starry night." He looked at Abigail. "That's what I want to do. With instruction and practice, I will."

For a moment Abigail couldn't speak. The sweetness of Seth's words, the satisfaction on his face mimicked Wade's. The temptation to concede defeat slid through her. But then she remembered the stakes. "Getting an education and a good job won't keep you from building furniture in your spare time. Maybe even selling a piece or two to bring in extra income."

Seth's brows beetled. "I don't want to do this in my spare time. I've prayed for this apprenticeship, dream about it at night. When I'm making furniture, I'm content, never in a rush. You can't hurry something beautiful."

"But, you can't make money if—"

"Abby, money isn't everything." Wade stepped closer. "You've said your piece, given Seth your advice. As his teacher, something you should do. But you don't know when to quit. You're stomping on Seth's dream."

"The decision he makes now is important. The lack of a high school diploma can cut off a path he might want to take later."

"I don't want to be a doctor, poking and prodding sick folks. I don't want to be a lawyer waiting for trouble to march in the door. I don't want to be a scientist concocting a formula for a better paint or a horseless carriage."

"Those are all good things, Seth," Abigail said. "Things that could make a difference, save a life, change the world."

Seth nodded. "For someone else, but not for me." He released a gust of air. "I've got a plan for my life that suits me fine."

"Seth, why don't you go on inside?"

"Yes, sir." Seth glanced at Abigail. "Goodbye, Miss Wilson." As if he couldn't get away fast enough, he sprinted inside.

Easing the door closed behind him, Wade walked out into the lawn, moving Abigail along with him until they stood in the Cummingses' garden. The soft buzz of bumblebees gathering nectar from delphinium and foxglove gave a misleading sense of harmony. But the look on Wade's face, his puckered brow and narrowed lips, predicted an impending storm.

"I won't have you badgering that boy."

"I want him to see he's making a mistake."

Wade let out a sigh. "I know you care and your intentions are good but you're bullying that boy. Instead of harping at Seth—" Wade pointed toward the house "—perhaps you need to remember the reason you're here and spend your time and energy on my father."

His rebuke stung like one of those bees. Straightening her shoulders, she gave him a curt nod as the truth sank inside her.

"You and I are miles apart. Worlds apart. I don't know why I expected otherwise." Abigail tilted her chin. "Whether you know it or not, we're in a battle. A battle I intend to win."

A muscle in Wade's cheek jumped. "We have nothing more to say." He turned and trudged to the shop.

Wade's opposition festered like a splinter under her skin. As she watched him go, Abigail tamped down her dismay at the impasse between them and made her decision.

She'd talk to Rafe. Surely he'd realize his life was going nowhere. And he had a negative influence on his son. If he knew funds were available to handle the cost, he might see he held Seth back from a better life.

If the attraction between her and Wade, the sense of connection, had evaporated like dew on a hot sunny morning, well, nothing could make her happier.

So why did she feel like crying?

Not that she would.

A Wilson never cried.

The image of Abby's face, of the disappointment she felt when Seth asserted his desire to apprentice, nibbled at Wade. She meant well, genuinely feared for Seth's well-being, he knew that, but whether she admitted it or not, she'd gone too far.

God wanted His children to use the talents He'd given them. To hone them, yes, with education, but also with practice. To use those talents to provide for one's family, as Seth wanted to do. As Abby did. Why couldn't she understand the boy's urgency to help out at home? Had her anger at him colored her thinking?

A lump formed in his throat. Losing the farm and her father had hurt her. When Wade had set her aside years ago, he'd done it to save her from losing her family. Yet his decision had hurt her even more. Had the combination of all those hurts caused her to put her trust in education? Not in God? He'd pray she could lean on God, leaving the future to the One in control of the universe.

Perhaps, just perhaps, he could find a way to mend the pain he'd caused her.

For now, he'd focus on the task of producing beds. The simple design had no turned legs or posts. No curlicue ornamentations. Just straight lines made from solid oak to withstand a lifetime of use.

To add to his growing list of problems, he'd received written notice that the equipment he'd ordered must be paid in full before delivery. To approve his own loan smacked of duplicity. Yet without equipment, he couldn't produce orders. He'd have to speak to his father about a loan. That meant revealing his plan to open the shop. News his father wouldn't take lying down.

With handling the bank, overseeing other holdings and constructing beds in the evenings, Wade would barely have time to eat and catch a few hours of sleep. Maybe before long his father could work from home or come into the office for an hour or two each day and slowly take over the reins.

Across the way Seth, eager to help the burned-out families, cut the slats for the beds. The peaceful look of concentration on the boy's face reminded Wade of the contentment he found creating furniture.

"Wade, why veneer the top of the buffet instead of using a solid piece of cherry?" Seth asked, glancing at the finished piece.

"With the uneven heat in many homes a veneered surface reduces the likelihood of cracking. Poorly dried wood increases the possibility. The mill supplying my lumber has gone out of business. I'm planning a trip to the Sullivan Lumberyard in Waterloo. Would you like to go along?"

"Yes, sir, I would," Seth said, a big smile on his face.

"Speak to your father. We'll go once we finish the beds."

"I will."

Wade wondered if Seth had a good solid bed to sleep on at home, but wouldn't insult him with the question.

Seth turned to Wade with troubled eyes. "Miss Wilson's been kind to me but now she's upset."

Seth called Abby kind. Wade had seen her kindness with George, the gentle way she spoke to Seth. Upon occasion, he'd even heard that tone connected to his name.

"Well, if that's true, Seth, she's upset with both of us."

The boy tilted his head, his expression puzzled. "Sometimes you and Miss Wilson sound like you're fighting over who you are, not over me."

Wade blinked. His grip on the saw slowed. Why hadn't he seen that? How could he and Abby find harmony and give Seth the help he needed?

Not that Wade wanted anything permanent with her.

Not that the Wilsons would allow it if he did.

He'd concentrate on his work, on Seth, and try to ignore the spitfire of a woman who occupied too many of his thoughts.

Yet he understood Seth's dismay. How could he ease the boy's mind? "I don't think Miss Wilson's so much upset with you as she is with your decision. She cares about you."

"Reckon you're right. I don't know much about ladies."

Wade chuckled. "You're not alone. Few of us men understand women."

"I figured you, ah, having a sister and all... Maybe you could help me understand Miss Wilson."

"Can't say that I can, but I'm willing to give it a try. What's bothering you?"

Earnestness rode Seth's features. "She takes care of her ma. Since the fire, she's providing for her whole family." His brow furrowed, as if trying to fit a piece into a puzzle that didn't fit. "So why doesn't she understand me wanting to look after my pa?"

No wonder Seth was confused. Abby's behavior contradicted her stance. "She probably does understand, underneath."

"Then why is she set on me going to college?"

"She believes college is your best chance for a good life."

The boy raised baffled eyes to Wade. "But that's what I don't understand. My life is good."

Not one whit of deception lurked in those blue eyes. Yet surely the boy's life wasn't easy with a father who drank too much. With a father who barely made ends meet. With a father who kept the community at arm's length. Except for an occasional appearance at church or the feed store, Rafe was a recluse.

Was Seth deceiving himself? Or did he even know what constituted what most would call a good life? "What's the best thing about your life?"

"Pa's always been good to me, drunk or sober, but he hasn't been himself since Ma passed." Seth sighed. "He looks…lost. Each morning, he gets down on his knees and prays to be a good man, pleading with God for strength to not take that first drink. Pa doesn't want to let me down." Tears filled the boy's eyes. "Even though he fails time after time, he never stops trying. One day, he won't fail. One day, my pa will win." Seth gave a dazzling smile like the sun bursting through an overcast sky. "Knowing with God's help, Pa will defeat this thing, that's the best."

The backs of Wade's eyes stung. This boy was like no other. Seth Collier loved his father. Believed Rafe didn't want to fail him. Believed his Heavenly Father would help Rafe find the courage and strength to stop drinking. That faith never wavered. Seth stood by his father as flawed as Rafe was, not out of duty, but because he loved his father totally, without conditions.

Wade was teaching Seth to know wood, to craft furniture, but Seth was teaching Wade something far more vital.

"You know, Seth, I want to be just like you—a man with God's own heart."

Instead of a man with a heart too damaged to love.

Sunday morning Abigail sat with her family in their usual pew, grateful to be back to church as a family, to know the days of uncertainty would soon end. Billy slept in his mother's arms. Ma held Donnie on her lap while the twins and Peter sat wedged between the adults.

Heart overflowing with thankfulness for God's healing and the town's support of those who lost everything, Abigail scanned the parishioners, asking God to bless each one as they'd blessed the Lessmans.

One of Joe's blessings had come from an unlikely source. George Cummings had insisted he no longer needed his wheelchair, a generous loan considering her employer still struggled with shortness of breath. Ma had been wary of George's motives, but when Joe hobbled down the stairs that morning, eager to get outside and into that wheelchair, Ethel had changed her mind.

Another blessing—Pastor Ted had set aside this Sunday to bring in used clothing, furnishings and items for those who'd lost everything in the fire. Chests of drawers, hall trees and chairs dotted the churchyard. A huge stack of linens, countless bags of clothing and several boxes of tableware all but filled the vestibule, proof of the congregation's generosity. The ladies auxiliary would meet Monday to divide and distribute the bounty.

As Orville Radcliff rose to lead the singing, everyone stood. A movement out of the corner of her eye drew Abigail's attention. Wade followed his father down the aisle to their pew on the far side of the church. The dark hair at

Wade's nape, damp and curly from a dousing, broad shoulders back, head high, he was an imposing figure, turning young ladies' heads.

Abigail's breath caught. Including hers.

A familiar cough proved the short walk from carriage to pew had taxed George's lungs. Why had Wade's father insisted on lending a wheelchair he obviously needed? Was he trying to assuage his guilt over calling the Wilson loan?

If so, God must be working in his life.

Her grip on the hymnal tightened. She prayed daily, read the Scriptures, loved the Lord with all her heart. Yet had she allowed God to work in her life, had she surrendered her will to God's? Had she trusted Him in everything?

Unable to examine that now, she tamped down her uncertainty, forcing her attention on the words swimming on the page then lifted her voice in worship.

At the close of the last song, the congregation settled onto the wooden pews. As Peter watched a fly crawl on his arm, Sam snuggled against her. Hugging him close, Abigail smiled down at him. Within minutes Sam's eyes closed and he slept. Children were such a blessing. The only reason she'd risk marriage.

Pastor Ted climbed the steps to the pulpit and asked them to turn to the fourth chapter of Ephesians in their Bibles. As he read the verses on unity, Abigail's heart stuttered in her chest. God didn't approve of strife among believers. That meant forgiving.

If she could forgive, how could she forget?

When George Cummings took the farm, his heartless actions changed Frank Wilson from a caring, fun-loving man into an unresponsive shadow. George made money selling Wilson land to the railroad while destroying her father, in essence killing him. How did George live with himself?

Her gaze traveled to Wade. The wide gap between father

and son revealed their relationship. Was Cora correct when she said the day Ernestine left shattered Wade and George's fragile bond? Or did Wade's aloofness come from disapproval of his father's business practices?

With every particle of her being, she forced herself to concentrate on the sermon and not on the man across the way.

After the closing song and announcements, people poured into the aisles, greeting one another and Pastor Ted.

In the foyer of the church, a cough slowed Abigail's steps. She turned to face the Cummings men. Two pair of indigo eyes looked back at her. Only one pair kicked up her pulse a notch. As Wade's dark regard rippled through her, her heart tripped in her chest then tumbled. No matter how much she tried, she couldn't be indifferent to Wade.

"I'm pleased you felt up to coming this morning, George," she said though her gaze remained on his son.

Wade's eyes twinkled. "Does that include me?"

"Are you feeling ill?" Abigail arched a brow.

"If sickness stirs your interest, I feel a cold coming on."

The corners of Abigail's lips turned up. A sudden longing to let go of the feud, to put that ugliness behind her, slid through her.

Orville Radcliff stopped beside them. "I was about to summon the feud police till I saw those smiles. If Cummingses and Wilsons sit in the middle pews next week, God will have worked a miracle in our midst. What I've been praying for."

That their behavior necessitated prayer scorched Abigail's cheeks.

George snorted. "Rome wasn't built in a day."

Orville grinned. "Good to see you out, Mr. Cummings."

With dogged steps, Lois pushed Joe with Billy on his lap

up the aisle. Ma herded the bigger boys along behind them. They stopped near George. What was this about?

"Thanks for the loan of the wheelchair, Mr. Cummings." Joe offered his good hand. "I feel less like a caged lion."

George took Joe's hand gingerly in his bandaged palm. "Does that make you his zookeeper, Mrs. Lessman?"

To Abigail's amazement, Lois and Joe chuckled along with Wade and his father. Ma didn't crack a smile.

"We men take exception to being laid up," George said. "I'm sure Abigail can verify I've been cantankerous."

A flash of antagonism sparked in Ma's gray-blue eyes. "*That* hardly needs confirmation, Mr. Cummings."

"Well, we'd better be going. The children are restless," Lois said then pushed Joe's wheelchair toward the vestibule. Everyone followed her out.

At the door the pastor talked to Seth. Rafe stood at a distance, turning his hat in his hands, eyes glued to the floor. They must've sat in the last row for Abigail not to have seen them.

Oh, this gave her an opportunity to speak with Rafe. "I'll be right back," she said, heading toward the door.

With long strides, Wade circled her, blocking her path. "Rafe hasn't been to church more than a couple times since his wife died. This isn't the time to waylay the man." His gaze softened. "Instead of pushing Seth to put his trust in education, why not assure him that God will take care of him, his dad too?"

Heat climbed her neck. "Are you implying I don't believe that?"

"I'm suggesting you could give that impression."

Abigail inhaled a shaky breath. He'd implied she didn't trust God. Yet he'd never had to trust God for one bite of food, one unpaid bill. She'd seen that God helps those who help themselves. "You believe preparing oneself for the future shows a lack of trust? What would you know about providing for your family? Seth's life is far more like mine than yours."

Wade reached out a hand and cupped her chin. She yearned to lean into the warmth of his touch, but she'd learned not to rely on anyone.

"Oh, Abby, you've had to carry a heavy load." His Adam's apple bobbed. "Because of my family. I'm sorry."

Unable to speak, she covered his hand with hers and soaked up the comfort he offered, and then stepped away.

"Well, my dad's waiting. I'd better go."

Wade returned to his father, who was sitting in the back pew of the now-deserted church. As the Cummings men moved through the open door, the Baggett sisters met them on the stoop. The sight of Wade surrounded by three gushing females sliced through her.

Why did she care?

Unable to examine the question, she skirted the circle of Wade's admirers and hurried down the steps as Seth and his father pulled away in their wagon. Wade had been right. Church was not the place to talk to Rafe.

Rachel strolled over. "Looks like the Baggett sisters are determined to reel in Wade."

"That's fine with me."

"Really? You look upset."

"I'm…confused." About Wade. About Seth. About most everything, but she couldn't say that, not even to her best friend.

As they walked toward Rachel's house, Abigail sighed. "I don't understand why Seth is in such a rush to grow up."

"You were just like him."

Abigail blinked. True, she'd pushed hard to attend Normal School so she could teach in the one-room schoolhouse. Summers she took additional classes enabling her to teach

English at the high school. "But I finished twelfth grade first."

"Maybe Seth's desperate for money now."

If so, Seth hurried to reach his goal for the exact same reason she had. Their families needed their income. She understood Seth perfectly. But that didn't mean she couldn't want more for him.

The reason she'd risk a visit to the Collier farm and Rafe's wrath. Even if that visit angered him, Rafe wouldn't harm a woman.

Would he?

Chapter Eleven

A small boy, shirtless under his overalls, bare feet, dusty and on tiptoe, struggled to choose from the selection of penny candy lined up in glass jars along the counter.

As Abigail waited for the youngster to make his decision, she inhaled the scent of coffee, molasses and pickles wafting from barrels on the floor. To celebrate her first payday at the Cummingses, she'd buy her nephews a rare treat.

The proprietor, Seymour Manning, wearing an apron over his clothing and a patient expression on his face, gave her a smile. Once a gambler, Elizabeth's father had turned his life around and like Pastor Ted had encouraged and counseled Joe.

His selection made, the boy plopped a penny down while Mr. Manning sacked his purchase. Bag clutched in a dirty dimpled hand, the boy whirled to the door. "Thanks!" he shouted.

Mr. Manning, an imposing man with a handsome head of hair and wide girth, chuckled. "Sorry for the wait. If all my customers were as indecisive, I'd be pulling out my hair."

Smiling, Abigail laid out her purchases. "The delay gave me time to think about buying candy for my nephews. Please add four red lollipops to my order."

"Well, in that case, I may hire the lad," he said with a wink, then popped the staples in one bag and the lollipops in another. "Appreciate your business."

Harrison Carder appeared at her elbow and tipped his hat. Blond and gray-eyed with a neatly trimmed beard, he looked dapper. "You look mighty fetching, Miss Abigail," he said in that charming Boston accent.

Smooth talk. Smooth manners. Smooth brow. "Thank you."

"Which penny candy is your favorite?"

Once Wade had given her the candy. "Peppermints."

Harrison dropped a coin on the counter. "Peppermints for the lady."

As Mr. Manning tunneled into the jar with a brass scoop, Harrison turned toward her. "Those peppermints are my way of softening you up. Hoping you'll take pity on a lonely bachelor and invite him for a home-cooked meal."

A snicker drew Abigail's attention to Cecil and Oscar Moore playing checkers beside the unlit stove.

"At least we don't have to beg for Elizabeth Logan's biscuits," Cecil said loud enough for Harrison to hear.

Oscar snorted. "Young whippersnappers today ain't got no clue on how to sway a female."

In an attempt to tamp down the chuckle shoving out of her mouth, Abigail coughed behind a gloved hand. "I'm sorry but our kitchen table is overflowing with nine of us in one tiny apartment."

That dejected look on Harrison's face tugged at her conscience. A Christian should be hospitable, especially to a newcomer. "Once my sister's family is back in their house, I'd enjoy preparing you a home-cooked meal."

All smiles, he clasped his hands together. "I'll look forward to it."

Elizabeth Logan marched up with Wade Cummings in

tow. Her wide-brimmed straw hat was adorned with silk flowers pretty enough to draw bees.

Elizabeth looked pleased with herself.

Wade looked…trapped. What was this about?

"Until then, Abigail, I hope you'll accept my invitation to dine at Agnes's Café." Harrison flashed even white teeth.

Wade glowered at Harrison. "What are you doing here?"

"Would you believe shopping? No? Well, I'm inviting Abigail to join me for dinner." He beamed at her. "Would next Saturday evening be convenient?"

"Yes, thank you."

"I'll come by for you at six o'clock, early enough for a leisurely stroll in the park afterward." Harrison tipped his hat to Elizabeth, gave Abigail a wink then tossed a smile at Wade before sauntering out the door.

"What a nice man," Elizabeth said.

Looking about as happy as a man walking the gangplank over high seas with the tip of a pirate's sword at his back, Wade emitted a low guttural sound, almost a growl.

Appearing not to notice Wade's reaction, Elizabeth pulled him closer. "Abigail, I saw you come in here and convinced Wade to leave his desk to discuss a project I have for you two."

Abigail opened her mouth to speak.

The pastor's wife lifted a dainty palm. "Now before you say you're too busy, let me assure you that the only folks with time on their hands are laid out in the church cemetery."

Across the way, Cecil and Oscar Moore guffawed.

"Ain't she something?" Cecil said.

Oscar nodded. "Yep, Elizabeth gets to the heart of things."

Indeed she did. Who in this town had the nerve to go up against Elizabeth Logan, including her husband? Whatever Elizabeth wanted, she usually got. In the two years she'd lived here, she'd done more good, worked harder than anyone in town.

"What do you have in mind?" Abigail heard herself ask. As if she had time to add one more task to her load.

"The bills for lumber, roofing, insulation—all the construction materials have been paid with auction funds. Yesterday George Cummings gave Ted a sizable donation, enough money to supply the essentials for our burned-out families. Once we ascertain their needs, we can purchase in quantity."

"That's wonderful news." Abigail couldn't earn enough money to purchase all Lois would need to run a home. The weight of that burden had been lifted from her shoulders by George Cummings, a man not known for philanthropy. She touched Wade's arm. "Thank your father for us."

Wade looked confused. "I had no idea he'd done that."

George Cummings had his faults, but bragging wasn't one of them. He hadn't even told his son. Perhaps merely proof he didn't share anything of consequence with Wade.

"The problem I'm seeing is a lack of coordination in the town's efforts," Elizabeth went on. "The Ladies' Club is working. The churches are working. Without someone overseeing how money is spent, some needs may be duplicated, others overlooked. That's where you two come in."

Wade ran a hand over his nape, as if Elizabeth's suggestion put a knot there.

"Why us?" Abigail hoped the question wouldn't elicit a homily on overlooking the feud and learning to work together.

"Who better to handle purchases than the banker son of the biggest donor and the sister of one of the impacted families, a competent woman who's seen needs firsthand?"

The pastor's wife knew how to use flattery to get her way.

Her way always benefited the community so no one minded. George Cummings could take lessons from Elizabeth.

"I have more good news." Elizabeth beamed. "Wade just told me he's making bed frames for the families."

Abigail had seen Wade as self-centered, his furniture making as a threat to Seth's education, yet here was a practical example of the good his work could do. "That's generous."

"Wish I had time to turn the bedposts on the lathe."

"Nothing fancy is needed," Elizabeth assured him. "Our families will be grateful for serviceable beds."

She handed Abigail and Wade a sheet of paper with the sum of all available funds then glanced around the store. "Obviously we'll purchase what we can from town merchants. The church and Ladies' Club are handling linens, clothing and smaller kitchen items. Major purchases like cookstoves and iceboxes will probably head our list. My father will order whatever he doesn't carry in the store and sell it to us at cost."

Wade nodded, never taking his eyes off Abigail. "I knew Seymour would do his part."

"All business owners are quoting the lowest possible price," Elizabeth said.

All too aware of the rise and fall of Wade's broad chest in rhythm with her own, the power in those wide shoulders and large capable hands, Abigail scrambled for footing. "Should we…ah…divide the funds by six?"

"The distribution doesn't have to be identical as long as crucial needs are met. Speak to the Andersons. I've heard their relatives are purchasing their cookstove."

Abigail stared into Wade's eyes, losing herself in those indigo orbs. "That's nice." Nice hardly described Wade's mesmerizing eyes, his—

"Are you willing to take this on? Abigail?" Elizabeth asked.

"What?" She forced her mind on the conversation and off Wade.

"Will you work on this committee with Wade?"

How could she refuse? A committee to coordinate efforts made sense. "Yes, as long as you understand my responsibility to Mr. Cummings comes first."

"Naturally. Wade, with your hectic schedule, would it be easier for you to meet during the noon hour over a late lunch?"

Wade appeared bewildered by the question. "What?"

"What's wrong with you two? If I didn't know better, I'd think you'd lost your hearing."

Heat climbed Abigail's neck and flooded into her cheeks.

Not waiting for an answer, Elizabeth drew Abigail and Wade together, one on each side of her. "I'm relieved to have you overseeing this. I'll leave you to work out the particulars."

And that quickly, Abigail and Wade had agreed to spend more time together. Had Elizabeth Logan just engineered her biggest coup yet—bringing a Cummings and a Wilson together?

Elizabeth walked over to the Moore brothers, the only men welcome in the Ladies' Club. "See you gentlemen at the meeting Saturday afternoon."

"Be there with sleigh bells on."

At the puzzled expression on Elizabeth's face, Cecil said, "We ain't got no other kind."

With a nod for the Moore brothers and a jaunty wave to her father, Elizabeth swept out the door.

Wade turned his gaze on Abigail, rooting her to the spot. As she peered into those sapphire eyes, caught his masculine scent, felt the warmth radiating from his skin, a surge of longing slid through her, snatching her breath.

"Look, Oscar. Miss Abigail's got a dinner invite from that lawyer feller. Now she's making eyes at Wade here," Cecil said.

Awakened from her trancelike state, she took a step back—almost as fast as Wade.

"Next thing ya know, we'll be playing harmonica and banjo at another wedding celebration," Oscar replied.

Nodding, Cecil pursed his lips. "Reckon so, but whose?"

Oscar cackled. "Ain't that the big question?"

Wade cleared his throat. "Will it…? Can you…meet at the bank tomorrow at twelve-thirty to formulate our plans?"

"Yes, I'll bring lunch," she said, sounding as breathless as Wade's father. What had gotten into her? She was reacting as if she'd never seen Wade before.

Where would all this togetherness with Wade lead?

Wade stumbled from the Mercantile. Everything around him, the shops, passersby, horses tied at the hitching posts, looked as usual. But back in the store, he and Abigail had stared into each other's eyes until he could barely breathe, leaving him as disoriented as a tourist on the streets of Boston. He took a deep breath and let his gaze travel the street.

Down the way, Seth handed Betty Jo Weaver a nosegay. Bestowing him with a sweet smile, she sniffed the flowers, gazing up at him. Seth smiled back, beamed really.

Wade hoped he hadn't looked that starry-eyed in Abigail's presence.

Paul Roger, his ruddy face twisted in a scowl, stomped over and took Betty Jo's arm. After a moment of hesitation, Betty Jo chose Paul over Seth and the two walked on.

The raw, wounded look on Seth's face served as a bucket of cold water, a splash of reality bringing Wade to his senses.

Abigail agreed to work on the committee and to take care of his father, but she had no interest in him.

Acceptance of that dinner invitation said her interest lay with Harry, a man who could offer her what Wade couldn't—freedom from a troubled past.

Weary of conflict, Wade needed the peace he found making furniture. But before he went back to the bank, to that desk strewn with work, he'd stop by Harry's office. Make sure he treated Abby right.

A slice of Agnes's sugar cream pie should calm Abigail's jangled nerves. Or so she hoped. To help Lois, she'd work with Wade Cummings on this committee, but she wouldn't be duped by that crazy reaction she'd just had to the man.

He'd broken her heart five years ago. No matter how much she tried to pretend the relationship had been juvenile, her heart hadn't healed. Worse, by falling for Wade, she'd been disloyal to her family. Her father had been right. A Cummings couldn't be trusted.

She'd rely on common sense, intelligence, even intuition. All of those warned her away from Wade.

Tantalizing aromas drifted from the kitchen as Agnes prepared for the dinner rush. But for now only one other table in the far corner was occupied.

Across from Abigail, dark hair swept up under her hat, Rachel cut off a bite of cherry pie, oozing filling through the lattice crust. "This is delicious."

Abigail's reason for inviting her friend had nothing to do with Wade or a desire for pie, and everything to do with making sure Rachel had no feelings for Harrison Carder.

"I'm pleased you'll be working with Wade." Rachel wagged her brows. "Never know where that might lead."

The bite of sugar cream, smooth and sweet, melted in Abigail's mouth. "You're incorrigible. Let me enjoy my pie."

"Use all the big words you want, but only love could drive a practical woman like you to eat dessert before supper."

"Not love. More like second thoughts." She cocked her head at Rachel. "I accepted Harrison Carder's dinner invitation before I had time to think. Are you sure you don't have an interest in him?"

"He's not my type, as I said after the box lunch social."

"Well, yes, but I had to be sure."

"I'm surprised he's yours."

"You sound like the Moore brothers. They behaved as if accepting a dinner invitation was comparable to accepting a marriage proposal."

Rachel giggled. "Probably is to those two." She sobered. "Why go to dinner with Harrison when Wade's far more appealing?"

Abigail's fork clattered to the table. "Do you have a crush on Wade?"

"No, but you do." She wagged a finger. "Look how you reacted when you thought I might have an interest in him."

"I don't want you to get hurt." Abigail sighed. "Please accept I'm not that starry-eyed girl who fell for Wade in high school. You're stuck in the past." Since then Abigail had learned to stand on her own feet, depending on no one, making her own way.

A reminder that Rachel should plan for the future. "Have you thought about preparing for a career?"

Rachel's gaze dropped to her plate. "I always thought I'd get married."

"I'm sure you will, but New Harmony isn't crawling with eligible bachelors. Have you considered attending Iowa State Normal School in Cedar Falls?"

"Train to teach?"

"Why not? You enjoy teaching Sunday school." Abigail planted an elbow on the table and her chin in her hand, smiling. "You might meet someone in Cedar Falls."

"The idea of something new, finding my place in this world is exciting." A smile bloomed then faded. "If I left, my dad would be sad."

"He'd miss you. But he might be relieved to know you could manage if something happened to him."

Her brow furrowed. "I can't imagine life without him."

Rachel had already lost her mother. "I'm sure you'll have your father for a long, long time."

The door to the café jangled open and banged closed as diners entered and took seats.

Rachel sighed. "I'll pray about it. Talk to my dad." She gasped. "Oh, Abby, he can't cook."

"Maybe he'll find someone who can."

Rachel's jaw dropped.

"Why not? Your dad's young enough to want another woman in his life. If you weren't there to fix his meals and keep his house, he might go to the trouble of finding one."

"I never thought of such a thing. My dad's…well, just dad. Not a man who'd want a woman in his life."

"Would a stepmother be okay with you?"

"Well, I suppose… If she's nice, that is." Lost in thought, Rachel spun the handle of her fork time and again. Then her gaze landed on Abigail. "You talk about me and my dad finding someone to love. God might have a plan for your life, a plan that includes a man. Give Wade a chance."

Abigail shook her head. "I can't."

Rachel leaned toward her. "I remember what you and Wade meant to each other. I remember the way you stared into each other's eyes, how you'd light up when he entered the room, how you'd talk and talk, forgetting I was even there."

"You think I don't?" Tears stung the back of Abigail's eyes. She blinked them away, red-faced she'd come close to weeping in the café. "You want to forget what happened, but I can't. One minute, he stuck to my side like a burr on knickers. The next minute he was gone."

"Maybe he had a reason."

The reasons Abigail had considered made her feel worse.

"If you could forgive him—"

"Forgiving him doesn't mean I could ever trust him." She shoved her plate away. "Since you're not interested in Harrison, I'm going to keep our dinner plans," she said, forcing a smile. "I consider that giving a man a chance, don't you?"

"I consider that a waste of time." Rachel frowned. "Why can't you see the good in Wade?"

"I admire things about Wade." She wasn't merely attracted though that pull was powerful. "He's talented, hardworking, loyal to his father and serves others," she said, ticking off attributes she admired on the fingers of one hand.

"With the Cummingses' money, he could've lived a life of ease."

"True." Abigail raised her other hand. "He's also aloof, stubborn, holds things inside and can't give his heart." She'd fight that unwanted admiration with everything in her. "He proved that five years ago and I've seen nothing since to make me believe otherwise."

"All right, I'll stop pestering you about him."

"Finally." Abigail laid her hand on Rachel's arm. "When you have a career, you're not forced to marry unless you want to. That's what I want for you. Talk to your father."

"Don't let your profession convince you that you can handle everything—anything—alone. We can make plans, but we can't control the future." Rachel gave her hand a squeeze. "Only God can do that. Trust Him with everything, including your heart."

Wade had urged her to trust God, now Rachel did the same. Abigail lowered her gaze to her hands. Losing the farm, her father, Wade…

Where was God in any of that?

A lump rose in her throat. The past lay behind her. The time had come to concentrate on the future. She'd go to dinner with Harrison, see where that led.

The glass on the door embossed Harrison Carder, Attorney at Law rattled shut behind Wade. The shelves of the small office were lined with law books. Surely a statute could be found in one of those tomes demanding a lawyer treated a woman right. Certainly God's Word did.

Across the way Harry sat at his desk, scissors in hand, cutting out a…chain of paper dolls. "You're obviously not busy."

Harry's eyes twinkled. "Actually I'm creating clients— important work, but I can always make time for a friend." He laid down the scissors and leaned back. "What can I do for you?"

"What are your feelings for Abigail Wilson?"

"I barely know the woman." Harry arched a brow and danced the strip of paper dolls. "I'm hoping to remedy that."

"At dinner Saturday night?"

"Exactly."

"You'll like her." He plowed a hand through his hair. "What I don't know is your intentions once you do."

Harry chuckled. "You're adept at talking gibberish. Have you considered law?"

Wade sat on the opposite side of the desk in one of the two empty chairs reserved for clients. "I have a vocation." Or soon would. "Are you looking for a wife?"

Harry's eyes popped wide, gray circles of surprise. "Tarnation, man. I've got to establish my law practice. Make some money. I'm in no hurry to marry."

A weight Wade didn't know he carried slipped from his shoulders. "That's sensible."

"If things don't improve, I may return to Boston. A small town may not be the place for me."

Wade nodded. "The social scene must seem quiet here."

Harry folded the paper dolls until only two remained, hands joined. "Since Abigail accepted my invitation, things are looking up."

Wade rose to his feet, planted his palms on the desk and leaned toward Harry. "Abby's not one of those paper dolls. She's flesh and blood and can be hurt."

Harry dropped the paper dolls and held up his hands, as if facing the barrel end of a revolver. "Don't get excited. We'll see where this leads."

Wade glowered at his friend. "Abby isn't a trail to follow. She's a wonderful woman who deserves a man who'll love and protect her."

"You're crazy. You know that?" He plopped his hands behind his head and leaned back. "Crazy in love with that woman, that's what you are."

"What I am doesn't matter. Abby will never get beyond the trouble between us." He leaned closer. "But that doesn't mean I'll stand by and let you—"

"Sweep her off her feet?" Harry winked, as if he thought Wade's warning a joke.

"Hurt her. If you do, you'll answer to me."

"You're smitten, all right."

Harry's laughter followed Wade to the door. Why had he bothered trying to talk to the swain?

Tarnation, the man cut out clients. And Harrison called *him* crazy.

Tomorrow, when he and Abby met over lunch, he'd warn her that Harrison Carder had about as much substance as one of those flimsy paper dolls he'd made, and even less heart.

Chapter Twelve

The feather on Abby's jaunty purple hat fluttered like a bird in flight as she unpacked the picnic basket on the table. Wade gaped at the gloves she wore, made of mesh of all things, surely useless for keeping hands either clean or warm. Nothing he'd expect to see this practical woman wear.

How well did he know Abby really?

One thing he did know—she looked more scrumptious and smelled better than the food she'd prepared for their lunch.

And that was saying plenty.

His gaze traveled the long line of her willowy neck, the defined yet delicate jaw then moved to full rosy lips, soft and kissable and—

Whoa, Cummings. Get a grip.

He forced his mind back to the reason they'd come to the conference room. A cheery spot to meet that didn't require Wade to clear his cluttered desk. "I've, ah, been thinking about the task ahead of us and…"

She leaned toward him, waiting for him to finish. A tendril of hair had escaped its moorings and hugged her neck. If she took down her hair, would those blond tresses feel soft and silky under his palms?

He cleared his throat. Twice. "Should we make a list of necessities? The families could prioritize their needs."

"I had the exact same idea." Her slender eyebrows rose. "Imagine a Cummings and a Wilson agreeing on anything?" she said with a grin.

Her smile left a hollow in one cheek. He found that tiny dent so intriguing he couldn't tear his gaze away.

What was getting into him?

Abby motioned to the table. Plates, glasses, napkins, silverware—everything laid out with the food. "Shall we eat?"

They sat across from each other.

"You remembered I don't like crusts."

"Yes."

Such a small thing but her remembering pleased him. Wade bit into the ham salad sandwich. "Delicious."

"Thank you."

As she ate, she captured a crumb with her tongue sending a thrill skittering along his spine. He gulped. Even with the trouble between them now, he couldn't stop reacting to her beauty. He couldn't stop admiring her spunk, her work ethic, that kind heart of hers, under the tough exterior she'd built around it.

Abby looked at him strangely, as if he'd made some faux pas. He supposed he'd been staring.

"Shall we get started brainstorming a list of necessities?" she asked.

"Ah, yes. Once the list is complete, I'll ask Miss Detmer to type and make copies." He handed her paper and a pen. "Would you mind? Miss Detmer struggles with my handwriting."

"Happy to."

Abby jotted down items needed for different areas of the home, obviously more aware of the essentials for setting up housekeeping than he. Or perhaps she merely had more ability to focus on the task at hand when all he could do was focus on her.

The list grew until she'd filled a handwritten page. The soft curlicues of her penmanship, unlike his scrawl—more scratches with a pen compared to her feminine flourishes. What would his name look like written by her hand?

The scent of her soap, her shampoo—the mysterious fragrance that was Abigail—invaded his senses. Without thinking, he reached out a hand, longing to cradle the curve of her cheek.

"We might want to divide the list into expensive and less costly purchases." She frowned. "Are you okay?"

His hand fell away. "I'm fine." What had gotten into him? Was that appendage sitting on his shoulders empty of every rational thought? "Why would you think I'm not?"

"You're not eating."

He looked at the half sandwich in his hand. He hadn't realized he held it. As he quickly ate a bite, he glanced at her plate, empty except for a few crumbs.

"I'll have time in the evening to take the list around to the families involved," Abby said, studying it for omissions.

Harrison Carder might be lurking about. "You shouldn't go unescorted at night. I'll go with you."

A pang in his gut chided him for such absurdity. No one in town, not even Harry, posed a threat to Abby. Truth was—

He was jealous. Jealous of Harrison Carder.

"If we make the home visits right after the dinner hour," he said, "I should be back in the shop by eight or so."

"That's late to start making furniture." She smiled sweetly. "I'll ask Harrison to accompany me."

All but foaming at the mouth like a mad dog in his final throes of death, Wade said, "No need to bother Harry. Visiting the families is my obligation as a member of this committee."

"If you insist."

"I do." Harry wasn't the right man for Abby. Perhaps now was the time to caution her. "I wonder if you should cancel your dinner plans with Harry."

Gentle blue eyes turned chilly. "Why?"

"Ah, he's nice enough but not ready for courtship."

"Why do you say that?"

"Well, he's not established in his career. Not ready to take on a wife."

"Like you are?"

"What?"

"Like you're established in your career?"

He thrust his fingers between his neck and his collar. Why was it so hot in here? "Well, no, I wasn't speaking of myself."

"I'm sure that's true." She gave a frosty smile. "You know, a wife might be exactly what Harrison needs to help him achieve his goals."

This was going all wrong. His warning appeared to have increased Abby's interest in Harry.

Abby studied the list, as if indifferent to him or his warning. "Every household needs a cookstove. If we purchased five at retail, we could ask the Mercantile to donate a sixth."

"You're savvy about business as well as a skilled teacher."

"We women wear many hats."

"My mom did." He chuckled. "She loved make-believe and often gave Regina and me parts in her little skits. Once she took the role of a man, wearing my father's tie and hat, speaking in a remarkably deep voice."

"She sounds like a fun mom."

"She was. Dad disliked her silliness. Upon occasion he'd come home early and catch us in our hilarity. His stern ex-

LOVE INSPIRED® BOOKS,
a leading publisher of inspirational
romance fiction, presents...

Love Inspired® **HISTORICAL**

A SERIES OF HISTORICAL
LOVE STORIES THAT WILL LIFT YOUR
SPIRITS AND WARM YOUR SOUL!

GET 2 FREE BOOKS!

2 FREE BOOKS

**TO GET YOUR 2 FREE
BOOKS, AFFIX THIS
PEEL-OFF STICKER TO
THE REPLY CARD AND
MAIL IT TODAY!**

Plus, receive two
FREE BONUS GIFTS!

We'd like to send you two free books to introduce you to the Love Inspired® Historical series. Your two books have a combined cover price of $11.50 in the U.S. and $13.50 in Canada, but they are yours free! We'll even send you two wonderful surprise gifts. You can't lose!

Love Inspired HISTORICAL
An Honorable Gentleman

Love Inspired HISTORICAL
VICTORIA BYLIN
Marrying the Major

Love Inspired HISTORICAL
ANNA SCHMIDT
Family Blessings

Love Inspired HISTORICAL
LAURIE KINGERY
Could love blossom before the spring?
The Rancher's Courtship

Love Inspired HISTORICAL
NOELLE MARCHAND
Unlawfully Wedded Bride
Married—by mistake!

Each of your **FREE** books is filled with romance, adventur and faith set in various historical periods from bibli times to World W.

GET 2 FREE BOOKS!

Love Inspired HISTORICAL

HURRY!

Return this card today to get **2 FREE Books** *and* **2 FREE Bonus Gifts!**

YES! *Please send me the 2 FREE Love Inspired® Historical books and 2 FREE gifts for which I qualify. I understand that I am under no obligation to purchase anything further, as explained on the back of this card.*

affix
free
books
sticker
here

102/302 IDL FMHT

FIRST NAME

LAST NAME

ADDRESS

APT.#

CITY

STATE/PROV.

ZIP/POSTAL CODE

If offer card is missing write to: The Reader Service, P.O. Box 1867, Buffalo, NY 14240-1867 or visit: www.ReaderService.com

BUSINESS REPLY MAIL
FIRST-CLASS MAIL   PERMIT NO. 717   BUFFALO, NY

POSTAGE WILL BE PAID BY ADDRESSEE

THE READER SERVICE
PO BOX 1867
BUFFALO NY 14240-9952

NO POSTAGE
NECESSARY
IF MAILED
IN THE
UNITED STATES

pression burst our high spirits faster than a pin to an over-inflated balloon."

"George takes life too seriously."

That Abby understood slid through him. Wade laid his palm on her hand. "Dad's relaxed some. I credit you for the change in him."

"I'm glad." She looked away. "A father's indifference hurts."

They shared that and more. Much more. If only...

No, he might be attracted to Abby, drawn to everything about her, but he'd never give his heart.

By the end of the hour they had a plan of action: to take the list to those impacted by the fire; to ask retailers in town to donate an item or give a discount.

Thankfully Abby didn't mention Harry accompanying her again.

She gathered the remnants of lunch. "We've got our work cut out for us."

Work he could handle. Work had been his way of coping with Abby's presence in his house. Now they'd spend even more time together. Keeping his distance would be difficult.

If only he could have what he'd missed all his life—a trustworthy love. But from what he'd seen no such thing existed. Even if it did, Abby had made it abundantly clear he'd destroyed any feelings she'd once had for him.

Still, he could try to forge a friendship. "Would you attend the Fourth of July picnic with my father and me?"

She looked him straight in the eye. "That would give the wrong impression."

To whom? To Carder? To the town?

A knot twisted in his throat. She was speaking about giving the wrong impression to *him*.

He'd concentrate on making those beds, immerse himself in getting his business underway and handle his job at the bank.

Keep so busy he'd put Miss Abigail Wilson out of his mind.

Abigail should've taken George Cummings's cold stare as a warning.

"Where have you been? I don't pay you to gad about town," he groused, sounding like a cranky toddler in need of a nap.

"I was at the bank with your son."

"Doing what?"

"Not taking out a loan." She bit back her sarcasm, determined not to argue. "We're overseeing the disbursement of the money you contributed to the relief fund."

With a wave of his hand, he dismissed the recognition.

If praise didn't warm him up, maybe exercise would. "Are you up to taking Blue for a short walk?"

With a wag of his tail the hound rose from the sunny spot on the carpet and ambled toward them.

The knot between George's brows vanished. "About time you earned your wages."

They left the porch and ambled down the street, greeting passersby. Blue trailed behind, sniffing the grass, circling bushes, his ears all but dragging on the ground.

Abigail glanced at George. "Your donation was generous."

"Foolish was what it was. Stupid smoke muddled my brain."

That smoke hadn't damaged his brain, but had harmed his lungs. Why had George risked his life to save another? That action didn't fit her image of him.

At the corner Abigail insisted they turn back, unwilling to risk taxing his strength or lungs. As they walked toward the house, Abigail realized what she'd once considered ostentatious she now saw as merely a lovely home.

Inside the parlor George dropped into a chair at the bay window. Yawning, Blue plopped down at his feet with a grunt. Abigail lowered herself into the chair opposite from his.

Across the way the grand piano stood. Keys forever silent, a memorial to the woman who'd played it. Much had happened in this house. Much about the owner, someone she'd seen as self-seeking, puzzled her.

Abigail pressed her palms into her lap, gathering courage. "Why did you go into that burning house?"

George shrugged, staring out the window at the robins fluttering their wings in the fountain.

"Some would call what you did risky."

"Getting out of bed's a risk."

"True, but to go inside took courage. Why did you?"

"I heard something. Didn't see anyone else around to do it."

"Your donations and risking your life to search a burning house—none of it fits my image of George Cummings."

"You've got me pegged. Don't let all that bamboozle you." He wagged his finger. "And don't expect I'd do that twice."

"Why? Because I might think you're nice?"

His gaze slid to the grand piano. "No one thinks I'm nice."

A twinge of guilt nipped Abigail's conscience. She headed the list of George Cummings's critics. "A lot of folks will, once they benefit from your generosity."

Shrewd eyes laced with curiosity turned toward her. "What are you and Wade wasting that money on?"

His crotchety tone contradicted the interest lighting his eyes. Not as indifferent as he pretended. She explained how his donation would be spent and the home visits they planned.

"You're organized," he said with the tiniest hint of respect. "Efficient. A hard worker."

"I try to be."

"Nothing like your dad."

"I can't believe you'd disparage my father!"

"I meant what I said as a compliment."

She huffed. Why had she tried to understand the man? He was cold, mean. "After what you did to my father—"

"If you're yapping about that loan, forget it."

"I'd expect you to avoid the issue, but now that we're being honest with one another, I want answers."

His dark brows lowered. "Are you sure about that?"

Fingering the chain around her neck, she glanced at Blue asleep in a patch of sunshine. No questions disturbed his peace. "Yes, I'm sure."

"What's to know? Transactions at the bank are aboveboard."

"Ha! You took our farm."

"I called the loan. The economy was shaky. Railroads overextended. Banks were failing. The times demanded drastic measures. I—" A coughing spell stopped his litany.

Or lies. "Don't you mean your greed demanded drastic measures? You made a fortune selling the partial of our land to the railroad."

"You exaggerate." He exhaled. "I didn't know of the railroads' interest before I called the loan."

"So you say."

"You're yapping at me for making savvy business decisions."

"This isn't about business. Calling that loan, losing our farm, killed my father."

Ears and neck red as fresh blood, George shook his index finger. "Frank's greed and guilt killed him, not me."

"Greed?" She leaned toward him, every muscle rigid. She wanted to shake some sense into him, make him take back the hateful things he'd spouted. "Lots of people borrow money."

"He borrowed to invest in a get-rich-quick venture. I warned him the deal was risky. But no, he wouldn't listen."

Abigail leaped to her feet. "How dare you smear my father's good name when he can't defend himself?"

George scowled. "*You* asked for this conversation, young lady. Plant people on a pedestal and you soon discover they're nothing but flesh and bone. If you can't handle the truth, then don't go looking for it."

"You call that truth? You're lying!"

As Abigail fled the room, Blue reared his head and bayed. The last sound she heard as she plunged out the front door.

She'd talk to Ma. Ma would set her straight. Destroy the destructive seeds George Cummings tried to plant in her mind.

The lullaby Ma sang to Billy trailed off. "What's wrong?" she said, shifting the sleeping baby in her arms. "Did that scoundrel fire you?"

"Worse. He claims Pa took out the loan to invest in a get-rich-quick gamble, that greed drove him to risk the farm." She stood over her mother, searching her uplifted gaze. "Tell me that's not true."

The rocker slowed. Ethel fidgeted with the thin blanket framing Billy's tiny face. She sighed. "It might be."

"Ma. How can you say that?"

"I… Well, I saw signs of greed in Frank. He raved about some business opportunity, getting in on the ground floor. 'This is our chance,' he said. 'We'll see the world.'"

Abigail wilted onto the worn sofa. Greed had motivated her father to risk the farm? George had spoken the truth?

In his sleep, Billy jerked. Ethel resumed her rocking. "We never left the state, but we had this dream to travel."

Ma hadn't deserved any of this. If only she could give her mother that dream. When Lois, Joe and the kids were settled in their house, she'd take Ma to St. Louis. See the Mississippi River.

"Well, no point in looking back," Ma said.

"How could he take out a loan on the farm without your consent?"

"We were married. The farm was as much his as mine. I'll admit I was unsure about the investment, but I went along."

Abigail's insides churned, yet Ma looked serene as if she'd long ago made peace with the loss. "How could Pa risk all you had?"

Ma stopped the rocker and shot Abigail a pointed look. "Don't be critical of your father. He made a poor decision but George Cummings took advantage of it, made money off it too."

Abigail cradled a sofa pillow to her chest. "Does it bother you that Pa shirked his responsibility after we moved to town, leaving you to carry the load?"

A flicker of dismay traveled Ma's face. "When Frank took sick, I got a job. Why shouldn't I? He'd toiled all those years for us."

"You said Pa took sick. What was wrong with him?"

"A broken spirit, I reckon. He never got over losing the farm."

"But he could've worked? Could've gotten a job?"

Ma's eyes glistened. "Oh, sweetie, what's the point in laying blame?"

Wasn't the feud all about laying blame?

Yet the conversation had left her mother pale and shaken. Abigail wouldn't push. She rose and gave her mother a kiss on the cheek. "I love you. Thanks for taking care of Lois and me."

Ethel laid a calloused palm on Abigail's cheek. "Love you, too. Together, with God's help, this family is strong."

Yet her father hadn't been. Ma had persevered for the sake of her family. Why hadn't Pa?

"Better get back to work." Abigail was breadwinner for her family. She wouldn't let them down.

George Cummings had been right. She wasn't like her father.

"Don't go thinking George Cummings is guiltless," Ma said as if she'd read Abigail's mind. "You'll never convince me that he didn't know the Illinois Central's interest in our land before he called the loan. That's greed." She huffed. "He's got no right to criticize your pa."

Abigail nodded. George had tried to take the scrutiny off him by turning it onto her father. She'd almost fallen for the tactic. "Where is everyone?"

"Out for a walk. Joe's practicing with that crutch. Lois was pushing the boys in the wheelchair when they left. I sure hope those younguns get out of that contraption and run off some of that energy."

"I checked their house yesterday. They're plastering. It won't be long before it's finished." She picked at a piece of lint on her sleeve. "I'm thinking about getting a second job this fall, maybe working evenings at the café."

"You'll work yourself into the ground."

"We need the money."

Ma frowned. "Stop fretting about money. We're getting by."

"I want to help Joe pay off his gambling debts."

"Give Joe and the Good Lord a chance to handle that.'

"Joe came to God eleven months ago."

"Are you putting God on the clock, like you believe you're the boss of God and this old world?"

Abigail dropped her head. "No, ma'am."

"Trust the Good Lord. We'll get through this. We always have."

She hugged her mother, a woman who'd held her family together with hard work and a strong will, and kissed Billy on the forehead, then retraced her steps, heading to the Cummingses' house and the man who'd ruined her family.

Perhaps George's claim that her father's greed brought about his downfall contained an element of truth, but as her mother said, the Cummingses profited from the Wilsons' misfortune. Power and money bred more of the same.

If George knew for certain her father's investment was such a risk, why did he make the loan? Clearly he'd seen a way to gain a foothold on their land.

If she wanted to keep the job, she had to let the accusations go. Like Ma, she'd do what needed doing.

As she passed Cummings State Bank, Wade strode out the entrance. Handsome in suit, vest and tie, the consummate professional, a role he despised but took for his father's sake.

Wade frowned. "Why aren't you with my dad?" His eyes roamed her face. "Has he done something to upset you?"

How did she explain how George had hurt her without smearing her own father's good name? "We got into an argument about the farm loan. I'd quit if I could."

"I'm sorry I roped you into the job," he said, his deep blue eyes kind, gentle. "He's not an easy man."

"He accused my father of greed," she said, voice shaky, barely audible. "Yet greed motivated everything he did— making the loan, calling the loan, selling off our land, all of it benefited him."

Wade reached a hand toward her then dropped it at his side, as if suspecting she couldn't abide his touch. "I'm sorry my father dredged up such painful memories."

"This isn't about memories! If George hadn't called the loan, our family would've gotten the railroad money. Enough money to pay off the loan and keep our farm. My father would be alive today."

"Abby, my dad said the railroad deal came after he'd called the loan. I've never caught him in a lie."

Her stomach clenched. She'd been ranting against Wade's father. To him. As if he could change the past. She'd vowed to try to heal Wade and George's relationship, yet everything she did seemed to widen, not lessen, the chasm between them.

"I'm sorry. You caught me at a bad time. I shouldn't have spewed all that on you."

"Should we postpone tonight's home visit?"

"I don't want to delay disbursing funds." She heaved a sigh. "Starting with Lois and Joe might be easier."

"Will seven o'clock work for you?"

"That's fine."

He cupped her jaw with his palm. "Only a few weeks until the job will end." His eyes dimmed. "I'm glad for your sake, but...I'll miss you."

At his gentle touch, a surge of longing swept through her and banged against her heart.

Giving her a tender smile, he strode off, leaving a disturbing emptiness inside her.

Wade's concern for her meant more than she wanted to admit. Still, she wouldn't get pulled into the family that had harmed hers. She'd guard her heart tonight.

Chapter Thirteen

Tonight Wade would ascertain the Lessman family needs, but more importantly, he hoped to ease the pain his father had given Abby that afternoon.

As he entered the cheerless entrance to the Wilson apartment overhead, the outside door squeaked on rusty hinges. In the dim enclosure he climbed the steep flight of stairs, appalled his father could rent such dowdy housing.

He'd once called Abby his princess. She didn't belong in this dismal place. Since graduating from college, he'd socked every cent he'd earned into savings, start-up money for his shop. Yet renovating this dingy rental couldn't wait. He'd talk to his father, set things in motion. Something practical he could do to ease the tension between the Cummingses and Wilsons.

So far he'd made no headway in healing the rift. If anything, since talking to Pastor Ted, the situation had deteriorated.

At the top landing, he knocked.

Abigail opened the door, head high, posture regal, her expression void of the anger he'd seen earlier. She wore a high-necked blouse adorned with a man's tie clinging to her feminine curves. At the sight of her, his chest squeezed, trapping the oxygen in his lungs.

She stepped aside to let him in, tendrils of her hair dancing above her collar. He couldn't take his eyes off that perky profile. "You're...you're beautiful," he stammered.

"Thank you." Her brisk tone dismissed his compliment. If he hoped to mend the feud, he had his work cut out for him.

Skirts rustling, she led him inside. He followed her slender form, aware of the faint fragrance of roses, that tiny waist, the gentle sway of her hips.

He swallowed hard and forced his gaze away from Abby to the cheerful but rudimentary kitchen they entered. Preparing meals here wouldn't be easy. Yet the lingering scent of meat loaf mingled with the aroma of fresh-brewed coffee. His stomach growled—a reminder he'd missed dinner.

In the small parlor the adults sat on a threadbare sofa with Peter reading a book beside his dad and Donnie curled up on his grandmother's lap. The twins sprawled on the floor, leaving chairs on opposite sides of the room for him and Abby.

Engrossed in scribbling with crayons on paper, the twins didn't look up. Drawings of stick figures wearing huge smiles cluttered a table—small boys' images of family. "Nice pictures."

Gary rolled onto his side to look at Wade then scrambled to his feet. "Donnie drew these."

Donnie popped his thumb out of his mouth. "Me."

"I like your family, Donnie." Especially his aunt but he wouldn't say that, not with Ethel watching every word and move.

"Aunt Abby bringed me a red lollipop," Donnie said.

"Me too," came from three other small mouths.

Abigail grinned. "All the lollipops were red. Prevents bickering."

"My sister thought girls should choose first," Wade said.

"We don't have any girls," Sam said, stretching like a contented cat on the bare floor.

Lois cocked her head. "What are Grandma, Aunt Abby and I then?"

Sam wrinkled his nose. "You're not girls, you're ladies," he said, eliciting chuckles from the adults.

Gary slipped a paper out from under him and held it out to Wade. This family had torsos, noses, clothes, as well as wide smiles. Wade identified each one, earning a nod of approval from the artist.

Sam waved a picture of a farm. "I'm gonna be a farmer."

Wade caught Abby's frown. Did she find a small boy's goal disturbing?

"You can have this." Gary handed Wade his drawing.

"Why, thank you. I'll hang it in my workshop where I can see it every day."

Grinning sheepishly, Gary toed the floor. "Welcome."

Even with their tragedies—the fire, Joe's gambling, losing their farm—this family appeared happy, content, filling Wade with longing for what they had, a loving home. Yet with Abby standing apart from him, he'd never felt more an outsider.

Ethel motioned to the youngsters. "Let's give the grown-ups time to talk. Come into my bedroom and I'll read another chapter of *Black Beauty*. Keep your voices down so you don't wake Billy."

"Do I have to?" Sam whined, pointing at Wade. "I wanna make a picture for him."

"Yes, you do." Ethel shooed the boys out of the room.

On his way, Gary gave Wade a quick glance, his smile shy, clearly curious about his visit, yet not upset by it either.

Wade's throat tightened. Thank God the feud hadn't touched these innocent children. He prayed it never would. Yet how likely was that? The feud had harmed him and Abby in a myriad of ways.

Abby excused herself, returning with a tray of steaming mugs. Wade handed a pencil and list to the Lessmans then took a seat as they skimmed the paper. As she offered coffee, Abby explained the purpose of his visit.

"Who provided the money to purchase this stuff?" Joe asked.

"Wade's father donated the lion's share."

Lois cleared her throat. "I'll be honest. I never thought I'd see the day I was grateful to George Cummings for anything, but I am for his donation." Her voice broke. "More than I can say. I intend to write a note and thank him personally."

The feud was never far from the Wilsons' thoughts. "I'm sure he'll appreciate it." Though Wade didn't know any such thing.

"What I miss most, we can't get back." Lois sighed. "Pictures of the boys wearing the Christening gown Ma made from her mother's wedding dress, a letter Pa wrote me on our wedding day. The pencil marks recording the boys' heights on the door frame of their room." Lois's face crumpled.

Joe draped an arm around his wife and pulled her close. "We have each other. That's what matters."

Lois gazed into her husband's face, love for him clear in her eyes. "I shouldn't mourn the loss of things." Swiping at her cheeks with both hands, she glanced at Wade. "I'm sorry. I'm emotional since the baby…and with all that's happened."

Wade spoke past the lump lodged in his throat, "No need to apologize, Mrs. Lessman. You've been through a lot."

Abigail sat on the other side of her sister. "Soon you'll

move into a new home and can put the worst of this behind you."

What the Lessmans had, the closeness, the love—the boys in the next room—tugged at Wade. What did he have, really? A house furnished with the finest things money could buy, yet not one shred of harmony. How could he hope to heal things with Abby when he couldn't heal his relationship with his own father?

"Not a day goes by I don't thank God that Joe made it out alive." Lois leaned against her husband, closing her eyes as if banishing something too horrible to contemplate.

"I walked through the shell of those houses, Joe." Wade grimaced. "With broken limbs, how did you manage to escape?"

"I'm not sure. The smoke was so thick I couldn't see and could barely breathe. The last thing I remember was plunging down the stairs." He shook his head. "Cecil and Oscar found me sprawled in the yard." His voice quavered. "By the grace of God I survived."

Joe appreciated the gift of life. Why didn't George exhibit gratitude for his survival?

The Lessmans returned to the list, marking items they needed. Lois glanced at Abby. "I feel greedy."

"Needs aren't greed," Abby said. "I'll purchase supplies for your kitchen, but the big items are beyond my paycheck."

Joe tapped the pencil on his knee. "Ab, I'd feel better if you put the money you planned to spend on us into the fire relief fund. Help others, not just us."

"Most of the families are bringing in an income. They can afford the smaller purchases I plan to buy."

Wade nodded. "Peter Anderson's burns keep him from working. The committee will see that his family's needs are met."

"Wade's making double beds for all six families, even supplying the mattresses."

"Nothing fancy," Wade protested, but he soaked up the approval he heard in her voice like sand soaked up rain.

Wade's and Abby's gazes locked. Something significant passed between them. Dare he hope something that spoke of forgiveness?

"You're a good guy, Wade." Joe struggled to his feet with the help of his crutch and shook Wade's hand, sling and all. "Trouble has a way of bringing folks together. Appreciate all you're doing for my family."

Wade said his goodbyes to the Wilsons. Good, hard-working people of faith. They, along with others like them, were the foundation of the country.

Abby walked Wade to the door. "Squeezing nine people into this apartment has to be difficult. Yet I feel the love between you. See it." He smiled. "Even smell it in the aroma of home cooking."

"Did you take time to eat?"

"No, but I will."

"I left a plate of food in the icebox." She smiled. "Don't stay up all hours building beds."

He took her hand, raising it to his mouth, sweeping his lips over her knuckles. She sucked in a breath, then she dropped her eyes, avoiding the heat in his gaze and took a step back. The hurt he'd caused erected barriers between them. Barriers he had no right to tear down, even if he could. He wasn't cut out for a family, for a wife and children.

Yet he craved every minute with her he could. "Shall we visit another family tomorrow night?"

"You're busy. I can manage by myself." She opened the door. "Goodnight, Wade."

As he plodded down the stairs and left by the back stoop, he wasn't fooled. Abby might not trust him, but he'd seen the flare of her nostrils, the hitch in her breathing. She fought the attraction between them with everything in her.

He remembered a time when she'd welcomed it. He'd never forget how a smile would light her face when he appeared. How special that smile had made him feel. She'd seen him, not his money, not his family—only him. Those few weeks spent with Abby had been the happiest of his life.

Who knew what would've happened if their affection had been allowed to mature as they did. Ending their courtship had been the toughest thing he'd ever done. But by giving her up, he'd ensured she'd keep what she valued most, the love and support of family.

In all the years since, he'd never found anyone like Abby. He felt certain she'd make a wonderful mother by the tender way she looked at her nephews. She'd grown into a caring, generous, determined woman. A woman he admired. A woman he'd do anything for. But a woman better off without him.

She wanted him to mend the rift with his father. This much he could do for her. To get what Abby's family had, he must take the first step with his dad. And leave the outcome to God.

Abigail wasn't fooled by Lois and Ma's desire for more coffee. They were fishing for her feelings about Wade. The only thing they'd catch was the dregs of the pot.

Ma shot her a pointed look. "Never thought I'd see the day when a Cummings would step foot in our home."

"Maybe we better get used to it." Lois lifted a brow. "Anyone could see Wade only had eyes for Abby."

Ethel gasped. "Lois, watch your mouth. I didn't raise a daughter of mine to fall for the likes of Wade Cummings."

"George Cummings donated the funds to furnish our homes. Wade's building beds, helping Abby on the committee and providing her a job. Reason enough to rethink your opinion of the man." Lois took a sip of coffee. "Besides, the father did our family wrong, not his son."

"Don't fret, Ma. I have no intention of getting involved with Wade." That should tell them what they wanted to know.

Lois set her cup down and met Abigail's eyes. "Because he broke your heart?"

"We were kids."

"I fell for Joe when I was sixteen."

That youthful romance led to years of misery. Lois of all people should understand Abigail's inability to trust Wade.

"Ab, I can read your face like a picture book. You're thinking about the years Joe's gambling tested our vows. I'll admit I fell for brawny muscles, a handsome face and a kind heart and married someone without faith. I prayed with every breath I took that Joe would come to God and he did."

With a blue-veined hand Ma patted Lois's sleeve. "In all those years of waiting, you never gave up. That's strong faith."

If Abigail had married someone like Joe, would she have stuck by him? Or would she have taken her children and walked out? Her stomach clenched. What would have happened to Joe if Lois had given up on him?

Ma rose. "I'm going to bed."

"Night, Ma," Lois and Abigail chimed in unison.

Once the bedroom door clicked closed, Abigail turned to Lois. "How were you able to hang onto your marriage vows all those years?"

"I knew God had the power and the desire to save Joe from gambling and for eternity. I prayed without ceasing and waited."

Abigail lowered her voice. "Was it hard to forgive Joe for all the heartache he caused?"

"After asking God to give Joe and me a new beginning, I couldn't very well hold a grudge. Besides, forgiving is a command."

Abigail fingered the chain around her neck. She had tried to forgive but she couldn't forget. Not when every day brought a reminder of all they'd lost.

Lois took Abigail's hand and squeezed. "God may have brought Wade back into your life for a more important reason than that job."

"Perhaps." How could she know God's will when it came to Wade? She faked a yawn and rose. "I'm going to bed."

"You're running from life, Abby," Lois said with a huff. "Running from love."

"No, I'm being realistic. Facing the truth and going on with my life." She gave Lois a hug. "Hope Billy gives you a good night's sleep."

In the room she shared with Ma, Abigail turned back the covers and slipped into bed, listening to Ma's even breathing.

Curling on her side, she waited for sleep.

Who knew what life could bring? What life could do to someone? Better to honor her teaching contract, to spend her life teaching children than take a risk on love. Ma and Lois might paint a pretty picture of their marriages, but Abigail had seen the heartache they'd endured.

She wouldn't give Wade a second chance.

Not that he'd asked for it.

Wade finished the plate of food Abigail had left for him. Even cold the meal was excellent, as delicious as Cora's. He suspected Cora's reason for leaving after all these years was a mutiny of sorts, her attempt to force his father to change.

As if anyone could force George Cummings to do anything.

He rinsed the plate, leaving it to drain then marched down the hall toward the parlor.

In the curve of the bay window George sat reading. Wade smiled at the title, *The Red Badge of Courage*. Abby had made huge inroads in expanding his father's interests and taming that temper of his. Though his coughing had eased, Wade could hear his ragged breathing. Proof his lungs weren't healed.

George glanced up then set the book aside. "You're home late."

"Abby and I met with the Lessmans tonight." He stepped to his father's side. "They're grateful for your donation."

George appeared not to hear.

"Joe was blessed to get out of that fire alive. You were too."

"Lucky, I guess."

Wade bit back his impatience. "Did you consider God had something to do with it?"

George shrugged. His father believed in God and in His power but somehow didn't connect that to events in his life.

"I'm curious why you made that huge donation to the relief fund."

"Generosity isn't what you'd expect from me, is that what you're saying?"

Shoulders hunched, hands in his pockets, Wade leaned against the window frame, feigning indifference to his father's caustic tone. Must every conversation end in an argument? Well, he wouldn't back down. Not this time. "I guess I am."

"Well, you'd be right."

A desire to walk out seized him, to leave his father in his self-imposed exile. Wade closed his eyes, remembering Seth. If he did, he wasn't the man a boy of seventeen was. Seth never gave up on Rafe, never stopped believing his father would be a better man and overcome what held him in its grip.

What overture could Wade make that his father wouldn't rebuff? Abby had suggested he find a common interest they could share. He glanced at the small table across the way, set up for checkers. What little time his competitive father had spent with his family, he'd chosen to play checkers or chess.

Not that Wade could afford time for games. He should be in the shop building those beds, but putting a job before his family made him no different than his driven father.

"Care to play checkers?" he said, using a casual tone like the answer didn't matter.

George blinked. "What?" Then nodded, slowly, not exactly eager, but then neither was Wade.

Before he had second thoughts, Wade repositioned the table in front of his father then pulled up a chair.

"I'll take black," George said. "Red goes first."

Appropriate for his father's mood.

Wade turned the board until the rows of black faced his father then pushed a red checker out of the front row, leaving behind an empty spot.

An empty spot like the hole his mom's desertion made in their lives. Ridiculous to see all that in a game of checkers, but the simplest things seemed to boil down to that defining moment.

Eyes gleaming with zeal to win—as if a game had significance in life—George slid a black checker diagonally to the left.

Wade made a move, then his father another, until red and black met in the middle, a standoff of sorts, much as the two of them lived. Ignoring the impasse like they did each day in this house, they took turns studying the board then moving another piece. Neither spoke, as if the game demanded their undivided attention. Or merely concealed they had no idea what to discuss.

As the game progressed they crowned each other's kings, enabling them to now move checkers back as well as forward.

If only they could move back in time. Help his mother see that running wasn't the way to handle her unhappiness.

Abby had accused him of running from confrontations. By keeping aloof, by avoiding talking about the past, he supposed he had. If he shared his feelings, perhaps George would open up.

He'd make the first move toward ending the stalemate.

With his king, George plucked Wade's checker from the board with a smirk, adding it to his growing pile. His father had amassed much in his lifetime, but at what price?

Another move, then another until only three red checkers survived. Even as an adult, Wade's father would defeat him.

Odd that he couldn't remember his mom ever losing a game. "I'd like to know how Mom managed to beat you in checkers."

George shifted in his seat. "I let her win."

"Why? You never let me win."

"Winning seemed to make her happy," his father said quietly. He fidgeted with his vest, smoothing a nonexistent wrinkle. "I wanted to give her that."

Losing opposed his father's instincts. That he'd lose deliberately revealed something about his parents' relationship Wade hadn't known with certainty. "You cared about her."

Dark eyes flashed. "Are you dim-witted enough to believe I'd marry a woman I didn't?"

"Your feelings must've changed." The reason love was risky.

His father thrust out a hand, obviously impatient with the delay of the game. "It's your turn," he grumbled.

Wade's move closed off a path to his last red king. "Did you love her when she left?"

Under the dark slashes of his brows, in stark contrast to his snow-white hair, George glared. "Why are you yapping about this? Instead of dredging up the past, get your mind in the game."

"My whole world collapsed when Mom left."

George's nostrils flared. "You think mine didn't!"

"How would I know?" Wade leaned across the board toward his father. "You didn't try to find her. You didn't try to bring her home. If you had, maybe she wouldn't have taken sick and died."

His father shuddered. Obviously that had occurred to him.

The time had come to uncover what went wrong between his parents. "I need to understand why she left. Your part in it."

"So you can lay the blame on me? Isn't that what this is about?" George jutted his chin. "*She's* the one who left."

Turning back to the game as if he considered the conversation over, George's scarred fingers poised over the board. His hands were healing. What about his heart?

"Mom's leaving hurt you. Well, she hurt me too. Why did the theater mean more to her than we did?"

Heaving a sigh, his father rose and plodded to the window, putting his back to Wade and distance between them as he'd done all these years.

In a couple long strides Wade reached him, turned him around, forcing his father to look at him. "Answer me!" he snapped, then said softly, "Please. I need to know."

"Your mother was a dreamer." He'd spoken the word as if dreamer was a curse. "There wasn't a stage in New Harmony big enough to hold her."

George pivoted to the grand piano in the corner. Did he see as Wade did, Ernestine sitting there, her fingers dancing across the keys? Did he hear her singing, the notes sweet to his ears? His mother's voice was extraordinary; even as a small boy Wade had grasped the brilliance of her talent.

Yet he'd also seen her unhappiness. Somehow knew she felt trapped, as if she lived a prison sentence without parole.

"Sometimes Mom performed scenes from *Romeo and Juliet*." Remembering, a smile curved his lips. "She'd come alive then, her beauty and skill dazzling." His smile faded as quickly as his mother's mood had. "When she thought we weren't looking, she wore a sad expression, a vacant look in her eyes."

His father's face contorted in a blend of anger and pain. "I'd come home and find the three of you laughing, running around in circles like overwound tops. If you noticed me watching, you'd stop, standing there silent and uneasy." Tears filled his eyes. "I was an outsider in my own home."

Wade reached a hand. "You could've joined in—"

As if unable to bear Wade's touch, George jerked away. "I had no time or energy for such foolishness. Can't you see that the success or failure of my businesses rested on my shoulders?"

His parents were such different people. Surely neither understood nor accepted what drove and energized the other.

Eyes blazing like a raging fire, George threw up his hands. "I gave Ernestine everything. I built this house for her, kept her in finery and jewels. I worked like a slave—for what? She never appreciated any of it." He slashed a hand, as if trying to dispel an image that haunted him. "I resented her discontent. Still do," he said in a raspy voice that ended in a cough.

"Why weren't you and Regina and I—enough?"

"You think I haven't asked myself that a million times?" He flailed an arm. "Stop going over and over this! Finish the game."

George stomped to the board, studying it, as if the answers to life could be found in wooden circles of red and black.

In essence cutting Wade off. His father didn't care about their relationship. Something inside Wade snapped.

With long strides, he reached the table, shoving it aside and sending checkers flying. "This stupid game doesn't matter!"

His father sneered. "Life's a game, boy. The moves you make determine if you win or lose. Time you learned that."

Did his father believe he could control life like he could maneuver a checkerboard?

Fighting for control, Wade sucked in a breath. "The day Mom left, you said you wouldn't let her come back. If she had, would you have allowed her to stay?"

"Ernestine ran off to follow her dream, leaving me to pick up the pieces. You grouse yet have no inkling of the strain. To work all day, come home to oversee you and Regina, to do it all. Yes, with Cora's help, but I…I barely hung on."

Wade took a step, then another, until he and his father stood toe-to-toe. "You didn't answer my question."

"I don't know the answer." Breathing hard, George dropped into his chair. "I wanted to hurt her like she hurt me." He leaned back and closed his eyes, his face pale. "Then she died…and I had nowhere to put my anger."

Wade's hands knotted. "I'm angry too. Angry she left. Angry you let her leaving destroy what was left of our family."

"I tried," George said. "I failed."

What could Wade say to that? Both of his parents had failed their children. Perhaps his mother had wanted it all— her dream and her family, and planned to return. "If she hadn't gotten sick, do you think she would've come back?"

"No," George said without one second of hesitation.

Bitterness kept his father from considering the possibility, but the wonderful times he and Regina shared with their mother made Wade believe she would've returned as she'd promised.

He had to believe that. He had to believe she'd loved them.

"What did she expect when she married me?" his father mumbled, as if talking to himself. "I gave her a good life. Yet she had not one whit of gratitude."

"Maybe she didn't need material things. Maybe she needed excitement, to feel alive, not caged. Couldn't you have taken her to New York or Chicago? Attended the theater, the opera?"

"I didn't have the time."

Wade snorted. "Why didn't you see Mom's happiness as important enough to sacrifice *your* agenda?"

"You've got all the answers. Or so you think," his father snarled. "Well, you're making a mess of your own life."

"What are you talking about?"

"All that sawing and sanding and hammering is a waste for someone like you."

Wade had hinted, but had never admitted his plans. The time had come. "Cabinetmaking is what I intend to do. Once you return to the bank, I'm opening a shop in town."

Looking dazed, as if Wade had slammed him with an uppercut to the jaw, his father stumbled to his feet. "I'm handing you an empire on a silver platter. You don't appreciate it! You're just like your—" He cut off his words and looked away.

"Mother. Isn't that what you were about to say? I'm just like my mother."

"Yes!" His father's dark blue eyes flashed like high seas in a raging storm. "She didn't appreciate anything I gave her, not enough to stay. You don't appreciate what I've built."

"I appreciate how hard you worked. But you did what you wanted to do. I want the same opportunity."

"You're tossing away your legacy, your future. For what? A pipe dream!"

"Why not be honest? You've never had confidence in my abilities—not as a banker, not as a businessman. Every word from your mouth attests to your lack of respect for me. Why would you want me running your businesses?"

"I've pushed you, sure, to…motivate you."

Did his father really believe disapproval motivated?

If he'd held his mother's dream in the same distain he held Wade's, Wade understood why she'd left.

"I need to do this." He stepped to George. "Hire someone to take my place. You could promote our cashier or bring back Regina's husband."

"You're throwing your legacy in my face like she did." Sighing, he dropped into his chair. "Nothing I've built matters," he said in a toneless voice.

Wade knelt beside his father's chair. George stared straight ahead, as if he didn't see him there. "That's not true. Look at the good your success is bringing others. Your generosity will provide six families a fresh start. You can be proud of that." He put his hand on his father's forearm. "I'm not like Mom. I'm not running out on you. I need to do what God gave me the talent and desire to do."

Eyes cold, remote, George turned toward Wade. "You're exactly like your mother." He waved a hand toward the bed. "I'm tired. You need to go."

Swallowing a protest, Wade rose, turned back the comforter then faced his father. "I'm sorry your life's been a disappointment. I'm sorry I've been a disappointment. But even with all that, if we wanted to, we could make a new beginning, you and I."

Silence.

Every muscle tense with hope, Wade waited, holding his father in his gaze.

"Leave me alone."

The dismissal slammed into Wade's stomach with the weight of a fist. Once he could speak, he said, "Good night."

Eyes stinging, Wade left the house and headed to the shop. He'd stood his ground with his father. He'd gotten to the truth. The truth hurt. More than he cared to admit. His father couldn't accept him, couldn't accept who he was, couldn't accept Wade's desire to do something else with his life.

If only Dad could be proud of him.

That would never happen.

Nothing between them had changed.

Nothing.

Chapter Fourteen

Chilled lemonade should put a smile on George's face. Or so Abigail hoped as she hauled the tray with two glasses to the front porch. Earlier, before he'd been aware of her presence, she'd glimpsed his dejection. As if something had broken his spirit. She preferred anger to this morose, haunted man, a painful reminder of her father.

George sat in a wicker rocker, staring off into space.

"I brought you a cold glass of lemonade," she said softly.

He jerked toward her. "A man could die of thirst around here."

Anger, she could handle. "Not when he's perfectly capable of walking to the kitchen he won't."

"Aha, just as I suspected, you moved my bedroom to the main floor to avoid waiting on me. A diabolical plan since I'm paying you for that very thing."

"No one hoodwinks you." She smiled.

He scowled—a vast improvement.

"Mind if I join you?"

"I'd prefer my own company."

"As you said, I can't accept wages if I'm not looking after your comfort."

"What about *you* can provide one shred of comfort?" he muttered under his breath but loud enough for Abigail to hear.

Good question, considering their past. "Normally you appreciate an adversary, even thrive on trying to best me." She chuckled. "I'd call that providing comfort."

George waved toward the empty chair. "Suit yourself."

Abigail sat, sipped her drink, fidgeting in the silence. If he didn't want to banter back and forth, he must be truly upset.

At least she'd enjoy the lovely landscaping, the puffy clouds floating overhead, chirping birds swooping in and out of the evergreens. "A beautiful day," she said.

He gulped half the glass. "They all blend together."

"You need to get back to work."

Dark eyes flashed. "Why? Everything I've built will die with me."

"You're a long way from dying."

"You a doctor?"

"Yes, a specialist."

A glimmer of humor lit George's eyes. "What kind?"

"Cardiologist. A doctor of the heart."

"My ticker's fine."

"My specialty is the seat of affection."

He snorted.

"My services are expensive."

"Why am I not surprised?"

She chuckled then swigged the last of her lemonade. "Let's take a stroll."

"Your second good idea. Lemonade being the first."

Unhooking his cane from the arm of his chair, George rose and trudged off. Just getting down the steps and out the gate appeared to tire him. Yet at the corner, he refused to turn back, insisted on going to town.

By the time they reached Main Street, his breathing was

labored, but he had a perkier look in his eye. "Well, would you look at that?" He leaned on his cane with both hands, studying six new houses, framed, roofed and sided. "They look solid, like good places to live."

Pleased he appreciated the humble abodes, Abigail shot him a smile. "There's work to do inside, but Lois and the others should move in by the Fourth of July—with furnishings, thanks to you."

"Maybe I'm good for something, after all."

"Feeling sorry for yourself this morning?"

He harrumphed then went into a fit of coughing.

A few storefronts down, Wade strode in their direction. Even from here, he looked handsome, in control, someone she could count on. Appearances were deceiving.

When Wade reached them, his gaze rested on her then slid to his father. He motioned to the bench near the park. "Sit over here, Dad."

Amazingly George obeyed, leaning heavily upon his cane but refusing Wade's arm. Settled on the bench, George pulled a monogrammed square of linen from his pocket and wiped his face.

A face that was ashen. "I don't like his color," Abigail said.

Brow furrowed, eyes filled with alarm, Wade huffed. "Are you trying to kill him?"

"You know how stubborn he can be when he gets an idea in his head."

"Was the walk his idea?"

"Well, no, but I visualized a short stroll no farther than the end of the block, the walk he handled well yesterday. I thought a change of scenery would do him good."

"Stop yapping about me like I'm not here," George said. His words cranky but his voice was weak.

"I'll get Doc Simmons to look you over."

"I've got my doctor with me." George glowered at Wade beneath beetled brows, as if daring Wade to challenge his claim.

"In that case, your doctor should've known to use the carriage instead of allowing you to walk."

Wade's tone had gentled, but her lack of judgment knotted Abigail's throat. "You're right. I'm sorry."

George flapped a hand. "No one makes my decisions except me."

Wade heaved a sigh. "I'll get the carriage."

As Wade strode toward home, Abigail sat beside his father.

"Pay him no mind." George reached over and patted her hand, then jerked it away as if he'd forgotten she was a Wilson and he was a Cummings.

She'd tried to lift George's spirits. The thanks she got—a scolding from Wade. At least he'd expressed concern for his father. She sighed. Not that the incident had narrowed the gulf—between father and son, or between her and Wade.

Well, she wouldn't accept failure. Not in this. For she knew without a doubt God wanted the same thing she did—healing between father and son. Between enemies. George had harmed their family but she now believed he hadn't called the loan maliciously. Neither side had been totally right or wrong. The time had come to release the feud.

She laid a hand on George's arm. "Feeling better?"

"Much."

"I'm glad."

"No matter what Wade claimed, I know you didn't want to kill me. 'Cause if you had, you'd have gotten the job done."

She met his twinkling eyes. "You're right."

"The reason I'm firing you as my physician. I'll stick with Doc Simmons."

Chuckling, she helped him to his feet. Wade was coming with the carriage. The laughter died on her lips. She'd forgive George for the loan, but that didn't mean she'd trust his son.

Only an idiot would accuse Abby of trying to bring his father harm.

At the first opportunity Wade would apologize, if she wasn't too angry to listen.

Alarmed by his father's pallor, he'd overreacted. That ridiculous response had been fueled by guilt. Guilt that his plan to open a shop had undermined George's fragile health.

With his father resting comfortably, Wade strode to the stable. Inside the dim interior, he inhaled the familiar odors and listened to the shuffle of feet, the whinny of the horses, their ears forward, alert, eager for food.

Wade fed them and added more water to their buckets, then grabbed a bridle from the wall and plopped down on a bale to clean the metal bit.

Abby appeared in the doorway, slowing his hand. Her features appeared chiseled from granite.

He rose. She stomped toward him, stopping mere inches away—within slapping distance. Wade took a step back.

"I made a bad decision and feel terrible about that, but how could you accuse me of trying to kill your father?"

"I'm sorry. I…" He ran a hand through his hair. "I know you'd never harm Dad or anyone. I'm to blame."

As if they'd doused it with water, his words smothered the fire in her eyes. "Well, thank you." She cocked her head, studying him as if evaluating a bullheaded student. "I suggested the walk because George appeared disheartened, like he'd lost his best friend. Any idea why?"

Unable to meet her intense gaze, he glanced toward the stalls. "We got in an argument last night. I blurted out my plan to open the shop. He accused me of being like my mom—putting a pipe dream ahead of duty."

"With the fragileness of his health right now, telling him your plans might not have been wise."

The weight of responsibility for bringing harm to his father sank inside him. "My temper hindered my judgment, but Dad needs to replace me at the bank."

"Your father isn't well enough to search for a replacement."

"He'll never replace me if I don't force him to." He lifted the bridle still in his hand. "A tight bit chafes, Abby. My father kept a tight grip on the reins. I've felt the pain of that bit in my mouth all my life."

She sighed. "George isn't an easy man. But under that tough hide he's wounded. Not all that different from you."

"What do you mean, not all that different from me?"

"Your mother wasn't the only one with a dream. Your father dreamed of building an empire. You dream of building—"

"Empire-style furniture," he finished for her, giving a weak smile.

"The dreams may be different but you Cummings men are alike. Alike and butting heads."

At her assertion Wade's jaw dropped. Were he and George alike? "If I'm like Dad, I've got to do more apologizing."

She laughed at his joke and he joined in. The sound settled within him, a balm to the raw hurt he carried inside. As he stared into those gentle blue eyes, got lost in their depths, the laughter died in his throat. "You're an amazing woman, Abby. I admire your intelligence, your feisty spirit, your compassion for my dad, a man who hurt your family."

He lifted a hand to a strand of her hair. The tendril curled around his finger like a newborn baby's hand. He gathered her in his arms. She fit him perfectly. They were two wounded people, harmed by the families they loved. Meant for each other.

As he leaned closer, gaze fastened on her mouth, she inhaled, all but holding her breath. He lowered his head and met her lips, soft and pliable under his. With a soft moan, she rose on tiptoe, hands encircling his neck, clinging to him. His heart hammered in his temples, pounded in his chest. Oh, how he loved her.

She pulled away, trembling before him.

He wrapped her hand in his and pressed her palm over his pounding heart. "Can you feel that, Abby? No woman affects me like you do."

Eyes searching his, as if deciding whether to believe him, she slowly nodded, then lowered her gaze. "That's what frightens me."

Her words, the panic in her eyes, drilled into him. He'd seen love die, seen what happens when it did, and had lived the consequences. He couldn't speak the words that would dispel her fear. How could he, when fear lived in him too?

Early that morning before the sun made it unbearable Abby donned work gloves and surveyed the plants she'd collected. Scattered around the Cummingses' garden, balls of dirt held black-eyed Susan, Shasta daisy, yarrow, sweet pea vine for the trellis, all awaiting homes.

To get George out of the house and hopefully lift his mood, she'd asked for his advice on where to place the new plants. He'd been surprisingly interested and had actually helped select their locations. Now he sat across the way reading the Bible with Blue dozing at his feet.

She hoped within those Holy pages, he found a fresh perspective and the wisdom he badly needed. And a remedy for the despondency plaguing him since Wade had revealed his plans to leave the business.

Wade had worked up the soil earlier, even offered to dig the holes. But he had to be at the bank and these plants couldn't wait.

As she bent over the handle, ready to shove the spade into the ground with her shoe, Wade strode out the back door wearing denims, boots, a rumpled shirt and a Stetson, looking more cowboy than banker, or even cabinetmaker.

He spoke to his father then strode toward her. "Hello, lovely lady," he said with a wide smile.

"Hello." The memory of last night's kiss was seared in her mind and sealed on her lips. Yet fear of trusting Wade held her in its grip.

He took the spade from her gloved hands. "This is a man's job."

"You'll be late for work."

"Work will wait. These wilted plants won't." He touched her chin with a finger, setting off a reaction that slithered through her. "I don't want you to get hurt."

His words doused her mood like a cold spring shower. Getting hurt was exactly what could happen.

With Wade's declaration percolating in her mind, she hurried to the pump, filled the galvanized sprinkling can then slogged to the garden with a lopsided gait, sloshing water on the hem of her skirts.

Wade relieved her of the burden, then watered the dirt clinging to the plant's roots. Setting the sprinkling can aside, he scooped the mound of soil into the hole, tamping it loosely in place with strong, capable hands. Perspiration beaded on his brow and he tipped his Stetson back, wiping his forehead on his sleeve, and then moved to the next plant, shoving the spade in the ground with a booted heel.

As she watched his muscles bunch beneath his shirt, her heart thudded in her chest. Abigail swallowed hard. The temptation to lean into his strength slid through her. She couldn't deny the appeal of those brawny muscles, of his strong work ethic, of his amazing kisses.

George meandered over. "A bench would be nice out here. A spot to drop down and watch the bees and humming-birds."

"That's a good idea, Dad."

"Could you build it?"

"Sure. How about a bench with a back and arms? Big enough to seat two?" he added, glancing at Abigail.

"Appreciate it," George said.

A smile wide on his face, Wade watched his father return to his chair. The garden and sunshine had apparently been what George needed to improve his outlook. Abigail could hardly believe that father and son were speaking cordially. And George wanted his son's handiwork. Perhaps time spent reading the Bible had made the biggest impact.

Wade finished planting the last perennial. "The garden looks good," he said, his gaze roaming the flower beds. "I'll take care of hoeing the weeds."

"I can do that."

"I want to help."

That he seemed to want to ease her load warred against her judgment. The verdict, Wade was a good man.

Trustworthy, kind. A man she could love. If she dared.

With a spring in her step Abigail entered the Cummings library, one of her favorite rooms in the house. Bookshelves stretched from floor to ceiling; the world globe hung in a wooden stand on the floor. The rich patina of the paneling, the scent of leather and George's pipe, now forgotten, perme-ated the room. When had she started to feel at home here?

She carried the copy of *The Red Badge of Courage.* George had finally finished the book and they'd spent most of the afternoon discussing that hideous war.

Crusty and stubborn as George could be, she'd also seen his vulnerability. Wade loved his father, obvious by his concern for his health. She suspected George loved his son but something kept them aloof, from admitting their feelings.

She wouldn't admit her feelings for Wade either, but the memory of his kiss scorched her cheeks. Countless times she'd relived the feel of his lips on hers. The power of the feelings he'd awakened told her she was falling for Wade again.

Could Rachel have been right when she said Wade deserved another chance?

As Abigail meandered toward the back wall to shelve the book, her skirts brushed against a file on George's cluttered desk, knocking it to the floor, scattering papers on the Persian rug.

Sighing, she laid the book aside and bent to gather the pages. A gilded letterhead caught her eye. *Illinois Central Railroad.*

Why would…?

Her heart skipped a beat. She reached for the paper, her hands trembling so badly she couldn't distinguish the words blurring on the page. She stumbled to the chair, laid the letter on the desk then read:

In response to your inquiry about possible interest in the *Illinois Central Railroad* providing a spur into New Harmony, Iowa, management has determined this enterprise would mutually benefit our company and your town.

She noted the date. This proved George Cummings knew the railroad's interest in Wilson land *weeks* before he called the loan on their farm.

Her throat clogged. Her father had spoken the truth. He'd

seen the Cummingses as enemies. This paper proved him correct. George Cummings was a blatant liar. Tears stung her eyes. She'd been a traitor to her father's memory. How could she have fallen into the Cummingses' snare? Again.

Anger pumping through her body, she grabbed the paper and sped down the hall toward the parlor. Wade and George stood near the window, conspirators in this travesty.

She marched to them, stuck the paper in front of George's face. "You lied! You knew the railroad planned a spur into New Harmony *before* you called the loan on our farm. You took our farm out of greed! Not to save the bank from failing."

George reached for the paper. "Where did you get that?" he asked, taking it out of her hands.

The shock in Wade's eyes turned guarded. "I unearthed a file on the Wilson transaction and left it on your desk. I planned to examine the contents later tonight," he said.

"So, Miss Wilson, you took advantage of my son's negligence," he said, nailing Wade with a pointed gaze. "And snooped through private papers."

"Dad, don't blame us. You claimed you had nothing to hide."

Abigail whirled toward Wade. "Don't pretend you didn't know about this."

"I didn't. You have to believe me." Wade took then scanned the paper. Stony eyes then lifted to his father. "She's right. You lied when you said you didn't know about the railroad's interest before you called the loan."

"I'd decided to call the loan *before* I got the reply to my inquiry. Nor was I certain the Illinois Central would buy Wilson land. That parcel wasn't the only way into town."

Wade huffed. "Crossing Wilson land was the direct route."

"Yes." George glanced at Abigail. "I'll admit the railroad's interest was a bonus."

"I can't stand the sight of you." She glanced at the opulence surrounding her. "That sale brought you an easy life. The money would have enabled my father to repay the loan and save his farm. Save his life!"

Unable to stay another minute in their presence, she lurched toward the door.

"Abby, wait! Let's talk about this."

"Whether you were aware of your father's treachery or not, you're a Cummings, cut from the same cloth as your father."

As she sped home, she faced the bitter truth. She'd opened her heart to the Cummings men. They'd shattered it into a million jagged shards that slashed with every breath she took.

How could she have enjoyed George's crusty company? How could she have fallen for Wade's phony charm?

She'd trusted emotion, not her head. What a fool she'd been. She recalled her father's edict. Never fraternize with the enemy. Yet that's exactly what she'd done. At her stupidity, a strangled laugh forced its way out of her throat.

Wade's kiss had convinced her she should cancel her dinner plans tomorrow night with Harrison Carder.

But now, nothing could make her happier. She'd show Harrison small-town hospitality.

And never let Wade Cummings into her heart again.

Business was booming at Agnes's Café. Diners filled every table. Their conversation and laughter easing those first awkward moments of the evening as Harrison seated Abigail then sat across from her. A tented hand-lettered RESERVED sign sat in the middle of the table.

A handsome, charming man, Harrison smiled at her. The

skin on her face felt stiff, even rigid, but she forced a smile. Determined to enjoy his company, she squared her shoulders.

What better way to forget how Wade had hurt her than to spend an evening with his best friend. To talk and laugh, share a meal. Keep too occupied to waste even one second thinking about Wade Cummings.

She'd show him that Abigail Wilson was made of strong stuff. Perhaps she'd even give Harrison a chance. Even if she'd never give her heart again, she enjoyed an occasional evening out. Harrison would be more entertaining than Leon, who hadn't come around since the box lunch auction. Probably afraid he'd lose his job. A valid concern.

"You look lovely tonight," Harrison said, his gray eyes sliding over her, an appreciative look on his face.

"Thank you. I must say you look quite dapper."

"As a successful lawyer should." He winked. "Not that I'm successful yet, but I must look the part."

Agnes appeared at her elbow. Round-faced, dark curly bangs clinging to her moist forehead, the proprietor looked exhausted. Perhaps Abigail would inquire about a job waitressing here. She'd like nothing better than to escape the Cummingses' house. But needed money until school started.

Once they'd ordered, Abigail spread her napkin on her lap. "I'm sorry your practice is slow. New Harmony doesn't have much call for lawsuits."

"True. I've written a couple wills. Handled a divorce."

"Really?"

"No one from here. Folks like to keep that quiet. Not that they succeed." He took a sip of water. "I yearn for a trial. A case I can sink my teeth into."

"You may need the big city to practice criminal law. I'm surprised you didn't stay in Boston."

"Eventually that's my goal. My grades weren't stellar so

no law firm hired me. I'll get some experience here—or if that fails to materialize, somewhere else—then return."

Harrison wouldn't be staying. Fine with her. She wanted to teach. She thought of Wade. He'd wheedled his way into her heart. She could teach anywhere. Even Boston.

"How's our friend Wade?" Harrison asked, cocking a brow.

Her stomach knotted. She'd had such hopes. "He's not my friend. Quite the opposite."

"How so?"

Before she thought of the ramifications, she'd told Harrison about discovering the Cummingses had prior knowledge of the railroad's interest in Wilson land. The whole ugly story.

"You might have grounds to litigate."

"Sue?"

"If I can find cases to establish precedence, we'd have a good chance of recouping some, if not all, of that money."

Her hands fidgeted with the napkin in her lap. That money could release Joe from the burden of his gambling debts. That money could enable her and Ma to purchase a small house.

That money...would be wrong.

As much as she despised what the Cummingses had done to her family, Scripture forbade believers from suing a fellow Christian. "I'm sorry. I can't sue the Cummingses."

"Why not? If they've wronged you—"

"God will have to take care of it." Abigail believed in handling things with the talent she'd been given, but she'd never knowingly take action that opposed God's Word.

Harrison gaped at her, as if she'd lost her mind. "If God was going to take care of it, He'd have done so by now. Think of the money you'd get if the court sided with us and found the Cummingses guilty of swindling your family."

The temptation for revenge slid through her. Heart pounding, her hands fisted in her lap. To see the Cummingses get what they deserved. To see them suffer as her family had suffered. To recoup the Wilson losses warred inside her.

She sucked in a calming breath then slowly released it. The advice wasn't in God's will. The place she wanted to be. "Money isn't everything."

Harrison leaned back in his seat. "I've got to hand it to you, Abigail. That faith of yours is more than talk. Most folks' principles collapse when money's in the mix."

"That's greed."

"Yes, ma'am, it is. I suspect lawyers would go out of business if not for greed. Greed, not money, is the root of all evil." Grinning, he lifted his glass of water. "Here's to greed."

"The reason I must refuse your offer."

And the reason she wouldn't be going to Boston.

Harrison Carder might be joking, but she hadn't seen evidence that he possessed a faith in God that guided his life. And he certainly hadn't hesitated to suggest suing his friend. Perhaps evidence of his own greed.

As the food arrived, pan-fried bluegill for her and steak for Harrison, Abigail resolved to concentrate on the evening, to put the Cummingses' deceit behind her. For now. If she didn't, she'd end the meal with a stomachache.

Perhaps she could interest Harrison in worship services. "I'd like to invite you to attend First Christian. Our pastor's sermons and the fellowship bless me each week."

Eyes wide and wary, he looked ready to refuse, but then nodded. "That would give me a chance to get acquainted. Let folks see I'm one of them."

Not exactly the reason she had in mind, but who knew what would come from hearing God's Word?

"What time?" he asked, slowing the fork to his mouth.

"Church is at ten. Sunday school at nine."

"I should be able to make ten."

She smiled. "I'll look forward to it."

He arched a brow. "Will you save me a seat?"

"Of course. I'll introduce you to my family."

"Perhaps I can talk one of them into suing."

"Not an acceptable topic in church with the Cummingses sitting across the sanctuary."

He laughed. "Suppose not. Don't worry, dear lady. I won't embarrass you."

Whatever motive Harrison had in mind for coming, she suspected he wouldn't appreciate hers. She wanted him to meet more than her family. She hoped he'd meet God.

Chapter Fifteen

With sweat slipping beneath the brim of his Stetson, Wade slammed the hoe into the soil, chopping at weeds springing up in the garden. Nothing he did eased his anger at his father's treachery. What he'd done to the Wilsons, to Abby, tore at him. The backs of his eyes stung. She hated him now.

She'd turned to Harry for solace. He supposed he couldn't blame her, but when he'd found Harry sitting beside Abby and her family in the pew yesterday, he'd wanted to grab him by his starched collar and escort him out the door.

Not the attitude a churchgoer should have toward a visitor. But Harry's jaunty little wave across the sanctuary had Wade grinding his teeth. Harry knew perfectly well Wade didn't appreciate his attentions to Abby. The man would go to any lengths to get close to her. After church, he'd let it slip—no doubt on purpose—that he and Abby had enjoyed a lovely evening the night before.

Smooth, good-looking and intelligent, Harrison Carder probably seemed like a good catch compared to most of the bachelors in this town. And Abby wasn't wasting time getting to know him better.

Seth rounded the corner of the house and moseyed toward him with the easy gait of a long-legged youth. "Can't stay to work on those beds. I'm meeting Betty Jo at the café for a glass of lemonade," Seth said, all smiles.

The boy's joy at seeing his girl reminded Wade of himself at that age. That girl was now a full-grown woman and couldn't stand the sight of him.

"I'll be in the shop first thing tomorrow to sign the paper for that apprenticeship."

Wade leaned on his shovel, his back to the house. "Sounds good."

To him. But Abby would not agree.

Within seconds he discovered how right he'd been. Because Abby had been standing right behind him, the frown on her face proof she'd overheard Seth.

A flush on her cheeks, her blue eyes icy, Abby was lovely, regal and angry. He'd keep his distance, though he yearned to pull her to him, to cradle her in his arms. But he could at least warn her about Harry.

By the time he'd repeated his concerns about trusting Harry, her frown turned into a scowl. "You have the nerve to warn me about Harrison."

"My father wronged your family. But I didn't have any part of that. Can we at least talk? See if we can find a way to get past this?"

"Too much has happened. I can't trust your dad or you."

He stepped away. "Is there anyone you'd allow yourself to trust?"

"Don't try to turn this mess around and make it my fault." She pushed by him, stomping toward the stable.

He dropped the hoe then followed her in.

She'd taken a bridle off the wall and now carried it to where Beauty waited, neck extended over the stall.

"What are you doing?"

Nose in the air, she ignored him, slipping the leather over the mare's ears, or trying to.

"Let me do that," he said.

She huffed and moved aside.

With the bridle in place, he led Beauty out of the stall. "Where are you going?"

"Your father gave me permission to use the rig. If that's not all right with you—"

"Of course it is." Did she think he'd deny her anything?

As he backed Beauty between the staves, Abby waited, arms folded, tapping her toe. Whatever she planned to do, she couldn't wait to be on her way.

What was she up to that she needed a conveyance? Did she have a clandestine meeting with that so-called friend of his? At the prospect jealousy roared through him and brought the words out of his mouth. "Are you meeting Carder?"

"Where I'm going is none of your concern."

"If something happened and you didn't return, I wouldn't know where to look for you."

She planted dainty hands on the hips of the riding skirt she wore. "If you're worried about your conveyance—"

"No! I'm…worried about you."

"Your concern is too little, too late."

The truth pressed against his lungs. He'd lost Abby's regard, if he'd ever had it. He'd failed to heal the feud. He didn't have the money to make restitution for the railroad deal and his father insisted they didn't have cash lying around. Wade knew in that at least, his father spoke the truth.

Grabbing Beauty's bridle, he walked the horse out of the stable, and then assisted Abby into the rig. "Be careful," he said, gazing up at her.

"I'm always careful."

He suspected this impulsive woman didn't know the meaning of the word. If she was meeting Carder, he knew she didn't. The man was a womanizer at Harvard. A desire to follow her rose up inside him.

If Abby was the right woman for him, as Pastor Ted had implied, then somehow the trouble between them would be healed. Spying on Abby would not help his cause. But he'd never been more tempted.

Well, he had a simpler way to determine if Abby was meeting Carder. He'd make a visit to his law office. The man better be playing with paper dolls and not off somewhere with Abby.

Abigail waited until Wade headed inside before setting off for the Collier farm. With Rafe's reputation, she didn't relish the errand, but she'd overheard Seth say he'd sign a agreement with Wade. She had to act quickly. The best way to influence Seth appeared to be through his father.

As she turned onto Main Street, she passed Harrison's law office. The glare on the window kept her from seeing inside. She wondered what Harrison thought about the sermon, the warm reception from the congregation. Next Sunday would reveal what, if anything, the service meant to him.

As she drove out of town, she breathed a prayer Rafe would listen to reason and take a stand for his son's education.

If not for her encounter with Wade and the purpose of the errand, she would have enjoyed the freedom of getting out of town, seeing some of the countryside. The blades of corn, almost knee-high in the fields, fluttered in the breeze. Across the way, wheat undulated like a calm sea. Crops looked good. Hopefully New Harmony's farmers would have a successful harvest, unlike last year. Within minutes, a storm, hail, high winds, could destroy their efforts. Another reason she had to encourage her nephews to go into another occupation. To get the education that would enable them to find employment with less risk.

She had no trouble spotting the Collier property. The only farm she'd passed with keep-out signs posted on every fencepost.

At the lane she tugged on the reins, stopping Beauty, then jumped from the rig and tethered the horse.

Only to find the gate securely locked.

Well, she wouldn't let that stop her. Hitching up her skirt, she found a toehold then heaved to the top and over the gate and then dropped to the ground. As she did, she landed wrong, twisting her ankle. Hissing with pain, she leaned against the gate, rubbing the ankle. Once the throbbing eased a bit, she hobbled up the lane.

A very long lane.

The sun bore down. Perspiration beaded on her forehead. Her ankle hurt worse, no doubt swelling from the exertion and heat. Well, she'd come this far. She wouldn't be deterred.

As she reached a cove of trees and the welcome shade it provided, she heard an ominous click.

"Stop right where you are."

Rafe stepped from the trees, toting a gun.

"Mr. Collier, it's Abigail Wilson, Seth's teacher. I'd like to talk about your son's education."

Silence.

"I'd like a chance to explain what Seth's options are and what that could mean for his future."

She moved toward Rafe. His face shaded by a wide-brimmed Stetson, she couldn't read his expression but smelled whiskey.

He waved the shotgun. "Get on home. You're trespassing."

"I'm not here to poach or abuse your land. I just want to talk—"

"Leave now or I'll fire."

"But surely, you care what Seth—"

An explosion from the gun blasted her ears. Heart pounding, she staggered, almost falling, a cry escaping her lips. The man was crazy. He'd fire his weapon near a woman who he surely knew meant him no harm. What else was he capable of?

"I'm leaving," she said, hobbling backward, keeping her eyes on him.

Rafe Collier was unstable, a threat to anyone coming onto his property. Perhaps even a threat to his son. The reason Seth refused to leave his father might have more to do with fear than loyalty.

As she reached the sunny patch, she turned around and limped to the gate and hauled herself over it with shaking hands. As she lowered herself to the ground, she heard the sound of ripping fabric.

If she could get her hands on Rafe Collier, she'd like to shake some sense into him. Safe on the other side, she looked back from where she'd come. No sign of Rafe.

Ankle throbbing, she untied Beauty and climbed inside the rig and examined her split skirt. The two-corner tear would be hard to repair. As she headed the horse toward town, she knew what she must do. She would stop at the Sheriff's Office and report Rafe Collier's behavior. He was a menace to the community. And more importantly might be to his son.

Wade made the rounds of the Cummings's rental properties, and then headed to the Carder law office. He found Harry at his desk. He released a gust of air, pleased to have paid the man for his business advice and the excuse for being in his office now. Still he had to wonder what Abby was up to.

"You look lonely without those paper dolls."

Harry grinned then shoved a paper across the desk. "I lost interest in clients who couldn't pay."

A quick look at the list confirmed Harry had done his research. "These strategies should provide my employees a safe, healthy workplace. Appreciate your advice."

"Underneath that courteous façade, I can see you're as mad as a hornet."

Wade harrumphed.

"Admit it. You're upset I'm seeing Abigail."

"You've seen her more than once?"

The door opened. Abby, of all people, entered the room. Hobbled, really. Her skirt was ripped, her hat askew, a smudge of dirt on her cheek. Wade lunged to his feet and covered the distance between them in three strides.

"Are you hurt? What happened?" Wade asked as Carder whipped around his desk and joined them.

"I twisted my ankle, my fault." Abby plopped her hands on hips and glared at him. "But I could've as easily been killed."

"Killed? Here, take my arm." Wade put his other arm around her waist and eased her into a chair. "Did you fall?"

Harry turned the wastebasket upside down. "Better elevate that ankle."

As she took his advice and gingerly propped her foot, Abby winced. "Rafe Collier is dangerous." Troubled blue eyes rested on Wade as she explained what happened at the Collier farm. "I spoke to Sheriff Howe. He refuses to do anything."

"That's…ridiculous," Harry sputtered.

"Why, the sheriff even blamed me for trespassing on private property. Said the Collier place is clearly marked Keep Out. I suppose he'd have been forced to take action if I'd been shot, but he claims firing a gun over my head doesn't prove intent to kill." She wrapped her arms around her middle. "Call me a coward if you want, but I felt threatened."

"You're not a coward." Wade's stomach tightened. What kind of an idiot brandished a gun around a woman? A moonshine-soaked recluse. "I'm sorry. I understand how Rafe frightened you, but he wouldn't shoot anyone, especially a woman."

She snorted.

"He *is* touchy about intruders. Not that I'm excusing his behavior. I'll ride out there and have it out with him."

"The man's demented." She glanced at Carder. "Sheriff Howe said I can file a civil complaint."

"I can help you with that," Harry said.

"Abby, think about this. You're talking about Seth's father," Wade said, squatting on his heels beside her.

She turned troubled eyes on him. "That's what frightens me most. I smelled whiskey. Who knows what Rafe's capable of when he's drinking heavily?"

Hovering over Abigail like a mother hen, Carder nodded. "If Collier's inebriated that could affect both his dexterity and his judgment. He's liable for a lawsuit."

Carder practically salivated at the prospect of a court case. Wade's image of the man slid from mother hen to bird of prey, a vulture or hawk circling overhead.

"Harrison, you know how I feel about lawsuits."

Abby and Harry had discussed the topic? Had Carder proposed Abby sue the Cummingses? If so, that schemer needed a drawn-out dunk in a horse tank. Wade squared his shoulders, finding himself in the mood to get the job done.

"After today, I suspect fear is the reason Seth refuses to say anything against his father," Abby said.

Wade shook his head. "Seth loves his father. He's not afraid of him."

Abby shook her head. "If he were, he'd never admit it."

"Let's address one concern at a time," Harry said. "Collier can't be allowed to wield a gun around a helpless woman, much less fire it, especially under the influence of spirits."

Though Wade agreed with Carder on this, he struggled to see Abby as helpless.

"Were you afraid of him?" Harry asked.

"Yes, Rafe is out of control. He's going to hurt someone."

Harry took Abigail's hand. "Why, you're shaking. Let me get my legal pad. I'll ask a few questions. See where that leads."

By the time Wade returned from the café with ice for Abby's ankle, Harry had finished his interrogation. The lawyer was beaming. "You have grounds for filing a complaint. To clarify, a complaint is not a lawsuit."

Wade laid the towel soaked with cold water and filled with ice on Abby's ankle. She flinched then tugged her skirt over her feet. If only he could take the pain away. Take away the worry furrowing her brow. But at least she allowed him to touch her.

She glanced at Harry. "Is there enough evidence to take Seth out of that home—at least until Rafe stops drinking?"

"Abby, don't do that. Seth could end up a ward of the court."

"That's better than laid out in the church cemetery."

"Rafe would never hurt his son."

"Perhaps not, when he's sober, but with enough moonshine in him, how can you be sure?"

"I'll talk to Seth. Get him to open up."

Harry rose and opened a file drawer, fingered the files, then pulled out a sheet of paper. He filled in the blanks then handed it to Abigail. "Read, then sign the complaint. If you wish to pursue removing Seth from the Collier house, I will file a petition in the county courthouse tomorrow."

"I most certainly do."

"Abby, why not think about this for a day or so. Give yourself time to calm down. I'll talk to Rafe. Make him understand that he could have his son taken from him. That'll frighten him enough to mend his ways."

"And risk getting your head blown off with a twelve gauge?" Harry said. "Collier's a hothead. Logic won't convince him."

"You don't know Rafe. Since he lost his wife, he's…"

"Off his rocker?"

"No. He's struggling. Lost his way, but if given time, he'll come around."

Harry raised a hand. "Enough time and someone could end up hurt. Or worse. I can't stomach he frightened Abigail. What man would do that to a woman? Only answer I have—a man who isn't in his right mind."

Abby smiled at Harry, no doubt grateful for his support. Wade wanted to slug the guy.

She leveled her gaze on him. "I'm not surprised we don't agree on this, Wade. We rarely agree on anything. My concern is for Seth. Or for anyone who might stumble onto Collier property. Not for Rafe Collier."

"Abby, you didn't stumble onto Collier property any more than I did. Rafe brandished a gun at me too, but—"

"Did he fire at you?" Harry asked.

"Well, not at me."

"Did he discharge his weapon?" Carder eyed Wade as if he were a witness on the stand.

"Only into the air." Wade ran a hand through his hair. "I believe Rafe's in his right mind and fired the gun to frighten Abigail off his property, not to harm her."

"No-trespassing signs are meant to keep hunters or

poachers off private property," Abby said. "Not to keep neighbors from coming for a visit. Something has to be done."

With that Abby wrote her name on the complaint with those lovely flourishes he admired. Her penmanship in stark contrast to the ugly intent of the document she'd signed.

Where would this lead?

One thing he knew. Rafe would rue the day he got crossways with Abigail Wilson.

Fists at the ready, Wade stood over Rafe Collier sprawled on his back in the lane. His shotgun and Stetson lay a few feet away. Rafe made no move for the weapon, telling Wade plenty.

Abby was right, but only to a point. He steered clear of confrontation—until Rafe threw the punch. Even a disciplined man like Wade had limits. Wade rubbed his sore jaw, the reason he'd reached his with Rafe.

"You treated Abby like a horse thief or worse! If you ever fire a gun at anyone again, man or woman, I'll haul you into jail."

Rafe lumbered to his feet. Head down, he rubbed the stubble on his no doubt aching jaw. "I didn't mean her harm."

The heels of Rafe's boots were run-down. The hem of his denims frayed. The brim of his Stetson stained and worn. Rafe and his son were going through tough times. Tough times weren't an excuse to frighten a woman.

"You've got trouble, Rafe. Miss Wilson's filed a complaint against you. Worse, Harrison Carder, the lawyer in town, is looking into taking Seth away from you."

Dark eyes widened with disbelief. "What? Why?"

"When you threaten a woman with a gun, you're seen as

crazy, even dangerous. That jeopardizes the custody of your son. What in tarnation were you thinking?"

"She's pushing Seth to go off to some fancy college. He doesn't want that, but no, she keeps harping on it."

"She only wanted to talk to you. Now that stunt's given her ammunition to take action."

Rafe's face fell lower than his knees. "You're saying by firing into the air, I've given her grounds to take Seth from me?"

"That's exactly what I'm saying."

"Don't those no-trespassing signs mean anything? It's my property. I say who comes on it."

"Rafe, you're not using your head. You haven't since Peggy died. I should've knocked some sense into you when you pulled that gun on me." Wade removed his Stetson and whacked it against his leg. "You passed up an opportunity to take a good-paying job. I suspect your drinking is behind all of this."

Collier toed the ground, the mannerism familiar. Wade had seen Seth do the same when he felt uneasy.

"You're a lousy example to your son of how to handle tough times. Moonshine impedes your judgment. Makes you unfit as a parent, as a man. Destroy that still, stop drinking."

Tears welled in Rafe's eyes. "Seth's all I've got."

"Then put that boy ahead of a jug of moonshine before it's too late."

Celebrating the nation's birthday was usually the highlight of Abigail's summer. But with George's deceit and the complaint against Rafe increasing the trouble between her and Wade, even Rachel's hug didn't ease the tension swirling inside her.

Rachel twirled her white parasol accented with blue and

red silk roses, festive with her blue dress and beribboned hat. "I've done my part by wearing the flag's colors."

Hands donned in her mesh gloves and wearing a plumed hat, Abigail's lace-trimmed pale-blue-and-white-striped dress swirled around her feet as she and Rachel set off to stroll through the park.

"Abby, one day I hope to go to New York City to see the Statue of Liberty. Imagine what immigrants must feel sailing into the harbor welcomed by that impressive lady."

"One day we both will. We'll travel, visit the oceans and desert, see the world."

"That takes money," Rachel said.

"True. Have you talked to your father about attending Normal School?"

"Yes. He's thinking about it."

"I'm sure he'll come around."

As they passed the Lessman family, she and Rachel waved to Joe and Lois sitting on wooden folding chairs in the shade of a spreading elm. Lois held the baby while Ma supervised the older boys tumbling on a nearby blanket. "Lois and Joe must be excited to get into the new house."

Abigail chuckled. "We all are."

"After sharing your apartment for weeks, I can imagine."

Joe hobbled to his feet, maneuvering with his crutch on the uneven ground to the row of six houses, freshly painted and close to occupation. Doors stood open, allowing the community to view the results of their labor.

"It won't be long now," Abigail said. "Cookstoves were installed this week. The mattresses and most of the furniture have been delivered. Wade's finishing the last bed."

Abigail hadn't seen Wade since the incident with Rafe. She missed Wade, a ridiculous reaction. She was far better off without him or his father in her life. Refusing to dwell on anything that would ruin the day, she swept her gaze over the park swarming with gaily attired neighbors.

Earlier a parade led by New Harmony's high school band and the veterans of two wars had passed to the cheers of onlookers, kicking off the day. Bunting of the stars and stripes, boasting forty-five stars, hung in swags around the gazebo. On the steps, their congressman, dressed to the nines in a suit and top hat, was just finishing his speech to polite applause.

Ice cream freezers dotted the gazebo. A baseball game was underway in a nearby field. Children waited in line for the swings. The town fathers planned a bonfire tonight. Everyone had brought what they needed to spend the entire day.

"Look, Abby." Rachel dropped her voice. "The Cummings men are arriving."

Abigail turned her head, following their progress. "With the food I prepared tucked inside the basket Wade's carrying."

Not far from the gazebo, Wade opened a wooden folding chair and got his father situated in the shade of an oak. Then carried the basket up the gazebo steps to the tables set up inside.

Discovering George had lied about the railroad deal had destroyed the likelihood of ending the feud. The last straw— Wade opposed denying Rafe custody of his son. Abigail prepared their food, kept that house in order and saw that George got fresh air and exercise. She was paid for her efforts, but the harm he'd brought her family made every chore onerous.

"You know, Rachel, I think Wade needs help unpacking that basket."

A smile curving her lips, Rachel searched the cloudless sky. "I sense a storm brewing."

An Inconvenient Match

* * *

Wade opened the basket, inhaling tantalizing aromas. Even mad enough to spit nails, Abby wouldn't taint food the entire community would share.

Certainly the fried chicken, coleslaw, potato salad and chocolate cake looked delicious. *Safe*.

Four weeks ago when he and Abby sat under that oak sharing her box lunch, she'd claimed that if she'd known she'd been cooking for a Cummings, she'd have seasoned the food with a laxative. Though she'd been teasing, the mistrust triggering the banter hadn't eased. If anything, things had gotten worse.

He lifted the basket, preparing to tuck it under the table when Abigail appeared at his elbow, a vision in white and pale blue. Even with the trouble between them, he missed her every moment they were apart.

Eyes gleaming like a Fourth of July sparkler, Abby cocked a brow. "You're a brave man, Wade Cummings."

That look, those words—she had mischief on her mind. "You wouldn't."

A sly smile stole across her face. "You don't know what I'm capable of."

"If you'd wanted to contaminate my food, you've had the opportunity."

Color dotted her cheeks. "You're mighty sure of yourself."

"With you? Never." He leaned toward her. "I'll promise you one thing. If you did taint my food, I wouldn't hire Harry to seek damages."

Fisted hands found her hips. Blazing eyes held his. Whoa, he'd riled her now. This woman battled him but deep down he knew she'd never run as his mother had.

She'd never looked lovelier, more alluring. No doubt about it, he was smitten. An urge to drag her to him, to kiss the sass off that enchanting face seized him. But he kept his arms pasted to his sides, choosing to finish the day in one piece.

"You're making light of Rafe's behavior and the grounds for my compliant. Why don't you share my concern for Seth's safety?" she said.

"Rafe's scared. Scared he'll lose Seth to college, to the courts. I warned him to change his ways, stop his drinking and threatening folks with that gun." Wade wouldn't tell her that he'd been forced to deliver the message with his fists.

"What kind of a father opposes a son bettering himself?"

"Seth's all Rafe's got."

"Rafe's the grown-up. Let him act like one."

She turned aside, fussing with the dishes she'd prepared, ignoring him.

Abby had no idea what Rafe meant to Seth. Odd when she clung to a steadfast loyalty to her father, a man who hadn't handled the blow of losing the farm any better than Rafe handled the loss of his wife.

Wade suspected underneath that faithful façade, Abby resented the father she claimed to adore—for shirking his duty, for losing his way when they needed him most.

To escape Frank's defeated life, had Abby latched on to education as a way to never have to depend on anyone or anything? Not on land. Not on a man.

"Abby, you'll break Seth's heart if that complaint you filed separates him from his pa."

"You've got all the answers, Wade, for everyone's life but your own."

Beard neatly trimmed, gray eyes dancing, Harry loped up the gazebo steps, wearing a navy double-breasted jacket, light slacks and straw boater cocked on his head.

Abby turned toward Harry with a smile, obviously welcoming the interruption.

"Thought you two might need my services." With a satisfied smirk, the attorney leaned back on his heels. "Perhaps a stay of execution's in order."

"I'm starting to rue the day you arrived in town."

"That you'd speak so callously about a fraternity brother wounds me, Cummings." Harry turned to Abby and held out his arm. "May I offer my protection from this brute and suggest a stroll of the grounds?"

Abby tucked a hand in the crook. "I'd love hearing more about your college days, Harrison."

Harry gave Wade a jaunty salute then sauntered off with Abby while Wade gnashed his teeth.

"Boston is a lively town, full of history, but also a place where history is made. Now Wade and I..."

As they moved out of earshot, Wade had no idea what nonsense Carder was planting in Abby's pretty head. The man loved to hear himself talk. If that rapt expression on her face meant anything, Abby enjoyed his spiel.

Paying Carder to leave town would be money well spent. With his practice languishing, Harry might actually go.

If only Wade had the funds.

He'd have a chat with Harry. Make a few things crystal clear. Just in case he didn't understand the lovely schoolteacher was his woman. Without a doubt, she'd deny it.

With all that stood between him and Abby, he had no idea how they'd make peace. *Lord, show me what to do.*

Before I lose her to that dandy.

Chapter Sixteen

A long and difficult day at the bank examining the books' low cash reserves and a delinquent loan confirmed the bank was at risk. Wade went home hauling that cold dose of reality to an equally cold dinner.

On the way into the house he'd dropped off the books in the office, leaving them for his father to dissect. Then stood at the kitchen counter eating the meal Abby had left for him and faced the truth. As much as he wanted to deny it, as much as he'd fight for any other option, more trouble loomed between Abby's family and the Cummingses.

With his stomach rebelling, he strode to the shop to meet Seth. He'd promised to assess the boy's design for the gift he wanted to make for Abby.

Why hadn't Wade thought to make something for her? Perhaps a present could bridge the chasm between them. He sighed. After tomorrow, that chasm would widen to Grand Canyon proportions.

Seth waited outside, excitement riding his face, a paper clutched in his hand. He'd never seen the boy look happier.

"If I make Miss Wilson something pretty," he said, "she'll see I'm good at this. See how much you've taught me. Maybe see I'm not afraid of my pa, that he isn't a threat to anyone."

Though he didn't see the connection, Wade said, "I hope you're right."

In the shop Wade studied the to-scale drawing of a wooden jewelry box, admiring the boy's creative attempt to soften Abby. Not that he believed a handcrafted gift would make her drop the complaint against Rafe. Still, the gesture couldn't hurt.

"What wood would you like to use?" Wade strolled to where he kept a stash of decorative wood.

"Cherry. Or maybe bird's-eye maple." His brow furrowed. "Which would she like?"

The rosy hue and soft grain of the cherry fit Abby perfectly. "I think the cherry suits her."

"Me too."

"I'll get you started." Wade helped Seth select a plank, laid it on the workbench to mark the dimensions.

Satisfied the design was feasible, Wade handed Seth the goggles. As he watched, Seth cut the wood into twelve-by-one-inch and eight-by-one-inch lengths.

"Wade, can a judge make me stay in school?"

"No." But he could remove Seth from the Collier home. "But you know, getting a high school diploma makes sense. Without it, you limit your options."

Seth sighed. "I don't see how I can manage to work on the farm, apprentice in your shop, attend school *and* study."

"Handling all that would be difficult but not impossible for a smart, hard-working kid like you."

A flush climbed Seth's neck. "Thanks, but I want to earn more money."

Wade heard the desperation in Seth's tone. "Sounds like you have a special reason."

"Without money I can't court Betty Jo."

"If she cares about you, money shouldn't matter." Still, Seth could barely afford to buy Betty Jo a soda at the drugstore. "Finish the twelfth grade and I'll give you an advance on your earnings."

"You'd do that for me?"

He'd do what he could to save Seth from the pain he himself had endured. "I remember how it feels to care about a girl and not be accepted." The problem had been his name, not money.

The door opened. Abby stood on the threshold. "Wade, your father wants to talk to you."

"I assumed you'd gone home for the day."

"I had grocery shopping to do. I thought I'd work in the garden for a while." She tilted her chin. "On my own time."

The implication he'd resent paying for her work slashed at his pride. He wouldn't grace the barb with a comment.

"Hello, Seth," Abby said, her voice soft, almost pleading, as if afraid of his response.

Seth leaned against the workbench, cutting off her view of the beginnings of the jewelry box.

"I hope you know I didn't file the complaint against your father to be mean. I'm concerned about him and about you."

"Pa fired his gun to run you off, Miss Wilson. If he'd wanted to hurt you, he would've, 'cause you see, Pa never misses."

Abby glanced at Wade, a flash of disquiet in her eyes. Most likely not pleased to hear of Rafe's prowess with a gun.

"Well…" Her voice trailed off. "Don't forget your father's waiting, Wade."

As Abby stepped out the door, Wade put a hand on Seth's shoulder. "Can you handle mitering those corners?"

"Yes, sir."

"Be careful of that saw. I'll be back later to see if you need help."

A faraway look on his face as he penciled lines on the wood, Seth didn't appear to hear.

"Seth?"

"Huh?"

"Be careful using the tools."

"Yes, sir."

The boy had worked at Wade's side for a year without incident, giving Wade confidence in his ability to work alone.

As he headed to the house, to his father's summons, he spotted Abby in the garden watering the resettled plants.

At his approach she turned toward him, her gaze filled with misgiving. "Seth's upset with me."

If she knew about the jewelry box, she'd worry less. "He doesn't hold a grudge."

"I hope you're right." She sighed. "Sometimes doing the tough thing is the right thing to do."

He hoped she'd remember those words in the coming days.

Some tough decisions had to be made before the bank examiner arrived. Wade rapped on the door then entered the library that also served as his father's office.

His desk strewn with accounting books, George sat staring off into space.

Wade cleared his throat, jerking up his father's head.

George motioned to the chair across from him. "Have a seat." He formed a steeple with his fingers. "I assume you agree the bank's in trouble."

Wade nodded. "Last fall's dismal crop forced farmers to borrow. The fire hurt us when those who lost their homes withdrew their savings." He expelled a breath. "Cash reserves are at a record low."

"The bank examiner could put us on probation, or worse, force us to close."

"Could you loan the bank some of your personal money?"

"Most of my cash reserves went to the fire victim fund."

"I could come up with a couple hundred." The start-up money for his shop. "But that money's already in the bank."

"We need *new* money. Talk to those leasing our buildings. See if anyone can come up with enough cash to buy us out. If not…" He cleared his throat. "You know what that means."

"We have to call a loan."

"The question is whose?" George ran a scarred finger along a column. "Five families owe the bank considerable money. But only one loan is delinquent. Delinquent loans don't please bank examiners."

Wade braced himself for what was coming. "I know."

"Lois Lessman borrowed money to pay off their creditors almost two years ago but they haven't paid one dime."

When Lois had come to Wade asking for a loan, she'd been desperate. Joe was gambling. Her income couldn't feed and clothe four boys. The grocer and Mercantile had refused to extend more credit.

"The Lessmans are just now getting on their feet. We can't add to their troubles, can't risk enlarging the feud."

"The feud is the reason I let that loan go unpaid as long as I did." He studied Wade under heavy brows. "If the bank fails, the entire town suffers." George shoved the tome aside.

"The Lessmans don't have money to pay off the loan. Joe can't work and he's still in deep with gambling debts."

"They'll have to sell their house."

His father's words sank to the bottom of Wade's stomach. Abby would never forgive him. Most likely the town would never forgive him. "That's heartless."

"Figure out another way if you can. But the Lessmans owe this bank hundreds of dollars. They're in arrears. The time has come to prove you're man enough to make the hard decisions. The bank examiner arrives in two weeks. This can't wait."

A knot formed in Wade's throat. *Lord, please let there be another way.*

He'd check with businessmen leasing Cummings's properties. Talk to the owner of the canning factory. Yet even as Wade made the plan, he doubted anyone in this town had the money to purchase the property they rented. Without a miracle, he knew what had to be done.

Calling the Lessman loan would pound the final nail into the coffin of his and Abby's relationship.

If he hoped to save the Lessman home, Wade had to bring more capital into the bank. Now. He'd saddle Rowdy and ride out to talk to Leland Owens, hoping the owner of the canning factory would have interest in buying one of the rental properties as an investment. On the way out Wade would mull over other money-making ideas.

Before he did, he'd see how Seth was getting along. A miter box was easy enough to use but Seth planned to dovetail the corners of the jewelry box, difficult for a novice.

"How's it going, Seth?" he called as he opened the door. Silence greeted him. Motes of dust floated in a strip of sunlight streaming in the window. "Seth?"

No answer. Wade took two steps. Stopped. His heart clutched, as if a mammoth hand wrapped around it and squeezed.

Blood.

On the tool bench.

On the floor.

"Seth!"

Wade spun around, searching the space. No Seth, only Abby coming in. "Have you seen Seth?" he asked her.

"No why? What's wrong?"

"Blood." Wade waved a hand toward the puddle on the

floor and cursed himself for leaving the boy alone. Why had he done that! "Oh, Lord, I pray he's okay."

"Are you sure?" Then Abby saw the glimmer of crimson and let out a gasp. "Where would he go?"

"I'm not sure, but I've got to find him. Make certain he got that bleeding stopped." Wade paced the floor, thinking. "Maybe he's at Doc Simmons. Or home."

"I'm going with you."

He was already halfway out the door with Abby at his heels. "Taking the carriage will slow me down."

She laid a hand on his shoulder. A touch of comfort, reason. "Wade, if Seth's lying along the way, bleeding, we'll need the carriage."

No point in arguing with the determined set of her jaw, especially since she was right. "Run to the house. Get gauze and antiseptic—in Dad's room—while I hitch Beauty."

A few minutes later, his mind racing with possibilities, Wade helped Abby into the carriage. What if the time he'd taken to hitch the horse had been too long?

Wade snapped the reins and Beauty jerked forward. The entire way to Doc's, Abby sat beside him, quiet, stoic, except for her white-knuckled hands opening and closing, opening and closing.

They reached the white clapboard house, Doc's office and residence, but found the door locked. Wade clambered into the carriage, dread coiled in his gut. "Doc must be out on a house call."

"He could be at the Colliers'," Abby offered, no doubt trying to reassure him.

"I hope you're right." Wade snapped the reins and turned Beauty east toward Rafe's farm. "What if Seth lost too much blood and didn't make it home?" He shook his head, trying to shake loose the horrifying images running through his mind.

Abby laid a gentle hand on his forearm. "He's going to be all right."

"I never should have left him alone. This is my fault."

"Seth's a smart boy. From what you've said, he knew what he was doing. Accidents happen even to experienced carpenters."

Wade turned to Abby, drinking in her quiet assurance, her soothing presence. "Thank you."

"For what?"

"For being here."

She smiled, and the tension in Wade's chest eased its iron grip. "He'll be okay, Wade."

"I pray you're right."

Out of town, Wade gave Beauty her head. Along the way, Wade scanned both sides of the gravel road for any sign of the boy or blood. The twenty-minute drive to the Collier farm took an eternity. But then finally the lane came into view. "The gate's open."

Abby looked at Wade. "Why?"

Dread squeezed his stomach as Beauty trotted up the lane. "I don't know."

No sign of Rafe and that gun of his. They drove through the stand of trees and into a clearing where the log cabin faced west. The logs were chinked tight. The roof was solid. The door was peeling paint, no doubt battered by rain and sun, but nothing suggested neglect. What had Wade expected? A dilapidated shanty?

As they pulled in front of the house, Rafe stepped out the door, the screen slapping shut behind him.

Wade leaped to the ground and tied Beauty to the hitching post then strode to Abby's side. They sprinted up the path to a stone stoop where Rafe paced. Brow furrowed, face pale, he looked terrible.

"Is Seth with you?" Wade asked.

Rafe nodded. "His hand. I stopped at Doc's. He wasn't there. I brought him home. Did the best I could, but…" He bit his lip. "I'm glad you're here." Rafe swiped a hand across a stubbly jaw. "It's my fault."

"Your fault? I shouldn't have left him alone."

He lifted bleak eyes to Wade's. "I wanted to see Seth work. I went to your shop and startled him. He cut his hand on the saw."

"No one's at fault," Abby said firmly, in control, keeping a cool head.

An example of how she managed a crisis in the classroom. Anywhere. Underneath that dainty, even fragile, façade was a strong woman who didn't fall apart. A woman he admired. A woman who had shared that calm and tenderness with him.

"Let's see that wound," she said.

Rafe threw open the door and they entered a small kitchen. Seth, pale with his jaw clenched, obviously in pain, slumped on a ladder-back chair, cradling his bandaged hand.

"I stopped the blood and cleaned the gash. He's got a ragged wound. He can move his fingers and feel pain." Rafe's eyes filled with tears. "My boy's hurting."

"Good signs, all of them. You'll be fine, Seth." Wade peeled back the bandages. The sight of the nasty gash flopped in his stomach. As ugly as it was, the wound would heal. "You'll have a scar to brag to your friends about."

Seth tried for a smile that faded faster than moonlight in the morning.

Wade redid the wraps then gave Seth's shoulder a gentle squeeze. "Good idea to let Doc take a look. Make sure it doesn't get infected."

"He's really going to be okay?" Rafe asked. "I did the right thing?"

Wade turned to Rafe, really looking at him. The lines

creasing his face had eased. Color had been restored to his face. But Wade also noticed Seth's father stood taller, had a new lucidity in his eyes. Eyes no longer bloodshot. He looked different. Sober. "You did a good job, Rafe."

"Thank God."

"Believe me, I already have."

Rafe dropped into a chair. "I need to thank you folks."

"We didn't do anything," Abby said. "You did all the doctoring."

"No, I meant about what you did before." Eyes glistening, he glanced at his son. "You...you made me see what a gift I had. Made me see I was ruining not just my life but Seth's too."

"Pa, I was fine," Seth said.

"No, you weren't. These two made me see...many things." He rose and stood before Wade. "When you were here last week, you said some difficult things to hear."

Wade opened his mouth to speak but Rafe put up a hand.

"Those things needed saying. After you left, I lined up and smashed every jug of moonshine then destroyed the still."

Wade glanced at Seth. The boy nodded. "You quit drinking?"

"It's been a week now." Rafe crossed to his son. "Seth stood by me through the nightmares and the shakes with prayers and a bucket and cold cloths. Now that I can keep food down and sleep, I'm seeing what I'd missed in that hazy world I'd holed up in. It's been a hard week..." Rafe exhaled a shaky breath. "But it'll get easier."

A week ago Wade had tried to knock some sense into Rafe. To persuade him to quit drinking; to leave his gun hanging over the door where it belonged; to treat a lady right instead of scaring her half to death. Rafe had taken those steps, had gone through torment. He'd done it for his son.

A week wasn't long, but long enough to rid his body of booze. Question was—would Rafe be strong enough to give up moonshine permanently? "That's a brave thing," Wade said. "I'd like to shake your hand."

"Not as brave as telling a man he was losing his son." Rafe clasped Wade's in his. "I'm grateful to you for taking Seth under your wing."

"Seth is a special young man." Wade glanced at his apprentice and sent him a smile. "But then you know that."

Rafe walked to Abigail. "Miss Wilson, I'm indebted to you too. Not just for all you done for Seth. But…" He cleared his throat. "That complaint you filed woke me up. Made me realize moonshine could rob me of the only thing I cared about. I've never been that scared." His eyes filled with tears. "After Peggy died, I… I wasn't a good father. Leastwise not the father Seth deserved. If you hadn't gone to the sheriff, I might've never found the courage to quit drinking."

Though Wade had taken exception to Abby's actions, she'd been right. Filing that complaint had spurred Rafe to straighten out his life.

Seth's prayers had been answered. His faith in his father and in God justified. Proof nothing was impossible with God.

The silence extended between them, their concern for the boy across the way connecting them while the fire crackled in the cookstove and the curtains danced back and forth in the breeze.

Wade clung to the hope that God would answer his prayers for his father, for the end of the feud and a new beginning for him and Abby.

"I'm relieved you've stopped drinking, Mr. Collier," Abby said. "You have a fine son."

"Yes, I do. And you're a fine teacher." His gaze found the

floor then rose to hers. "I apologize for scaring you. I used that gun to keep folks away, folks just being neighborly. I thought if someone saw the sorry state I was in, got wind of that still hidden in the woods, they'd take Seth from me."

"I'll drop the complaint, Mr. Collier." Abby reached out a hand.

Rafe shook it gently, as if he thought Abby might break. "I'm beholden to you."

"Thanks, Miss Wilson," Seth said, tears in his eyes.

"If the job offer stands, Wade, I'd like to tackle that warehouse," Rafe said, fighting tears of his own.

"Sure does."

"Now that you no longer need to play nursemaid to your old man, I'm hoping you'll have some fun, Seth." Rafe grinned. "Invite that gal, Betty Jo, to the ice cream social next month."

"I just might, Pa." Seth rose then wobbled. "I feel kinda woozy."

Rafe gently pushed his son back into the chair then filled a dipperful of water from a white enameled bucket on the counter and handed it to him. "This'll help."

Seth gulped the contents. "I'm mighty proud of you, Pa. All you did, all you went through made me think." He turned his gaze on Wade. "I still want to be your apprentice, Wade, but I've decided to finish high school."

"That's a good decision, Seth."

"Miss Wilson's right. I might want to go to college someday. Pa has taught me a man can change his path if the one he's on is going nowhere."

"You both have taught this teacher a thing or two," Abby said, eyes misty.

Wade believed the cabinetmaking shop would succeed, but whatever happened, by finishing high school, Seth wisely kept his options open.

"Truth is, son, things change. When that change hurts, a man doesn't hide behind anything. Not behind meanness, not behind a bottle, not behind a gun."

Was Wade's father's gruffness a façade meant to keep people away as surely as Rafe's gun?

Abby's father hadn't accepted change, hadn't been able to find another path when he'd lost the farm. Slowly Frank Wilson had withered and died, impacting his daughter forever.

George hadn't been able to move beyond his wife leaving, what he saw as rejection of himself. Perhaps, in time, with prayer, and with Wade refusing to give up on his dad—as Seth hadn't given up on Rafe—Wade's father would appreciate what he had—a family.

But whatever happened, Wade would never stop hoping and praying. Love meant never giving up. Love meant never losing faith in others. Faith that with God's help people could change, could be what God wanted them to be, had created them to be.

Wade's gaze drifted to Abby. For the first time in a long time he imagined a future. With her.

But not yet.

He had one more mountain to climb. Though Abby didn't know it yet, that mountain loomed between them, a barrier of massive proportions.

If he didn't save her sister's home, Abby would despise him as surely as her father had despised his.

Her hand in the crook of Wade's arm, Abigail strolled down the lane toward the carriage, no longer carrying the weight of her concern for Seth.

Wade squeezed her hand. "Want to know something? I resented the time I spent in college, but the courses I took will help me run the business end of my cabinetmaking shop."

She cocked her head. "At last you see things my way."

Chuckling, they neared the carriage. He leaned over and brushed his lips across her cheek, his gentle touch tender, healing, then helped her inside.

As they rode toward town, their sleeves brushing, Abigail was aware of those broad shoulders, the capable artistic hands holding the reins. She leaned into his strength, inhaling his masculine scent, trapping the oxygen in her lungs until she could barely breathe.

When had Wade become her life?

Wade slowed the carriage as they neared the bank. "It's a lovely night. Would you mind walking to your house?"

"I'd enjoy that."

Wade drove past the bank and her apartment overhead, then on down the street until they reached the edge of town.

"We're home," he said.

Home.

The last word Abigail had expected to associate with the Cummingses' residence. Yet she did.

With the conflict over Seth ended, another layer of the barrier between her and Wade had been stripped away. Wade had no part in his father's corrupt business dealings. She'd seen his kind heart with Seth, the effort he made to connect with his father, the love he had for God.

All of this proved Wade had matured into a good man, someone she could trust.

Wade drove through the roofed portico at the south end of the house and around back. He stopped Beauty then rounded the carriage and helped Abby out, his eyes searching her face. "Do you remember me telling you that a tight bit chafes?"

"Yes."

"Rafe held the reins loose, giving Seth his head, giving his son the freedom to choose his own way."

"And Seth made the right choice." She lifted her face to Wade. "You were right about that, you've been right about a lot of things."

"It's not about who's right or wrong. You and I need to trust each other in that same way." He laid a palm on her cheek. "I care for you. I believe you still care for me."

She did care. But caring was a risk.

"When we were kids, I called you my princess. Let me be your prince, Abby." Cupping her jaw with his palm, he leaned close, pulling her to him, eyes asking permission.

Abigail gazed up at him and lost herself in those dark blue depths. This man would not harm her. Here in his arms was where she belonged. No matter how hard she'd pretended otherwise, she'd never purged Wade from her heart.

With a soft whimper, she slipped her arms around his neck and her hands into the hair at his nape. His lips met hers, in a soft, lingering, leisurely kiss that sent shivers clear to her toes, leaving her unsteady on her feet.

When had she ever felt like this?

As the kiss ended Wade pulled her into his chest. She sagged against him, clinging to the solid strength of him and felt the galloping beat of his heart.

And knew she could love this man.

Uninvited, the pain of the breakup rose inside her. Could she trust his words, his kiss? Hadn't he claimed the very same thing before?

Chest heaving, she lurched from his arms. "I...I'd prefer to walk home alone."

The grim expression on Wade's face tore at her, but until she understood why he'd discarded her in high school, she couldn't let herself fall in love with him. If she did, and he rejected her again, she couldn't bear it.

Her stomach knotted. Could she end up like her father?

She stiffened her spine. She wouldn't give Wade the opportunity. As Cecil said, a Wilson and a Cummings were oil and water. They did not mix.

She'd do her job and keep things impersonal. She'd devote herself to teaching, to helping children reach their potential, whatever that might be.

And guard her heart from this man.

Chapter Seventeen

Wade put one foot in front of the other toward the parlor and the nightly game of checkers with his father, reliving the fear he'd seen plain on Abby's face. She didn't trust him. The past clung to her like a frightened child clung to its mother.

But she was no longer a child. And neither was he. He was a man ready for the woman he loved. Yet she wanted no part of him.

In the parlor Wade's father stood staring out the window. Steeling himself for George's usual snarly attitude, Wade crossed the room. His father turned toward him, face haggard, eyes weary.

Wade frowned. "You okay? You look tired."

"I haven't been sleeping well."

"Are you having trouble breathing? I'll speak with Doc Simmons, see— "

George raised a palm. "Doc has no remedy for what ails me."

"What's bothering you?"

His father turned away, putting his back to him. "An uneasy conscience."

That his father had given his behavior a thought, much less lost sleep over it, settled inside of Wade. *Lord, what do*

I say to that? "We've all made mistakes," he said finally. "My list's a mile long." Abby would no doubt double his estimate. "Would talking about it help?"

"Yapping can't fix this." He dropped into a chair. "All I've worked for leaves me…" His father's voice shriveled like an overripe peach in the noonday sun. "Empty."

Wade took the chair opposite him. "Why's success so important to you?"

George dug a handkerchief out of his back pocket and blew his nose. Had he been crying?

"I know your family was poor," Wade said.

"Dirt poor. Eight of us crammed into two windowless rooms in a rundown tenement in Chicago. Pa worked in the stockyards. The conditions and pay were dismal. I vowed then that no family of mine would experience such hardship."

"I'm sorry you had a miserable childhood."

George's gaze grew distant, as if traveling to another place. "I, ah…forgot something about that time."

"What did you forget?"

"When Pa came home at night, he'd clean up then gather us kids to him. Tell us to work hard, to look out for one another. He'd ask how we were doing in school. You see, Pa couldn't read and wanted better for us." His voice turned raspy. "I may have gone to bed hungry, but I went to sleep loved."

Wade heard the uncertainty in his dad's voice. The uncertainty anyone cared. He wanted to tell his dad he cared, but couldn't seem to shove the words out of his mouth. "I wish I could've known your parents. I only remember Mom's dad."

"Ernestine was an only child. I could hardly imagine that." A smile curved his dad's lips. "When I met your mother and we fell in love, I felt ten feet tall, the luckiest man alive. Ernestine hadn't grown up poor. Not that her folks were rich. Her dad loved working with wood." He glanced at Wade. "That's where you get your talent."

His father's acknowledgment that woodworking took talent eased the trouble between them.

"I wanted to give Ernestine everything. So she'd never regret marrying the likes of me." His voice trembled. "That's what happened. She didn't stay."

Even all these years later, Wade couldn't think about that day without bringing a lump the size of Gibraltar to his throat. He swallowed hard. "Dad, I understand how Mom's leaving hurt you. She hurt Regina and me too." He took a deep breath, knowing what he was about to say might trigger his father's temper. "But after she left, you never comforted us, never showed us you cared." That lump shoved up his throat. "We lost both our parents that day."

His father fiddled with his handkerchief, rolling the edges round and round between his fingers. "I guess in a way you did. I see that now."

"Why now?"

"Credit Abigail. That gal made me take a hard look at myself. I don't like what I see." He glanced at his Bible on his bedside table. "While I was building bigger barns like that farmer in Scripture, I was hurting others, hurting my family." He cleared his throat. "I resented you for rejecting what I'd spent my life achieving. Now I realize my legacy is you and Regina. You're all I've created that matters."

Tears welled in Wade's eyes. His father might not be able to speak the words, but he cared.

"Live your life the way you must to be happy. That's what I want for you and your sister. If that means cabinetmaking, well, then that's what you should do."

Wade groped for words. None seemed adequate to express the emotion swirling inside of him. "Dad," he said, his voice rough, uneven and laden with the tears running down his face.

A moan escaped his father's lips. "I'm sorry for trying to run your life, for treating you badly. I'd like a second chance."

George reached a hand.

Wade met his father halfway. Weeping, they embraced, a broken man, a mended son.

Ice cream and Cora's cookies, a combination Abigail hoped would tempt George into getting out of the office he'd been hibernating in and into the fresh air. The daily prescription Doc Simmons recommended for healing his lungs.

That morning Cora had returned to the Cummingses' kitchen, explaining Wade had stopped at her daughter's house on the way to the bank and announced he and George had made peace. Abigail and Cora had hugged, first crediting God, then each other for the healing between father and son. With Cora back to stay, Abigail had more time to devote to George's physical well-being.

The sooner Wade's father could return to his duties at the bank, the sooner Wade would be freed from that chafing bit he despised and open his cabinetmaking shop.

Not that Abigail had supported Wade's dream in the past, but since the visit to the Collier cabin, she wanted Wade to have the freedom of choice and the happiness he deserved.

She couldn't give Wade her heart but in many ways she understood him. Understood the importance of that peace he valued. Just as soon as Lois and Joe settled in their new home and the burden of Joe's gambling debts was lifted from their shoulders, she'd find that peace too.

Abigail rapped on the door then entered the library. At

the interruption, George's brow furrowed, but she paid him no mind.

"Time for recess," she said breezily. Tail wagging hello, Blue ambled over for a scratch to his ears. "I'm serving ice cream and Cora's cookies on the back veranda."

"Can't you see I'm busy writing a letter?"

"Teachers have rapped knuckles for far less defiance."

"Is that a threat?" he said, eyes twinkling.

"Indeed. But since I'm merciful, your punishment shall be fresh air and small talk."

He grinned. "At my age being treated like a kid is fun."

Blue followed them to the kitchen where Cora was loading a tray with goodies.

"Join us, Cora," George said.

"Not this time. I'm off to the grocer's. How's pork shank and sauerkraut sound for tomorrow's supper?"

"Delicious." George took Cora's hand. "I'm glad you're back. We missed you."

"I'll stay as long as you treat that son of yours right."

"I'm not sure I know how."

"Figure it out. Or I'll return to my daughter's." With that, Cora grabbed her pocketbook and sashayed out of the kitchen.

With a grin, George met Abigail's gaze. "Bet you didn't know anyone could be grumpier than I am."

Abigail chuckled and reached for the tray, but George insisted on carrying it. Though the effort made him breathe harder, he no longer gasped for air. Her time here was almost over. She'd have to find another job but she wouldn't think about that now.

On the veranda they sat side by side in wicker chairs as they ate ice cream and cookies, enjoying the gentle breeze, the call of the birds. George tossed Blue a cookie. He gobbled it down, then plodded down the steps and sniffed his way around the lawn.

"We need to get outside more if for no other reason than to give Blue exercise. He's getting fat."

"Better fat than sassy," he said arching a brow, "like some people I could name."

"Cora?" Her chuckle seemed to please him. "You're healing, George, your lungs and your heart."

He lowered his spoon. "Does that mean you're quitting?"

"Do you want me to?"

"Suit yourself." Though the cheerless look in his eyes suggested George didn't relish seeing her go.

Maybe she'd have this job through the summer after all. That she didn't want to quit jolted through her. Perhaps the trouble between them was healing along with George's injuries.

Joe was healing too. He'd helped clean up the new construction, doing what he could. Soon the Lessmans would be moving into their new home. Everything was working out.

Thank You, God, for creating us with the power to mend, mind and body and soul. Thank You for saving Joe when he needed You most.

The thought of Joe broken and battered, lying at the bottom of the steps in that fire tore through her. "George, what was being in that burning house like?"

"Like hell."

She shivered and not from the ice cream. "What did you hear that made you think someone was inside?"

George's tongue darted in and out of his mouth like a bad liar on the witness stand.

"You must've had trouble seeing with all the smoke."

His Adam's apple bobbed. "Yes."

"With the smoke you inhaled and your burns, I'm amazed

you got out alive. I keep going over and over it in my mind, trying to figure out how Joe made it out with a broken leg and arm."

George shifted his gaze away, but not before Abigail glimpsed the uneasiness in his eyes. "Stop yapping about that fire. It's over and done. I want to forget it."

She understood not wanting to remember the terror of that night, but why was George getting huffy? Surely he had to wonder how Joe made it. Yet his wary expression and nervous conduct reminded her of a student with something to hide.

Her breath caught. Could it be? "You know how Joe got out, don't you?"

George blinked rapidly. "Why would I?"

"You know because you rescued him. The cry for help you heard was Joe's."

George's gaze remained on his hands. He didn't admit it. Didn't deny it. Didn't say a word.

"What happened that night?"

He rose to his feet. "Recess is over."

She blocked his path. "You're not fooling me. Why are you so secretive? If you saved Joe, you're a hero."

Closing his eyes, he sighed. "I did no more than any man would."

"You saved Joe!" She threw her arms around him. "Thank you! With the feud dividing our families, I'm…"

A sad smile sagged on his lips. "Did you believe I'd let a man die because he was married to a Wilson?"

"No! What I don't understand is why you kept your heroism secret."

"I didn't want gratitude. Don't want it now."

"Whether you want it or not, you have my gratitude."

Tears welled in his eyes. "A man pays his debts."

Had guilt over the feud, over the railroad deal, kept

George silent? Whatever reason he had for his silence didn't matter.

Abigail led George back to his chair. "Tell me about that night."

His scarred fingers trembled as he wiped the tears trickling down his face. "I heard a scream. Stayed low trying to find him but couldn't see for the smoke. Thank God I stumbled over his body. He was out cold, dead weight. Flames lapped closer, the heat so intense I thought we'd burn alive." He looked at Abigail. "Some supernatural strength shot through me. I grabbed the bib of Joe's overalls and crawled in the direction I'd come in, dragging him with me." He stopped, his eyes glazed as if seeing it all again. "A burning timber had fallen, blocking the door, jammed in tight. I shoved it aside."

"And burned your hands."

"Yes," George said, sucking in a breath. "Outside, I saw two men heading toward us. I slipped away, easy with the smoke and confusion." He coughed, as if reliving the smoke impacting his lungs.

"Joe is alive, thanks to you." She laid a hand on George's shoulder. "You have my undying gratitude." He looked uncomfortable with the praise, but she wanted to shout it from the rooftops. "God brought you to rescue Joe."

Her heart swelled with gratitude not only to George for saving her brother-in-law, but to God for using the tragedy to heal wounds.

George looked drained of energy. "I'm going in to lie down," he said then walked off, Blue at his heels.

As she gathered bowls and spoons onto the tray, a wind kicked up, carrying cooler air. The line of dark clouds moving in from the west promised rain.

Odd she could read the clouds yet couldn't decipher the actions of others or even her own heart. She saw now that

her view of her family and the Cummingses had been dis-
torted. The Cummingses' sins were no worse in God's eyes
than the Wilsons'. As Joe had said, a feud wasn't God's will.

How must God feel to see His children lash out at each
other, instead of living in unity as His Word commanded?

Through difficult circumstances and tough times, God
taught the lessons she needed to learn. She hadn't forgiven
him in obedience to God. The command to forgive others
didn't hinge on *their* behavior. Only hers.

Unable to wait until evening to share the joy bubbling
within her, she'd go to the bank. Tell Wade about his father's
heroism and the end of the feud.

Where that would lead she didn't know. But for the first
time in years she was optimistic that her future might include Wade.

Umbrella angled against the wind, Abigail hurried along
the rain-slicked walk. At the entrance to Cummings State
Bank the redbrick looked solid, dependable, exactly as
a bank should. She closed and shook her umbrella, then
stepped inside.

As she moved through the lobby, treading carefully on
the slick tile, Leon scuttled around the partition. "Abigail,
may I have a word with you?"

"Certainly."

With his auburn hair slicked back and parted in the
middle, wire-rimmed glasses perched on his nose, Leon
reminded her of an owl, intelligent and watchful.

"I haven't seen you since the auction," he said, his tone
accusing.

As if the fault was hers. "I've been…busy. I suppose
you're the same."

"I heard about your job." His eyes narrowed. "Heard you

were seen holding hands with Wade Cummings. Considering the feud, I gave the rumor no credence."

Abigail scanned the few people going about their business, paying no attention to them. Thankfully word hadn't gotten out about Wade's kiss. Yet.

"George Cummings pulled my brother-in-law out of his burning house. George saved Joe's life! The feud is over."

As if her news were of no consequence, Leon's mouth turned down. "So the gossip's true."

"You and I— Well, you wouldn't call our relationship courting, would you?"

"What would you call it?"

"I'd say we're friends. Comfortable with each other but not romantically involved."

"Feelings aren't a good basis for a relationship."

She might've agreed once. But now that she'd experienced Wade's grown-up kiss—

She gulped. Those kisses had shifted her world on its axis. Romance might not be everything, even the most important thing, but those feelings mattered. "I'm sorry. I didn't realize you thought we were serious. I like you but not that way."

Behind his spectacles, hazel eyes hardened. "I'd be careful. Wade hurt you once. I remember."

"That was a long time ago."

"If he discards you, I won't be waiting," he said, then stomped to the barred teller cage.

Surely Leon wasn't in love with her. She'd never seen evidence or given him encouragement. Still she hadn't wanted to hurt him. Not when she knew the pain of a broken heart and had struggled since with mistrust.

Lord, heal Leon's heart.

Outside the bank president's office, George's secretary looked up from her desk. "Hello, Miss Wilson."

"Good afternoon, Miss Detmer. Is Wade in?"

As if she'd conjured him up, the door to his office opened. "Miss Detmer, would you—"

Seeing her standing there cut off Wade's words and Abigail's breath. Remembering their last time together, remembering that kiss, heat climbed her neck and flooded into her cheeks. His warm gaze swallowed her up. In his eyes she saw proof he cared. Why had she been afraid to trust Wade?

"Hello, Abby."

The warm caress of his tone, the scent of his essence, those indigo eyes enveloped her. She could barely find her wits to tell him. "I have amazing news," she said, her voice tremulous with excitement.

A quick glance toward the lobby furrowed his brow. Then he stepped back with a welcoming smile, allowing her to enter the office ahead of him.

"What a pleasure to see you here in the middle of the day, with a smile that would light up a room."

The urge to hug him, to kiss him, slid through her, but she merely laid a hand on his lapel. "Wade, the feud is over."

His eyes lit. "What's happened?"

"Your father—"

A knock on the open door. "Miss Detmer's not at her—" Lois gaped. "Ab, I'm surprised to see you here."

"Lois, you're in time to hear the best news!" She clapped her hands. "The night of the fire, Wade's father heard a scream and went into a burning house. That house was yours. God brought George to save Joe! Can you believe it?"

Expressions blank, Wade and Lois stood unmoving, speechless, as if struck dumb.

"How do you know that?" Wade finally said.

"George told me, just minutes ago."

Tears filled Lois's eyes. "I wondered how Joe got out with broken limbs."

"Isn't that incredible? After this, the feud seems...well, trivial. I'm sure you agree, Lois, that all should be forgiven."

Lois's eyes darted to Wade. The expression on her face wobbled in Abigail's stomach.

Lois should be overjoyed, not somber. Abigail moved toward Lois. "What's wrong? Why are you here?"

"Wade, I'd like Abby to sit in on the meeting."

Nodding, Wade ushered Lois and her to chairs opposite the desk. Why these somber faces when she'd just shared the best, most astonishing news.

Did Lois need money? "Are you asking for a loan?"

"The loan I'm here to discuss isn't new. Two years ago bills at the grocer and Mercantile had piled up. I couldn't handle them."

"I thought Joe paid off those debts right before the fire."

"He did."

"Then I don't understand what this is about." Abigail laid a hand on Lois's arm.

"When I borrowed that money, Joe was still gambling." Lois sighed. "He found where I'd hidden it before I could pay our creditors. He..."

Abigail swallowed against the bile shoving up her throat. "He lost the money at the poker tables."

"Yes."

One small word tinged with sorrow changed everything. Abigail looked at Wade. "Who made that loan?"

"I did. I was home from college that summer."

"How could you loan Lois money, knowing Joe gambled?"

"Lois came to me asking for help. Surely you can see that with the trouble between our families and the desperation of her situation, I couldn't refuse to loan her the money."

Lois took Abigail's hand. "This isn't Wade's fault, Abby. I should've gone to the stores immediately and settled up with them then and there. But Donnie was crying, needing his nap…" Tears brimmed in her eyes. "I blame myself."

The fault was Joe's. But to say as much would only wound her sister more. "Why are you here?"

Wade rose from the desk and stepped toward her, the look on his face knotting Abigail's stomach and filling her with dread.

"That loan is delinquent. I'm asking for payment."

Abigail stood on shaky limbs, threw back her shoulders, ready for battle. "You know they've lost everything and Joe can't work."

"I had no choice. Please believe I didn't make this decision out of spite. In less than two weeks, the bank examiner will inspect our books. Low cash reserves and a longstanding delinquent loan won't meet state bank standards. That loan must be paid and off our books."

Wade reached for her. She swatted at his hand. "How do you suggest they do that? Lois and Joe don't have money to pay off that loan. No one in our family does!"

Lois rose and put an arm around Abigail. "Ab, folks in this town depend on the bank. Wade's trying to protect their money."

"Fine, but how will you pay the loan back?"

Lois sighed. "I used our house as collateral."

"Your house burned to the ground."

"The new house is finished. We'll have to sell." Lois's face crumpled and she let out a soft moan. "My poor boys."

Abigail gasped.

Wade took her sister's hand. "The new house should bring more than you owe. Perhaps you can apply the rest of the money toward rent."

"Just like that?" Abigail's hands curled into fists. She wanted to pound them into that broad chest, to hurt Wade as he was hurting Lois. "When they're finally getting on their feet!"

"Stop blaming Wade. Joe and I brought this on ourselves."

"Who's to blame doesn't matter." Abigail had to persuade Wade to change his mind. If he had a heart, he'd find another way. "The boys need a yard. A room of their own. Please, Wade, please don't hurt those children."

Dark eyes glistening, he met her gaze. "I'd pay off the loan myself if I could." He placed a hand over his heart. "I'm sorry, Abby. I didn't have a choice."

"We always have a choice! You criticized your father for valuing money more than people, but he risked his life for Joe." Abigail flailed a hand. "What have you done for anyone?"

At his silence she gave a strangled laugh. "I thought you cared about me."

He jerked up his head. "I do care about you."

She'd thought he loved her. Though until this moment she hadn't admitted how much she cared, even to herself. Now the possibility for a future tumbled away, an avalanche she couldn't stop.

"You can't possibly care and be this cold and unfeeling to my family." She closed her eyes as memories came rushing back. Memories of the pain Wade had given her all those years ago. But this time he was hurting innocent children.

The Cummingses had money. She didn't believe Wade couldn't help. Did greed drive him as it had his father?

She took her sister by the arm. "Let's get out of here."

Lois pulled back. "I need to stay and sort out the details."

Abigail turned on Wade. His face was ashen, his brow furrowed. His eyes locked with hers.

Eyes she'd foolishly admired, gotten lost in. Those connections she'd felt between them... Wade Cummings was an actor, just like his mother. Well, she couldn't abide one more moment working in the Cummings house. "Consider this my notice. I quit!"

With one last glance at Lois, Abigail stormed out the door, slamming it behind her.

What could she do to help her sister? She had a pittance in the bank. Another job, even a second or third job, couldn't solve this.

She'd never felt more helpless.

And more like a fool.

Why had she let down her guard with Wade?

Chapter Eighteen

The glass in the office door rattled in the pane, the vibration jarring. Hurting Abby had ripped a hole in Wade's heart. A hole only she could fill. By calling the Lessman loan, he'd lost his chance with Abby. She'd never forgive him now.

From the condemnation he'd seen on her face, she didn't believe he'd had no choice. The survival of the bank had to come before his personal life. No matter what Abby believed, his motive wasn't greed.

Wade met Lois's troubled eyes. "I'm sorry."

"I know you didn't call the loan out of spite. Give Abby time to calm down. When she does, she'll know it too."

He plowed a hand through his hair. "She doesn't trust me. Her distrust goes beyond the feud."

"I know." Lois's eyes narrowed. "I've always wondered why you ended the relationship."

He dropped his gaze and shrugged.

"You're hiding something."

Nothing could make him tell her.

"One thing I've learned through the nightmare with Joe—as ugly as the truth may be, we have to look facts square in the face. Look ourselves square in the face. When we do, with God's help, we can overcome the mess we've made of things."

Wade slumped onto the corner of the desk. "Please tell Joe I explored every alternative." He swallowed hard. "But even if I could have brought more money into the bank, a bank examiner would see a delinquent loan as a red flag."

"Loans have brought about the Wilson downfall. I'll be glad to have this one paid." She gave a wobbly smile. "Don't look so grim. God will work this out." With that encouragement, she gave him a hug then walked out the office door.

With everything in him, he prayed God would do what he couldn't and somehow bring good from this mess. He couldn't imagine his life without Abby. The shop, his plans, nothing mattered if he couldn't share them with her.

Oh, Lord, comfort Abby. Help her to trust me, to trust You.

Even if she never spoke to him again, even if he couldn't have her in his life, he wanted her happiness.

An idea latched onto his mind. One thing he could do. He hoped he wasn't too late.

Heels clicking, Abigail marched through the bank lobby, looking neither right nor left, yet sensing Leon watching her. If she looked his way, he'd see the anger, the pain in her eyes.

Once again Wade had proved he didn't have a heart. Why had she thought otherwise? He was a Cummings after all.

The outside door swung closed behind her. With no plan except escape, she raised her umbrella against the driving rain and stumbled along, sloshing through puddles. At the alley leading to their apartment she hesitated. She couldn't go home. Couldn't face her family's unspoken but nonetheless real, I told you so.

Nor could she talk to Rachel. Rachel would urge her to

give Wade another chance. She didn't have another chance in her.

Even Elizabeth, a woman with many solutions, didn't have an answer for this. Abby had never felt more alone.

Without considering her destination, her feet took her to the park. Inside the shelter of the gazebo, hidden by a curtain of rain, she dropped onto a bench, then hunched forward, shivering.

By now Lois would be home, telling Joe they'd have to sell the house. Visualizing his face, Ma's, the boys', she moaned.

Only moments before she'd been excited about the future. With the feud behind them she and Wade might have found a way to build a life together. That hope had blown up in her face.

Why had she trusted him?

She straightened. She'd survive. She'd teach, work in the community and at church and spend her time with friends and her family. She needed nothing more.

No one else.

Not even a man with indigo eyes.

As the rain continued to fall, she shed no tears. A stone did not weep.

With his every step spraying water, Wade slugged home, rain sluicing off the brim of his hat. The temperature had dropped twenty degrees, matching his dismal mood.

He hoped Abby wasn't walking around in this weather, but he suspected she was. She didn't have a carriage house or shop to hole up in as he did. The crowded apartment provided not one iota of privacy or comfort. Comfort he'd like to give her but knew she wasn't ready to accept.

His only hope of bringing Abby and the Wilsons happiness, of making up for what the Cummingses had taken from them rested with Wade's father. A few weeks ago he wouldn't have given his errand a chance but George had softened. With the incentive Wade would offer, his father, a savvy businessman, just might agree.

Not wanting to track through the house with wet feet, Wade entered through the kitchen door. The aroma of corn bread and stew greeted him. An orderly house, a well-cooked meal—he appreciated what Abby had done, what Cora did now to make the Cummingses' house a home.

Her salt-and-pepper tresses twisted into a bun at her nape, Cora stood at the stove, an anchor in the storm, or so he saw her. How many times had she comforted him as a boy? Did she even know what she meant to him?

She looked over at him and smiled. "Supper won't be long."

Though he had no appetite, he could pretend. He moved to the stove and glanced at the bubbling stew. "My favorite."

"Appropriate for a day like this."

A day of damage he would undo. "Do you know where Dad is?"

"In the library. I just told him ten minutes till supper."

"Can you hold off a few minutes?"

Nodding, she studied him. "Is everything all right?"

The last time Wade could remember everything feeling right was five years ago, when he'd first given his heart to Abby. "No, but I hope to…make things better."

"Sounds serious. I'll pray for you. You and the mister."

"Thanks." Abby had taught him to express his feelings, to stand up for himself. From now on he'd share what was in his heart. "I hope you know you're family, my second mom."

Tears sprang to Cora's eyes. She laid a gentle palm on his cheek. He'd never known Cora to be at a loss for words, but she'd lost hers now.

He gave her a peck on the cheek. "Thanks for the prayers. Those prayers helped Dad and me to forgive each other."

Cora's eyes twinkled. "I knew God could knock some sense into George's hard head. He used Abigail Wilson to do it."

"God knocked some sense into me too."

Abby had shown him that someone had to take the first step. Someone had to stop running and do what they could to make things right. He headed toward his father's library, praying for wisdom, for strength. If his father agreed to his proposition, he'd rectify the damage the Cummingses had done to the Wilsons.

George sat at his desk, fiddling with his pipe, cold, unlit. He glanced up and studied him. "You don't look too good."

"I just called the Lessman loan."

With a grimace, his father set aside the pipe. "Not easy doing the hard thing."

"No, sir, it's not. Having to call that loan was one of the hardest things I've ever had to do." Hurting Abby all those years ago was worse.

Wade took the chair across from his father and met his gentle gaze. Verification of how much his father had changed and giving him hope George would accept his offer.

"Dad, I'm asking you to return the Wilson farm to their family."

His father's jaw dropped. "What? I—"

"Hear me out. The Lessmans are losing their home in order to pay back the delinquent loan. I've been in the shabby apartment over the bank, barely adequate for Abigail and her mother, much less the Lessman brood. If we return the land and farmhouse, we'll restore Joe's livelihood, the family's roots, and give them a good place to live."

"You're asking me to *give* the Wilsons the farm? Because

they have needs? If that policy guided me, I'd be providing for half the people in this town."

Wade shook his head. "I'm asking you to restore what we took from them."

"Calling that loan was aboveboard."

"Once you knew the railroad's interest in the Wilson land, and kept that information to yourself, you crossed a line." Wade waved a finger. "If you'd waited a month or so to call the loan, the Wilsons could've sold that partial to the railroad, giving Frank the money to repay what he'd borrowed." He leaned toward his father. "Face the truth. We owe them."

"If waiting another month had been an option, then why didn't you give the Lessmans more time?" He released a gust. "I'll tell you why. Conditions at the bank demanded action. Now."

"I'll give you that, but once the railroad deal was finalized, you could've returned what remained of their farm."

George picked up his pipe. "Returning the farm makes as much sense as putting this unlit pipe in my mouth. We can't restore assets to everyone who's made bad decisions. Besides, Frank would've risked that farm in another foolish venture."

"What he would've done isn't the point. The point is what *you* should've done."

George's nostrils flared. "Money is tight. Income from that farm helps us meet expenses." He sighed. "Truth is my lungs haven't yet healed. With your plan to open a shop," his father said, stumbling over the words, "I've got to hire someone to replace you and perhaps even myself. Giving the Wilsons that farm will add to my concerns about money."

Wade looked his father in the eye. "I have an offer that will handle your concerns. An offer you won't want to refuse."

"What's that?"

"Give the Wilsons their farm and I'll continue filling your shoes for as long as you need me."

"You'd give up your dream?" He blinked. "The only reason you'd do that…" His eyes softened. "You love her. You love Abigail."

More than life itself. "Yes. Without Abby, all my plans, the shop, none of it matters."

George rose and walked to the globe, spinning the orb, watching it swirl round and round. "I wish I'd seen that years ago, before I lost Ernestine."

Wade walked to his father. Put an arm around his shoulders. "Dad, it may be too late for Abby and me. But whatever happens between us, giving the Wilsons the farm will please God and show this town and the Wilsons that the Cummings name stands for integrity."

Fierce eyes turned on Wade. By questioning his father's integrity, had he destroyed the possibility that he'd accept the offer?

"Will you do the right thing?" Wade asked.

"I'll think about it. That's all I'm promising."

Three days passed, one rainy, bleak day after another. Abigail filled those days scrubbing the woodwork and walls, washing the windows, preparing family meals. Each night she fell into bed limp with exhaustion, but inside she was frozen hard. A person she didn't like but didn't know how to change.

That afternoon Wade had come to the house, wanting to talk. She'd refused, asking her mother to pass along the message. Ma had shot her a penetrating look, but complied.

Why had Abigail believed, even for a moment, that she and Wade could find happiness? They came from different worlds. The Cummingses' wealth enabled him to live in a cocoon. He didn't understand the average person's struggles. Didn't grasp the hardship, the pain he'd brought her family.

Now crowded around the table in a sparkling kitchen for a supper of beans and corn bread, Joe thanked God for the meal and for their blessings. Blessings in short supply.

Aghast at her lack of gratitude, Abigail begged God for forgiveness. They were healthy. They had food on the table and clothes on their backs. All blessings she appreciated. She just couldn't seem to overcome this crushing sense of sadness.

As she picked at her food, across from her Joe and Lois ate with abandon, gazing into one another's eyes, laughing and talking like newlyweds. Her nephews imitated their parents' good mood, giggling and chattering like magpies. The little guys didn't comprehend they'd lost their home. But how could Lois and Joe be this carefree?

Once they finished eating Joe gave his sons permission to leave the table. They scampered off like frolicking puppies.

Joe turned to Abigail, then Ma. "Lois and I've been saving our news until we could talk in peace. The Johnsons bought our house this afternoon, a wedding present for their daughter and her future husband."

"Stay here as long as you need," Ma said.

A sick feeling in her stomach, Abigail stared at her hands knotted in her lap. She'd prayed and prayed for God to step in and save their house. Now the house was sold. Gone. Too late for a miracle.

"The Johnsons gave us our asking price. Joe and I paid off the loan at the bank this afternoon," Lois said, then looked at Abigail. "Wade asked about you."

Abigail dug her nails into her palms. Why couldn't she be indifferent to him?

"The best part—Joe took the remaining money and paid

off his gambling debts," Lois said. "Thank You, God, for freeing us from that burden."

"That's mighty good news." Ma glanced at Abigail, arching a brow, obviously wanting her to congratulate them.

But no words would come.

"The door to that ugliness is closed." Tears flooded Joe's eyes. "I can hold my head up in this town."

Lois handed Billy to Joe. "Your son is proud of his papa."

As Joe took the baby in his arms, Billy burped, loud. "Your pa is proud of his son," Joe said.

Ma and Lois chuckled.

"I rented a rig and drove out to the Harper farm. Got some work lined up. In a few weeks, I'll earn enough to rent a place of our own." He bent and kissed Billy's forehead. "I'm blessed with a wonderful wife and five healthy sons. What more could a man want?" He looked from Ma to Abigail and sobered. "I can never thank you enough for taking us in."

"We're family. You'd do the same for us," Ma said.

"I would. I'll always be there for you and Ab." A screech brought Joe to his feet. "I'd better check on those little wild men before they tear up the place." He carried Billy into the parlor. "Quit bouncing on that sofa, Donald William."

The women rose to clean up from the meal. "Ab, you've done nothing but work around here. I'll help Ma with the dishes."

"Thanks, I think I'll take a walk."

"In this weather?" Ma said, glancing out the window.

Lois grinned. "A little rain would probably seem downright peaceful after listening to my rowdy boys."

The idea of being alone to think things through had Abigail grabbing her umbrella. Outside she set off down the alley to Main. As she ambled through town she passed the freshly painted row of houses. Crisp curtains hung at the windows. Petunias bloomed in window boxes. Barefooted children splashed in mud puddles.

Except for one house.

Her nephews had no yard. No bedroom of their own. No friends nearby.

Unable to abide the reminder, Abigail turned away from the sold sign in the window of what should've been Joe and Lois's house and moved on.

At the corner of Main and First Street, New Harmony First Christian beckoned. She'd attended the church all her life. Here she'd find a quiet place to think and pray.

She entered the sanctuary, closing the heavy door, muffling the sound of thunder rumbling in the distance, as if God wouldn't permit distraction in His house of worship. She sagged onto a pew in the last row.

Why had Lois been composed at losing their house, while Abigail couldn't accept the loss, couldn't see the good that had come from it? She carried an anger and emptiness that scared her. Was she becoming her father?

God felt far away. Did He hear her prayers?

She bowed her head.

"Miss Abigail."

Her eyes flew open. "Cecil. I didn't see you."

"Reckon you wouldn't." Without an invitation he sat down beside her with a soft groan. "I was up front and on my knees thanking God for a problem."

Had she heard him right? "You've what?"

"My rheumatism is acting up again. I call it rheumatisn't. 'Cause it tisn't gonna get me down."

She glanced at his gnarled hands, folded gingerly in his lap. "You thanked God for your pain?"

"Don't come natural to thank God for my troubles, but I'm learning He'll give me a big ole blessing if I do."

"You still have your rheumatism."

"Rheumatisn't," he corrected, then rubbed the pad of a thumb over the base of the other. "God don't promise to take my thorn away, no more than He done for the Apostle Paul. But God sees me through. Stopping in here on days when the pain kicks up, like here lately with all this rain, keeps my eyes on Him and off the hurt." He smiled. "Reckon iffen every day was sunny and free of pain, I 'spect I'd think I didn't need Him."

Cecil's faith in God's provision brought tears to her eyes. Her faith wasn't strong like his.

He studied her with his tender gaze. "Iffen you got troubles, Miss Abigail, you're in the right place. Thank the Good Lord for 'em. Then let Him work 'em out as He sees fit. You and me, we're His sheep." He chuckled. "Ain't the smartest critters, but sheep know the Shepherd's voice and trust He'll lead 'em to safe pastures." He patted her hand. "Reckon they ain't so dumb after all."

Lord, did You bring me here for just this moment?

"Thank you, Cecil, for saying what I need to hear."

"Is that so?" A smile lit his kind face. "Well, better mosey on. Let you chat with the Almighty." He lumbered to his feet, a slight groan on his lips.

"I'll be praying for your rheumatisn't."

"'Preciate it." He steadied himself with a hand on the pew. "I'm sorry Joe and Lois had to sell that house. I'm praying for 'em. Reckon you could use prayer too."

Cecil shuffled out the door, leaving her alone for that chat with God.

As long as Abigail could remember, she'd prayed. Read Scripture. Yet she'd fretted over bills. Over Joe and Rafe's compulsions, Joe's gambling debts, Seth's future. The list was endless. Why hadn't she seen that trying to save the day for everybody wasn't in her power? Or even in God's will.

"Lord, You are in control of this world. Forgive me for trying to rip control out of Your capable, powerful hands."

Her faith was shaky. Why?

The answer—she'd wanted a rosy world, a world without trouble, pain or sorrow.

"Lord, I've been afraid You would give me more than I could bear. Yet Cecil accepts life as it comes, handling his troubles and pain by keeping his eyes fixed on You."

If she didn't trust God, what did she have?

A miserable existence. Fear, worry.

The words of the Twenty-third Psalm filled her mind. Her heart. Sheep follow their Shepherd. God didn't promise a life without troubles. He promised He'd walk through the Valley with His children. He'd never forsake her, any more than she could forsake her family.

"Forgive me, Father, for not trusting You." She slid off the pew onto her knees, weeping tears she'd bottled up for years.

When she raised her eyes, a beam of sunlight had broken through the clouds, coming through the stained-glass window behind the altar, shooting prisms of color through the sanctuary. She felt cleansed. A blessed peace enveloped her. The love of God. God loved her even when she was most unlovable. He didn't love according to what she deserved. He loved according to who He was.

He loved her, loved her family.

He loved Wade. George.

All mankind.

If only she could love like God did. Yet how could she forget the hurt Wade had caused? How could she trust him when he'd tossed her away years before?

She rose and left the church. The rain was a mere shower now. As she popped up her umbrella, a smile sprang to her lips. Across the way a rainbow hugged the heavens, the sign of God's promise to never flood the earth again.

As if God had planted the thought, she knew what to do.

She'd give Wade a chance to explain why he'd declared his affection one moment and walked away the next. Would his explanation enable her to forgive how he'd hurt her?

Or drive them apart forever?

Chapter Nineteen

Even getting soaked to the skin, a ride into the country had restored Wade's flagging hope. *Lord, if it's in Your will and what's best for Abby, have her come to me.*

Filled with peace he couldn't explain but knew came from God, he rubbed down Rowdy and watered both horses, then turned them out to graze.

He scrubbed debris off the bit then tackled the bridle and saddle. Once they were clean and dry he rubbed heated oil into the leather. Dry rot could break a cinch, sending a man to the ground. Or sever the reins, losing a man's control of the animal.

The oil penetrated the thirsty cinch. Once he'd wished for an ointment to make him soft and pliable like this leather. He'd taken a while to learn the balm he sought could only be found in God's Word and in the power of prayer.

As his thoughts drifted with the repetitive action, he released the shop—his dream—to God. Whatever happened, he trusted Him with the outcome.

Tonight he'd get his father's answer. If George accepted Wade's offer, they'd return the farm to the Wilsons. And restore the Cummingses' tarnished good name. Only then could they truly move beyond the ugliness of the feud. And find harmony, even if that harmony came at the cost of his dream.

He'd still instruct Seth, pay him too. Perhaps one day he'd help Seth open a shop of his own.

Not that Wade would quit crafting furniture. Transforming wood into objects of function and beauty was as much a part of him, as vital as the air he breathed. Yet the prospect of spending his life behind a desk didn't distress him as he'd expected.

The difference—*he'd* made the choice, not had his path mandated. He'd made the decision out of love for Abby. Out of fairness to the Wilsons. Out of obedience to God.

Maybe if the farm was restored to the Wilsons, his future could include Abby. He'd fought his feelings for her, afraid of traveling the same road his parents had, but no longer. He loved Abby, completely, totally, with every particle of his being. He'd fallen for her years ago at a high school picnic. Back then too much stood in the way. Now, he'd ensure nothing did.

His father's mistakes had taught him the importance of establishing priorities. He'd never put anything ahead of God, ahead of Abby, if she'd allow him in her heart. Yet he wouldn't push. She'd have to want him as much as he wanted her.

A cricket chirped from somewhere in the straw. An owl hooted from his perch in a nearby tree. All was tranquil. Yet a sudden death grip on the rag in his hand shot tension into his neck and shoulders. What if everything he'd done to prove his love to Abby wasn't enough? What if—?

He gulped a calming breath and reminded himself the outcome was out of his hands and in God's. God had a plan for Wade's life. For Abby's too. A plan that would be best for them both. If he wasn't what Abby needed, he'd be man enough to let her go. Or so he hoped.

He felt her presence before he saw her.

Abby.

Silhouetted against the overcast nighttime sky, she waited in the open doorway, as if asking permission to enter.

His pulse hammered in his temples. God had answered his prayer.

Heart in his throat, he walked toward her, meeting her halfway, thanking God she had come.

"I'm sorry I had to call your sister's loan. I—"

She brushed her fingertips over his lips, stopping the apology. "I'm the one who's sorry. I blamed you for an action you had to take. The shock of Joe and Lois losing that house hurt." She gave a sad smile. "More me than them."

"I know."

"Wade, I haven't put my trust in God. I've tried to fix everything. Some of those things aren't my business or even in my power to fix." Her smile wobbled. "I've come from talking with God, really talking to Him, listening too." Her eyes filled with tears. "I confessed my sin, asked for His forgiveness and turned my life over to Him." She sighed. "Knowing me, I'll be tempted to snatch it back, but the only thing I'm to manage, with God's help, is me and my classroom."

Wade lifted a hand to her hair, touching her, wanting to pull her to him with a desperation that left him shaken. "Oh, Abby, I love you."

At his declaration she stiffened, silencing him as effectively as a muzzle. He'd let her have her say.

"I don't want to hurt you, Wade, but trusting God isn't the same as trusting you." She looked away, then back. "Why did you toss me aside in high school? Were you only pretending to care?"

"No! Please believe me. You were the best thing that ever happened to me."

"Then why?"

The owl hooted again. Time ticked to the beat of his racing heart. "Some things are better left in the past."

"Nothing stays in the past, Wade," she said gently. "Those things creep into the future. I have to understand." She swallowed hard. "Be honest and tell me why."

She was right. If they had any chance for happiness, they had to face facts and share their feelings. The reality—he hadn't been honest with her or with himself. He'd convinced himself he had to protect Abby from the ugly truth. But another reason kept him silent. Mistrust. Underneath, he'd feared telling her the truth would shatter the last hope of a future with Abby. Yet that fear revealed a lack of confidence in Abby and God to work it out.

He took her hand and led her to the bale of straw, tugging her down beside him. "The reason I broke up with you..." he inhaled, exhaled, breathing a silent prayer "...involves your father."

"My father? How?"

"Frank found out we were spending time together. You know small towns—everything's public knowledge." She nodded, so he went on. "On the way to school one morning he stopped me. Livid at me for what he called sneaking around behind his back. He...warned me to stop seeing you."

On her face surprise changed to shock then shock to horror. If only he could take back his words, but he couldn't. The truth stood between them, stark and cold.

She bit her lower lip, then sighed. "Go on."

"He said that if I didn't stop seeing you, he'd send you back East to live with relatives."

"To Aunt Gertrude's?"

"I don't know."

"Why didn't you tell me?"

That question had sat on his chest for a long time. "I grew up without a mother. I knew how much you loved yours. I couldn't take the risk that your father was bluffing. Or be the wedge between you. Lest one day you'd hate me for what I'd cost you."

Her eyes turned distant, focusing over his left shoulder. "Pa died three years ago. Why didn't you explain this then?"

"You loved him. I didn't want to hurt you."

The tears welling in her eyes spilled down her cheeks. "He would've done it. He would've sent me away." She shivered.

He drew her close, wanting to ease her pain.

She pulled away from his arms and scrambled to her feet. "I have to go."

"Abby—"

"If I don't get home to help with the picnic preparations, Ma will send a posse to look for me." She laughed but the sound held no humor. "We'll…talk about this later."

With that flimsy excuse she shot out the door.

He wasn't fooled. Abby was running from the information, from him, from the future they could have.

Despite all she'd said, she still didn't trust him. Like a blow to the chest, that truth walloped him hard, shattering the hope he'd clung to. As he'd feared, the truth about the breakup had cost him Abby. Frank Wilson had won, even from the grave.

Wade had his father's answer. Now he needed Abby's. And he would get it today.

After he'd had time to think and pray about Abby's reaction last night, he'd realized he shouldn't have expected her to fall into his arms when she'd just been told the tough truth about her father. She needed time to digest the facts. To see how she felt about her father's actions, how she felt about Wade keeping the truth from her.

The congregation of New Harmony First Christian spilled

out of church, carrying picnic baskets and blankets, abuzz with speculation about what had happened to end the long-standing feud between the Wilsons and Cummingses. The two families had sat in the middle of the church, not shoulder to shoulder, but separated by only a few pews.

Oscar Moore sidled up beside Wade and his father, grinning like a Cheshire cat with a secret. Tugging on his suspenders, he leaned in. "Glad to help you out today," he said in a stage whisper then with a wink, he ambled on.

"What's that about?" his father asked.

"A plan. A plan for my future."

George grinned. "I hope that plan includes Abigail."

Wade hoped the same. But where was Abby? She hadn't come out of the church.

Before he could go inside to look for her, Joe stopped in front of his father, both men leaning on canes.

With a wide smile on his face, Joe shook George's hand. "I'm beholden to you for saving my life, Mr. Cummings."

"The Lord put me there at the right time and the right place for that very purpose."

"I'm mighty grateful for His care and for yours. If I can do anything for you, ask."

Across the way families carried baskets to tables constructed from sawhorses and boards, dropping off dishes, then spread out, searching for shade. He needed to set his plan in motion before the picnic began.

"Excuse me, gentlemen, I have a lady to see," Wade said then took the church steps two at a time.

With Wade's assertion that he loved her roiling inside, Abigail sat beside Ma. Her hand sought her neck, then she remembered she'd removed the baby ring she'd worn on a chain all these years. She still loved her father but she saw him and herself more clearly. She wasn't Pa's baby girl anymore. She was a grown woman at a crossroads. She fiddled with her skirt, pleating the folds with shaky fingers.

Ethel covered Abigail's hand with her own. "Tell me what's on your mind before you ruin your Sunday best."

Would what she had to say hurt Ma as it had hurt her? Her breath caught. Or did Ma already know? "Wade said Pa threatened to send me to Aunt Gertrude's if he didn't stop seeing me." Her eyes filled with sudden tears. "I can't believe Pa would have been so cruel as to send me away."

"Abby girl, what your father did, he did out of love."

Ma had known all along. The knowledge pressed against her lungs.

"He truly believed Wade Cummings would break your heart." She lifted Abigail's chin, forcing her to meet her eyes. "With all that happened, can you understand why he felt he had to do everything in his power to protect you?"

"Was that love? Or revenge?"

"Your pa never stopped loving you, Abigail Louise. He believed the Cummingses couldn't be trusted." Ethel squeezed her hand. "He laid his feelings about the father on the son."

"But Wade was just a boy when Pa lost the farm and the railroad money."

"I know. What Frank believed isn't the gospel truth. Trust your heart, Abby girl."

Abigail wasn't sure what her heart was telling her. She only wanted to get through the picnic, to escape the anguish of seeing Wade.

Ethel motioned to the back door. Wade stood in the opening. "I'll leave you two alone," she said then marched up the aisle, said a word to Wade then left the church.

As Wade's long strides ate up the distance between them, Abigail's heart pounded in her chest with every step. She couldn't take her eyes off him.

He sat beside her in the pew and took her hand. "Are you hiding from me?"

She swallowed the sudden lump in her throat. "Maybe."

"Why? You have nothing to fear from me."

Desperate to make him understand, she said, "Love brought terrible heartache to my mother and sister. You and your dad were hurt by love too."

"You're afraid to love me."

"The problem isn't you. I believe with all my heart that you're a good man. I'm the problem. I've spent my life half living, fretting. I'm not sure I'm ready."

"I know what life is like without love. It's empty, Abby. Lonely. Is that the life you want?"

Shaking her head, she studied her hand wrapped in his.

"I'll risk pain over that awful emptiness." He brushed his lips over her knuckles. "Love is stronger than fear. When we love God and each other fear is defeated."

Hadn't she seen that yesterday when she'd talked to God right here in this church? Felt the peace that truly loving God brought her. Rachel had suggested God might've brought Wade back to her, a man to his woman. Wasn't giving herself permission to love part of trusting God's plan for her life?

"Do you believe that?" he asked gently.

"Yes. Yes, I do."

"I think you'll appreciate this," Wade said then reached inside his suit jacket.

Her heart tumbled. Was Wade going to give her a ring?

He pulled out a document. Not a ring.

She bit back a sigh laden with disappointment. Perhaps she wasn't as afraid to love as she'd thought.

"Abby, this is the deed to the Wilson farm." He handed it to her. "It's legal, free and clear. Harrison looked it over."

Had she heard him right? "You want us to have the farm?"

"The land rightfully belongs to your family."

"Your father agreed to this? Why?"

His expression turned evasive.

"We're going to be honest with each other, remember?"

"I told my father I'd work for him, give up my shop, if he'd return the farm."

She shoved the deed away. "I won't let you do that. You're talented, a craftsman—"

"I didn't have to." His voice clogged. "Dad wouldn't hear of my giving up the shop."

Her jaw dropped.

"I can barely believe it myself. He says he'll ask Regina's husband to run the bank. I hope he agrees so they'll move back."

"I think he'll agree once Lawrence sees your dad's changed."

"You're a big part of the reason." His fingers curved around her cheek. "Abby, don't ever doubt I'd give up my dream. I'd give up anything on this earth for you." His gaze darkened. "I saw what happened when my father put the success of business above my mother's happiness. I won't make that mistake."

He took her hand. "Joe can work the Wilson land and provide for his family. For your mother."

Momentarily unable to speak, Abigail squeezed Wade's hand, fighting tears. "The farm is the perfect place for five boys to grow up. I see God's provision in all of this. Your dad's willingness to give us the farm isn't the business decision he usually makes."

"He feels guilty about the railroad deal. Returning the land to your family is his way of an apology." He grinned. "Likely the only apology you'll get."

"As cantankerous as George can sometimes be, your father owns a piece of my heart."

"I'm hoping I own the largest piece." He gulped. "Do I?"

With a teasing grin, she cocked her head at him. "What do you think?"

"I think we're missing the auction."

"What auction?"

"Wait and see." Eyes twinkling, he pulled her to her feet then tucked the deed back in his jacket. "I'll keep this for now."

Outside they walked to the Wilson blankets where he left her with a mischievous grin. What was going on?

It was time.

Wade threw up a hand, his signal to Oscar.

Oscar shuffled to the main food table, let out a shrill whistle. The crowd quieted, no doubt expecting Pastor Ted's prayer.

"Been asked to hold a small auction, folks." Oscar leaned back on the soles of his feet. "Way I hear it, Wade Cummings wants another chance to bid on Abigail Wilson's basket. Not sure what he's up to, but I'm curious to find out."

A grin on his face, Oscar shuffled to the Wilson blanket. "Apparently, she's already unloaded it." He turned to Wade. "What's my bid? What's my bid on this empty basket?"

As folks moved closer to watch, heat climbed Abby's neck and flooded into her cheeks. Her wary gaze bored into Wade.

"I'll bid fifteen dollars," Wade said.

"Not much of a bid from a man in love," Oscar groused.

Grinning, Wade stepped forward. "In that case, let me change my offer." He tugged the woman he adored to her feet.

Blue eyes flashed with alarm. "What are you doing?"

"Trust me," he whispered.

Then he turned to the crowd. "You see, Oscar, I've discovered man doesn't live by bread alone." He took Abby's fisted hands and knelt on one knee, gazing up at the most beautiful woman he'd ever laid eyes on. "I'll bid everything I own, everything I am and a lifetime of love for Abigail Wilson's hand in marriage."

Oscar hooted. "Now that's more like it! The second time Wade Cummings's bid would curl a pig's tail."

Abby raised trusting, love-filled eyes to Wade, walloping him in the heart. "Abby, you know I'm in love with you. Are you willing to spend your life loving me?"

"Oh, Wade, I can't imagine life without you." She threw her arms around him. "I'm in love with you! I always have been."

Oscar cupped his ear. "Is that a yes I hear?"

"Yes! I'll marry you, Wade Cummings!"

Cecil whistled. "A Cummings marrying a Wilson—folks will talk."

"Let them," Abby said. "I've never been surer of anything."

"Well, then, I think there's only one thing to say." Oscar slapped his hands together. "Sold! Sold to Mr. Wade Cummings for the price of a lifetime of love!"

The entire Wilson clan rushed to them, hugging and talking at once. As the hubbub died down, Pastor Ted strolled to the table. Again Oscar whistled for quiet.

"Let's pray." Ted bowed his blond head along with the congregation. "Father in Heaven, we thank You for working in our midst and for the blessing of this newly promised couple. We give You all the glory. Bless the food for our use and for Your service. In His name, amen."

Everyone lined up to fill their plates, then returned to

their blankets to eat. The sun shone, the birds sang, the aroma of fried chicken and meat loaf drifted on the breeze, a perfect day for a picnic.

Her heart overflowing with love, Abigail couldn't stop smiling. Elizabeth bustled over. "Once you set a date, the Ladies' Club is available for the party. We'll help with decorations, cake, whatever you need."

Abigail gave her a hug. "Thank you."

"You've got a good man. Ted thinks highly of Wade."

Abby turned to her future husband, not one bit frightened by all the talk about the wedding ceremony and party. She couldn't wait to be Wade's wife. She knew with deep certainty that she could trust Wade with her heart, with her life.

As Elizabeth joined Ted and the children, Rachel took Abigail's arm. Eyes swimming with tears, Rachel gave her a fierce hug that made her squeak. "I'm thrilled for you and Wade!"

"You knew I loved him before I'd admitted it to myself."

Rachel leaned closer. "And you knew I'd love teaching before I did."

"You've decided to attend Normal School!" Abigail sobered. "Was your father okay with it?"

"He's unsure, but he agreed."

"Your dad wants to see you happy."

Wade tugged Abigail close. "If I have my way, Abby will continue teaching. Denying a married woman a contract is archaic. I intend to talk to the school board."

"You'd do that for me?"

"You're a born teacher. You should teach."

"Until the babies start coming," Rachel said.

Wade looked dumbstruck, then grinned. "I'd like a big family."

Babies. The idea slid through Abigail. She glanced at the children, the families around them and imagined the future. "I hope we have little boys with brown hair and indigo eyes, exact replicas of their father."

"No, I want little girls with blond hair and forget-me-not-blue eyes exactly like their mother," Wade protested.

Boys or girls, Abigail wanted Wade's children with every fiber of her being.

George strolled over and clapped Wade on the back. "Abby will make you a wonderful wife. And a sassy second daughter to me." He chuckled. "My favorite kind."

Abigail hugged Wade's father. George had opened his heart to others, to his son, maybe even to Cora, if those furtive glances between them meant anything. And to her. If he considered her a second daughter, she saw him as a second father. Nothing like the first, but a man she now respected.

"Will you walk me down the aisle?" she asked.

Wade's father blinked. His eyes welled with tears. "I'd be proud to."

Beaming, Cora gave Wade a big hug. "My boy's getting married." Then she turned to Abigail. "I knew you'd make the difference in this family." She tossed a grin to George. "I love being right."

"Cora, a man doesn't like hearing he's wrong."

"I'd think you'd be used to it by now."

George chuckled. "If you can behave yourself, Ethel asked us to join them for the meal to give these two some privacy," he said, offering Cora his arm.

Wade shrugged out of his jacket, grabbed the deed out of the pocket and handed it to George. "Why don't you tell the Wilsons the good news, Dad?"

"My pleasure, son," he said.

Cecil sidled up. "Iffen you need music for a wedding party, Oscar and me are offering."

"We'd have no one else." Abigail laid a hand on his arm. "How's that rheumatisn't?"

"No rain. Never better. But don't you fret. Ain't no rheumatisn't in my lips to keep me from playing harmonica at your wedding party."

Finally the crowd of well-wishers dispensed. Wade pulled Abigail into his arms. "I love you, Abby." He spoke near her ear. His eyes locked with hers, everything around them faded, leaving them aware of only the two of them. "You've made me the happiest man alive. I hope you don't make me wait long to be your husband."

"I don't want to wait either," she said, then leaned into him, lifting her lips to his before realizing what she was doing. She quickly stepped away. "We should eat."

"Afraid you'll shock some folks if you kiss your fiancé?" he teased as they made their way to the tables and gathered their food.

With all the giddiness swirling inside of her, Abigail could barely eat, while Wade wolfed his down. "Proposing must make a man hungry," she said drily.

"I couldn't eat last night or this morning, worried you'd turn me down." He chucked her under the chin. "You're not a woman a man takes for granted."

"I like the sound of that." She laid her fingers against his lips. "But never doubt you've made me the happiest woman alive."

Wade set his plate aside. "After we're married, how would you feel about living with Dad, giving us a chance to get closer and help Cora look after him?"

"I've come to love that grand house and its inhabitants. I'd live anywhere as long as I'm with you."

"Where else would a princess live?"

Sudden moisture filled her eyes. "I had my life all mapped out, but God's plan is far better than anything I could've imagined." Abigail threw her arms around his neck. "I'll live in a castle, married to Prince Charming—my dream as a little girl."

"Aw, Abby, dreams do come true. Mine have in you."

She laid a hand on his jaw. "Will you fill our room with your beautiful furniture?"

"I'll build anything you want."

She slipped into his arms and lifted her lips to his. "You already did, Wade. You already did."

She thanked him with her kiss.

* * * * *

Dear Reader,

Today women—married or single—have a multitude of career options, but in Abigail Wilson's day, teaching was one of the few accepted careers for single women. Marriage often terminated the teaching contract, since married women were expected to stay home to rear children. As Abigail came to realize in *An Inconvenient Match,* security rests with God, not with anything in this world, including intelligence and education.

Yet, education is very important and I hold teachers in high regard. Not surprising with three generations of teachers in my family. My father began teaching in a one-room schoolhouse, moved on to junior high and then spent most of his career teaching high school social studies and art. My daughter and I taught in the elementary grades. Since my days in the classroom, much has changed in society and in the schools. Problems are difficult to solve and require students, parents, teachers and administration to work together. A favorite Scripture of mine urges: "Whatever you do, work at it with all your heart, as working for the Lord, not for men." Colossians 3:23. Think how different our world would be if we all took that Scripture to heart.

Thank you for choosing *An Inconvenient Match*. I enjoy hearing from readers. Write me through my website, www.janetdean.net, or by mail at Love Inspired Books, 233 Broadway, Suite 1001, New York, NY 10279.

God bless you.

Janet Dean

Questions for Discussion

1. The trouble between the Wilson and the Cummings families began over money. What other issues frequently cause trouble between families or individuals?

2. What besides the feud stood between Abigail and Wade? Do you understand how the breakup could affect Abigail years later?

3. Abigail valued honesty. Yet she was unable to examine her father's part in the feud. Why? Do you understand this?

4. George accused Frank Wilson of greed, yet was guilty of greed himself. He excused himself for profiting from the railroad deal by saying he'd done nothing illegal. Are Christians called to a high standard?

5. Abigail resented George, but then came to understand him, feeling sympathy and finally affection for him. What changed? What did George admire about Abigail?

6. Wade dreamed of opening a cabinetmaking shop, yet something held him back. How did both his father and mother impact his hesitancy? What did Wade fear?

7. What did Seth Collier teach Abigail and Wade about love, about hope?

8. What factors were involved in ending the feud?

9. Though Abigail had faith, she struggled with trusting God with her life and the lives of those she loved. What did Cecil Moore teach Abigail?

10. What ways did you see God at work in Abigail's and Wade's lives?

INSPIRATIONAL

Wholesome romances that touch the heart and soul.

Love Inspired.
HISTORICAL

celebrating
15
YEARS

COMING NEXT MONTH
AVAILABLE FEBRUARY 14, 2012

THE COWBOY FATHER
Three Brides for Three Cowboys
Linda Ford

HOMETOWN CINDERELLA
Ruth Axtell Morren

THE ROGUE'S REFORM
The Everard Legacy
Regina Scott

CAPTAIN OF HER HEART
Lily George

REQUEST YOUR FREE BOOKS!

2 FREE INSPIRATIONAL NOVELS
PLUS 2
FREE
MYSTERY GIFTS

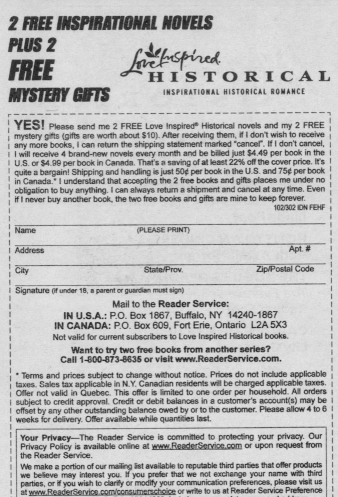

Love Inspired
HISTORICAL
INSPIRATIONAL HISTORICAL ROMANCE

YES! Please send me 2 FREE Love Inspired® Historical novels and my 2 FREE mystery gifts (gifts are worth about $10). After receiving them, if I don't wish to receive any more books, I can return the shipping statement marked "cancel". If I don't cancel, I will receive 4 brand-new novels every month and be billed just $4.49 per book in the U.S. or $4.99 per book in Canada. That's a saving of at least 22% off the cover price. It's quite a bargain! Shipping and handling is just 50¢ per book in the U.S. and 75¢ per book in Canada.* I understand that accepting the 2 free books and gifts places me under no obligation to buy anything. I can always return a shipment and cancel at any time. Even if I never buy another book, the two free books and gifts are mine to keep forever.

102/302 IDN FEHF

Name	(PLEASE PRINT)
Address	Apt. #
City	State/Prov.	Zip/Postal Code

Signature (if under 18, a parent or guardian must sign)

Mail to the **Reader Service:**
IN U.S.A.: P.O. Box 1867, Buffalo, NY 14240-1867
IN CANADA: P.O. Box 609, Fort Erie, Ontario L2A 5X3
Not valid for current subscribers to Love Inspired Historical books.

Want to try two free books from another series?
Call 1-800-873-8635 or visit www.ReaderService.com.

* Terms and prices subject to change without notice. Prices do not include applicable taxes. Sales tax applicable in N.Y. Canadian residents will be charged applicable taxes. Offer not valid in Quebec. This offer is limited to one order per household. All orders subject to credit approval. Credit or debit balances in a customer's account(s) may be offset by any other outstanding balance owed by or to the customer. Please allow 4 to 6 weeks for delivery. Offer available while quantities last.

Your Privacy—The Reader Service is committed to protecting your privacy. Our Privacy Policy is available online at www.ReaderService.com or upon request from the Reader Service.

We make a portion of our mailing list available to reputable third parties that offer products we believe may interest you. If you prefer that we not exchange your name with third parties, or if you wish to clarify or modify your communication preferences, please visit us at www.ReaderService.com/consumerschoice or write to us at Reader Service Preference Service, P.O. Box 9062, Buffalo, NY 14269. Include your complete name and address.

LIH11B

Louisa Morgan loves being around children.
So when she has the opportunity to tutor bedridden Ellie,
she's determined to bring joy back into the motherless
girl's world. Can she also help Ellie's father open his
heart again? Read on for a sneak peek of

THE COWBOY FATHER

by Linda Ford,
available February 2012 from Love Inspired Historical.

Why had Louisa thought she could do this job? A bubble of self-pity whispered she was totally useless, but Louisa ignored it. She wasn't useless. She could help Ellie if the child allowed it.

Emmet walked her out, waiting until they were out of earshot to speak. "I sense you and Ellie are not getting along."

"Ellie has lost her freedom. On top of that, everything is new. Familiar things are gone. Her only defense is to exert what little independence she has left. I believe she will soon tire of it and find there are more enjoyable ways to pass the time."

He looked doubtful. Louisa feared he would tell her not to return. But after several seconds' consideration, he sighed heavily. "You're right about one thing. She's lost everything. She can hardly be blamed for feeling out of sorts."

"She hasn't lost everything, though." Her words were quiet, coming from a place full of certainty that Emmet was more than enough for this child. "She has you."

"She'll always have me. As long as I live." He clenched his fists. "And I fully intend to raise her in such a way that even if something happened to me, she would never feel like I was gone. I'd be in her thoughts and in her actions every day."

Peace filled Louisa. "Exactly what my father did."

Their gazes connected, forged a single thought about fathers and daughters…how each needed the other. How sweet the relationship was.

Louisa tipped her head away first. "I'll see you tomorrow."

Emmet nodded. "Until tomorrow then."

She climbed behind the wheel of their automobile and turned toward home. She admired Emmet's devotion to his child. It reminded her of the love her own father had lavished on Louisa and her sisters. Louisa smiled as fond memories of her father filled her thoughts. Ellie was a fortunate child to know such love.

Louisa understands what both father and daughter are going through. Will her compassion help them heal—and form a new family? Find out in
THE COWBOY FATHER
by Linda Ford, available February 14, 2012.

Love Inspired Books celebrates 15 years of inspirational romance in 2012! February puts the spotlight on Love Inspired Historical, with each book celebrating family and the special place it has in our hearts. Be sure to pick up all four Love Inspired Historical stories, available February 14, wherever books are sold.

Love Inspired

SUSPENSE

RIVETING INSPIRATIONAL ROMANCE

FITZGERALD BAY

Law-enforcement siblings fight for justice and family.

Follow the men and women of Fitzgerald Bay as they unravel the mystery of their small town and find love in the process, with:

THE LAWMAN'S LEGACY by Shirlee McCoy
January 2012

THE ROOKIE'S ASSIGNMENT by Valerie Hansen
February 2012

THE DETECTIVE'S SECRET DAUGHTER
by Rachelle McCalla
March 2012

THE WIDOW'S PROTECTOR by Stephanie Newton
April 2012

THE BLACK SHEEP'S REDEMPTION by Lynette Eason
May 2012

THE DEPUTY'S DUTY by Terri Reed
June 2012

*Available wherever
books are sold.*

www.LoveInspiredBooks.com